D1505503

NIGHTWALKER

**Center Point
Large Print**

**This Large Print Book carries the
Seal of Approval of N.A.V.H.**

NIGHTWALKER

HEATHER GRAHAM

CENTER POINT PUBLISHING
THORNDIKE, MAINE

This Center Point Large Print edition
is published in the year 2009 by arrangement with
Harlequin Books S.A.

The text of this Large Print edition is unabridged.
In other aspects, this book may vary
from the original edition.
Printed in the United States of America.
Set in 16-point Times New Roman type.

ISBN: 978-1-60285-434-5

Library of Congress Cataloging-in-Publication Data

Graham, Heather.
  Nightwalker / Heather Graham.
      p. cm.
  ISBN 978-1-60285-434-5 (library binding : alk. paper)
  1. Single women--Fiction. 2. Private investigators--Nevada--Fiction.
    3. Las Vegas (Nev.)--Fiction. 4. Murder--Investigation--Fiction 5. Large type books.
    I. Title.

PS3557.R198N56 2009b
813'.54--dc22

2009002772

For friends in Vegas,
Dan Frank, Adam Fenner, Shelley Martinsen
and Dick Martinsen,
and with special love for
Lance Taubold and Rich Devin

Prologue

Nevada, 1876

Smoke from a dozen cigars and cigarillos filled the saloon, creating a gray mist that hung over the patrons' heads. George Turner, a man with a curious mix of races running through his blood, was playing the piano. Milly Taylor, a soprano who survived by prostitution in this godforsaken hellhole, was singing about being in a gilded cage. The desert dust, which never seemed to really settle, joined with the miasma of smoke, and it was only the fact that the fiery red ball of the sun was finally setting that made it bearable to sit at the poker table.

John Wolf was holding a flush, aces high. He leaned back easily in his chair. There was a fair amount of money on the table, but if he appeared casual, it wasn't just his customary stoicism that made him so.

He didn't give a damn about the money at stake. He'd just returned from a trip that could change the lives of everyone around him. Now he was waiting for Mariah.

"I'll see your dollar, breed," Mark Davison said.

John didn't bat an eye. He knew Davison was trying to rile him with the remark. The man should have known better. If there was anything John had learned from being raised between two worlds in this lawless sandpit, it was to control any outward display of emotion.

"I'll raise you two," Davison continued.

Davison was an ass, a would-be gunslinger.

He'd come from the East, with family money and an attitude. Whether he won or lost, he tipped the bartenders and the girls, so that, at least, was good. But he'd taken up with Frank Varny and his crowd, and that was bad.

"Two bucks," Davison repeated. There was color in his cheeks.

"Two bucks," John said, smoothly sliding the sum onto the pile.

He could tell by Davison's expression that the other man had expected him to fold.

"This is a friendly poker game, fellows," Grant Percy, the so-called sheriff said, fidgeting uneasily in his seat and folding his cards. He might wear a badge, but the truth was, Frank Varny owned the town.

He had muscled his way in, and he had kept his power in the usual way: by intimidation. You joined him—or you went out into the desert with your mule and pickax, and only the mule and pickax came back.

But today, John Wolf knew, things were going to change. Mariah would come, and whatever happened to him after that wouldn't matter. She was the one good, honest human being he'd come across in his life, and he was going to give her the information she needed to ensure that the people here—not just the tribe but all the people in this town who'd suffered for too long under Varny's corrupt rule—found life worth living again.

"I'm out, so lay down your cards," Ringo Murphy, the fourth and last man at the table, said. Murphy was a wild card himself. He'd been an opinionated rancher down in Missouri, so the story went. Just a kid when his world had gone to hell. He'd become a sharpshooter during the War Between the States, and now that it was over, he was chasing a dream of wealth and comfort. He was gaunt but well toned, a fellow with a devil-may-care attitude, and he wasn't quick to bend to any man's brutal tactics. He leaned back in his chair with his guns visible, nestled into the shoulder holsters he wore. Names were etched on the barrels: Lola and Lilly. "Come on, Davison," Ringo said impatiently. "I'd like to get back into this game."

Davison was a lean man, as skinny as a string bean—letting his muscle come from the two Colts he wore holstered on his hips.

John was armed himself. Always. He, too, carried Colts. Six-shooters, each one double-barreled, providing him with an extra shot per gun. He also carried two knives, sheathed at his ankles. It wasn't out of meanness. Out here, it meant survival.

"Call," Davison said gruffly. John laid his cards on the table.

That was when the swinging doors to the saloon burst open. The sun was setting, painting the sky a deep red hue. Against it, a man was silhouetted in the doorway.

Frank Varny had come, just as John had known he would. But the timing was bad; Varny shouldn't have made it in from his "office" in the hills until nightfall.

"Wolf!" he said, the single word sounding like a roar.

John didn't twitch. He cursed silently and didn't acknowledge the newcomer. He'd had it all planned down to a crossed *T,* but someone had betrayed him. Varny shouldn't have known he was back. Not until Mariah had come.

The smoke in the air began to dissipate as most of the crowd scattered hurriedly, like dry leaves caught in a high wind, heading out the backdoor.

Even the bartender disappeared. Milly Taylor croaked out one last note, then froze, as her accompanist scrambled up the stairs.

Only John paid no attention to the other man's arrival.

Frank Varny didn't like being ignored. He strode across the room, so accustomed to being a law unto himself that he didn't see the flicker of annoyance in Ringo Murphy's black eyes.

Davison looked up nervously, though, barely

noticing anything as he set his cards down by reflex alone.

John had won. "My flush beats your straight," he said, and scooped in the gold dollars piled on the table.

"Good. Now the rest of us can get back into the game," Ringo Murphy muttered.

"The game is over," Frank Varny announced. By then, four of his henchmen had followed him into the saloon. They were all resting their hands on the guns holstered at their hips.

"Deal," John told Grant Percy.

"Now, now," Sheriff Percy said, licking his lips nervously. "Seems like Mr. Varny needs to have a word with you first, John Wolf."

John looked toward the swinging doors and saw a tumbleweed dance by in the breeze that had suddenly lifted. He looked upward, not at Varny, but at the red sky that was darkening to crimson, deep as a dead man's blood. From the corner of his eye, he judged where Varny's men were standing.

Varny planted a fist on the table, leaning down. "You found the vein, didn't you? Well, it's my land. And it's my gold."

John stared back at him and smiled slowly. "It's Paiute land," he said calmly. He drew the cards toward himself and started to shuffle. "I brought a claim into Carson City, and I took ownership, on behalf of the tribe, of the land that once belonged to the Paiute nation, before you white men came

11

and took it all away. Up in those offices in Carson City, they're not afraid of you, Varny. They believe in something called the law. So now the claim is on *Paiute* land, my friend."

Ringo Murphy let out a snort and stared from one man to the other. "What the hell? Are we playing cards here or not?"

"Shut your mouth," Varny said. "We're doing business here."

"Get the hell out of my sight, Varny," John said. "I told you, that gold is mine."

It was amazing, John thought, that Varny didn't die of apoplexy on the spot. He looked as if he was about to explode. "That's my gold, and you're going to tell me where to find it, you red bastard."

"Is anyone going to deal?" Murphy demanded. "I would like to win my money back."

"We'll get right back to it," John said to Murphy. He turned back to Varny. "Actually, I'm only half-red. My mother was white. She was working in this very saloon when she was captured, and she soon realized she had a better life as a Paiute captive than a white barmaid."

"Barmaid? Whore, more like," Varny spat out.

John looked evenly into the other man's eyes. "Whatever she might have done in life to survive, she was a far better person than you. Hell, Varny, you murdering scum. That makes her pretty damn fine in comparison, no matter what the hell she did."

Varny drew his gun, and his men drew theirs. Left with no choice, John Wolf rose, kicking the table over and using it for cover, as he drew, himself. He noticed Murphy drawing his own gun, evening the odds at least slightly.

As the shots began to explode and ricochet, the sheriff and Davison dived for cover, and Milly Taylor ducked behind the piano and screamed.

To John Wolf, the world seemed to slow down, letting him see every little detail of what was happening.

Murphy was good. Faster than lightning, even in John's slowed-down view. As the sheriff threw himself under a nearby table for protection, Murphy held his ground, both guns blazing. John heard the sickening thuds as first one bullet struck home, then the other, as Murphy took out two of Varny's men, saving John's hide.

John Wolf took that in even as his own guns blazed against Varny's other two thugs.

Another thud, and a spray of brilliant color as one man was struck in the heart. A moment later, the other took a bullet in the lung. Blood streamed across the floor, matching the sunset.

Varny's men were dead, all four of them, but Ringo Murphy been hit himself. He looked at John before he died. "Sorry, partner," he said, and fell. Hiding under a table hadn't helped the sheriff; he was sprawled out under it now, his eyes glazed in death. It hadn't saved the skinny fool from the

East, either. Davison was bleeding out on top of the sheriff; his jugular had been hit, his geysering blood turning into a deep, dark river as it mingled with the dirt on the floor.

Milly Taylor wasn't dead, though. She had wilted against the piano and was sobbing. The wall was blown out behind her. Varny had been hit in the right arm, but he was still standing.

Now it was just the two of them.

They stood in the midst of the carnage and stared at one another.

"You're a lucky son of a bitch," Varny said. "Your buddy there took down Riley and Austin. Without him, you'd be dead. You couldn't have shot all four of them."

"The world is full of what might have happened," John said softly.

Varny grinned slowly. "I'm going to kill you, you know. Thing is, why the hell are you holding out? Give me the gold and I'll let you live. Are you going to give me some cock and bull about your father's people? You said that it was your land now. So which is it? Misplaced heroics or personal greed?"

John shrugged. "Misplaced heroics? Those who came here first, my father's people, they need it. They'll share. And you, you already have more than any man needs in a lifetime. You know, there's a rumor out there that you have Indian blood, too."

"The hell I do."

"Thank God. The Indian nations don't need your kind."

Varny knew how to hold his temper, and he grinned, even if there was a tic at the vein in his throat. "What about your white half, boy?"

John hiked a brow slowly. Boy? "Well, *Pops,* my mother is dead. And what folks she had, I never knew about. But this isn't about red or white. It's about greed. Yours. You've managed to cause a hell of a lot of trouble since the Paiute War, kidnapping women from the villages, discarding them like garbage. And when their husbands, fathers and brothers have come after you, you've managed to shoot them down or get them hanged. All you've wanted for as long as I've known about you is gold. Paiute gold. And you're not going to get it. This land—and any gold that's on it—is the tribe's now."

Varny's eyes filled with rage, but he kept his distance. John couldn't be sure, but he thought Varny might be out of ammunition. It had been hard to count when a half-dozen guns were blazing, but if Varny carried the old army Colts he always had, he was most probably out of bullets.

Then Varny smiled coldly. "I've got something you want as much as I want that gold."

John didn't allow any sign of wariness to show on his features. He waited. What the hell did he have to lose at this point? Things hadn't gone the way he'd expected, but now it was down to Varny and himself. He might die, but he would take Varny down with him if he did.

"Did you think I'd play all my cards so quickly?" Varny asked. He never looked away from John. "Tobias! Get in here!"

Tobias was a big man, like some corn-fed Nebraskan. He didn't look happy as he came in, straw-colored hair flying, denims held up by suspenders.

But that didn't give John pause. What caused his heart to skip a beat was the fact that Tobias was dragging a terrified captive.

Mariah.

She was in deerskin and moccasins, her hair braided, as befitted a Paiute maiden. But her eyes were bluer than a clear sky at noon, and her skin was as pale as porcelain. She was one of those rare creatures who found happiness and harmony wherever she went; she adored her Indian stepsiblings as much as she had loved her white father, before he died and the Paiute took her in. She was a voice of sanity and peace, and Varny must have grabbed her as she had hurried here to meet him.

"I'll kill her," Varny said flatly. There was no emotion in the man's voice at all. "I'd have fun with her first, except she's such a timid little mouse, and that's no fun at all. But who knows? I might give it a try. I actually prefer my women wild and wicked, like Milly over there, but I'm willing to put up with a lot for that deed and that vein of gold. Then again, there's nothing like blowing off someone's kneecap. That would hurt like hell, and I'm betting it would get you to talk."

The first thought that occurred to John was that he would do anything, anything at all, to save Mariah's life. He would give up all the gold in the universe, salvation for the world, just to see her free. He should drop his weapons and give Varny everything he wanted.

But it wouldn't help. Varny was going to kill them both, possibly torture them both, no matter what he said to the contrary, once he had the gold.

"Well?" Varny pressed.

It was amazing, John thought, that Varny hadn't realized the truth about the gold.

"Don't give him anything!" Mariah cried, fighting the hold Varny's lackey had upon her. "Don't give him anything at all."

Her eyes flashed with her fury and her hatred, which only seemed to amuse Varny—and appeal to him.

"Maybe the lady isn't so boring after all," he mused.

With only split seconds before the choice was no longer his, John weighed his options. And they were few. No aid was coming. Ringo Murphy was dead on the ground, and he was the only fool who would have dared to help.

How good was he? John asked himself. He could

take down Varny, but could he do that *and* save Mariah? Maybe. If he tried negotiation, if he stalled, if Varny was the first to draw . . .

No help, no hope.

He drew.

He fired like lightning; both guns blazing. One bullet for Tobias, one for Varny.

But Varny was fast, too.

John's bullets struck both men, but Varny hit John in the chest, dead center, as well. Oddly, he didn't feel pain. Just the punch of the bullet, and then . . . cold.

Cold like ice.

They always said this kind of death was instantaneous.

But it wasn't. He was aware of far too much as he died.

He saw Mariah's face, her mouth the O of a silent scream, as he fell. He tried to say what he needed to tell her, but didn't know if his lips moved, didn't know if he made any sound. He wasn't sure it mattered.

At least she was free. She would live. He tried again to tell her the things she needed to know, but he couldn't tell if she under-stood him or not.

But death trapped the final words in his throat, and death came with its white light, then darkness, and after that he was aware of nothing more, not even the ever-present dust as it sifted down and mingled with his blood as his life ebbed away.

1

Tension was high around the table, but then, there were thousands of dollars strewn out across the board, represented by colorful plastic chips.

Because this was Vegas, where men and women could rise like meteors to the top of the world, then plummet to the bottom just as quickly.

Jessy Sparhawk could feel the pressure, could feel the eyes of the other gamblers on her.

Some people were playing big money.

Others—idiots like herself—were taking a desperate, edgy, ridiculous chance, playing to beat the odds. To defy the gods of Vegas, who always proclaimed that the house won.

Oh, yes, she was an idiot. Why in God's name had she taken the last of her savings to the craps table? She worked in Vegas, she had grown up out here. She'd seen the down-and-outers. She'd seen the poor, the pathetic, the alcoholics, the junkies, all trying for a big win when they knew the law of averages.

"Ten, baby, roll a hard ten" a man called from the end of the table. He wasn't one of the down-and-outers. He was a regular all over town. She had seen him over at the Big Easy, and he had a deep Southern accent, but one with a Texas twang. His name was Coot Calhoun. All right, so his real name probably wasn't *Coot,* but that was how he was known. Nice man. He'd inherited one of the biggest oil fields in Texas. She liked him. He had a wife named Minnie—though Jessy was doubtful about *that* name, too—who he genuinely loved, and he tipped well because he was generous, not because he was expecting any favors.

"I'm trying, Coot, I'm trying," she assured him, praying for a hard ten not for Coot's sake but for Tim's.

She was here, gambling at the Vegas Sun, because she wasn't allowed to gamble in the casino where she worked, which usually didn't bother her, since she wasn't a gambler. The Sun was owned by a billionaire who had been in the casino trade a long time. Her own Big Easy was owned by Emil Landon. A rich man, yes. A very rich man. But he hadn't been at the casino game long. Even though she wasn't a gambler, she knew the games. She'd been a dealer, a hostess, a waitress, a bartender, a singer, a dancer—even an acrobat for a brief period of time. She knew Vegas in and out, backward and forward, and she had learned long, long ago, not to gamble, because the house always won.

"Baby, baby, baby, *bee-you-ti-ful* baby, do it. Hard ten," another man called. He was young. Drunk. Probably had too much money on the board, and definitely had too much alcohol in his system.

She was aware of so many people watching her.

It had been kind of fun at first, but now she felt the tension. Even Darrell Frye, one of the Sun's pit bosses, was watching her with a measuring stare, as if afraid she was on one of those long rolls that totally outweighed the odds.

"Ten, ten, ten," a nearby woman repeated fervently. She was haggard looking, thin, and her dress had been stylish twenty years ago, back when she had been pretty. Now her features bore the weight of time, but she offered Jessy a smile, and Jessy smiled back.

"Get on with it," someone else insisted. "Just roll."

She did. To her horror, the dice bounced off the table.

"Hey, it's all right, just a game," said a deep, smooth, masculine voice.

She looked up. The man who had spoken was several people away to her left, and she had noticed him earlier. He was the kind of man it was hard not to notice. He wasn't typically handsome, and certainly not a pretty boy, but he had what she could only call presence. Tall, with broad shoulders, he managed to be simultaneously casual and elegant, and rugged on top of that.

She flashed him a smile. He wasn't drunk; he had been sipping the same drink since she had started watching the table. She was five-ten and wearing heels, but he towered over her by several inches. His eyes were so dark that to call them brown would be an injustice. His hair, too, was almost ebony, and the striking cut of his cheekbones made her think there had to be Native American blood in his background, and maybe not far back. He was simply striking, dressed in a white pin-striped shirt open at the neck, a nicely fitted jacket and black jeans. He hadn't been risking big money, but he had played as if he knew something about the game, and he'd been playing the same money since she first noticed him. And he seemed to be watching for more than just the roll of the dice.

He lifted his glass to her and looked over at the dealer as he tossed out two hundred-dollar chips. "Hard ten for me and for the roller," he said.

"You don't need to—" she began.

"Jessy, just roll, sweetie," Coot called to her, then turned to the croupier as he picked up two chips himself. "My money is on the little lady. Throw this on the hard ten, one for me, one for her, please."

His hundreds went down.

More chips were thrown down on the hard ten, plenty of them for her, and she knew that she was blushing. "Thanks," she murmured, looking at the man who had started it all. The pressure was really on now. A so-called "hard" bet paid really well.

But there was a lot of money to be lost if she failed.

Her handsome benefactor said, "Don't worry.

It's going to be a hard ten. And if it's not, it's all right. I never put down what I can't afford to lose."

She wished she could say the same thing. But at this point, she was desperate. If she didn't come up with the money, she couldn't pay to keep Timothy in the home. She could see Mr. Hoskins' face now, as he calmly told her, "I'm sorry, Miss Sparhawk, but there's nothing we can do. I've been as patient as I can, but if I don't have that three thousand dollars by tomorrow morning, you'll have to find another facility."

She hated Hoskins. He was a thin-lipped, nose-in-the-air jerk, but he only ran the Hawthorne Home; he wasn't the one who spent time with Tim. And Tim loved Jimmy Britin, the orderly, and Liz Freeze, his nurse. And Dr. Joe, who was a wonderful man, who worked at the home in order to be able to afford to donate his time at several local shelters.

A hard ten. If she rolled a hard ten, two fives, she made not just her own hundred-dollar bet, but . . . ten times that hundred. Plenty of money to keep Timothy where he needed to be.

She swallowed hard and rolled the dice.

"Hard ten, hard ten!" It became a chant.

She had never seen dice roll for so long on a craps table. A four and a three . . . and groans went around the table, because a seven meant that she would crap out. But the dice were still rolling. . . .

A five and a three.

A five and a two.

A five and . . .

A five. A hard ten.

The screaming and shouting was deafening. Hands clapping, high fives all around. She wasn't sure who picked her up and swung her around, but she didn't protest that any more than she protested the hugs and backslaps that came her way, or even Coot's enthusiastic kiss on her cheek. She was simply too stunned.

The one man who didn't grab her or go insane was the tall, dark-haired stranger. He just watched her, pleased, and yet somehow grave.

Jessy couldn't believe the number of chips coming her way.

"I'm cashing in," she told the dealer.

He gave her an odd look. "You're still rolling," he reminded her. "If you leave, these folks will lynch me. Don't pass the roll. Go until you crap out."

She glanced to the side, looking for the dark-haired stranger.

He was gone; of course. He wasn't rolling. Still, she missed him. And she had the oddest feeling that things weren't going to go right, now that he was gone. And she was right, because it wasn't long until she crapped out. Still, as she collected her chips, which were still worth far more than the three thousand dollars she needed, everyone regaled her as if she were a celebrity. She thanked them, then turned, eager to escape as quickly as possible.

That was when the huge man plowed into her.

Huge. Bodyguard huge. He was bald and built like a wall of solid rock. His eyes were hazel and streaked with red.

"Hey!" Coot yelled indignantly.

It didn't stop the man, who hit her so hard that he knocked her flat onto the craps table, then fell on top of her.

She was pinned, and when she tried to budge his weight, she couldn't. She started to ask the onlookers for assistance, but her words were cut short by someone's shrill, hysterical scream.

And then she felt the blood trickling down on her as she struggled under the man's weight.

His *dead* weight . . .

His glazed and frozen eyes stared at her, and then his mouth moved.

He spoke one word.

"Indigo."

And then his lips stopped moving and something, some light, went out in his eyes.

She tried to twist out from beneath him, and that was when she saw the knife sticking out of his back, saw the blood, and began to scream herself.

Dillon Wolf heard the screams just seconds after he had stepped into the special "high-roller" section of the casino. He spun around, returning at a

25

breakneck speed, and arrived back at the craps table just as casino security descended on it. He saw the beautiful redhead he'd staked earlier, desperately trying to push the weight of the huge man off her, and he saw the man's face almost as quickly.

Tanner Green. Hell.

He'd spent most of the night keeping track of who was coming and going, trying to get a handle on who was frequenting the new casino, and the last damn thing he'd imagined was Green turning up dead. The man was a pro. *Had been* a pro. Not only that, before rejoining the world, he'd worked as a mercenary; there was no way in hell he should have been taken by surprise by anyone. But a knife in the back? That pretty much screamed *surprise*.

The fact that the police would want the body left *in situ* didn't prevent him from diving in to help the redhead free herself as quickly as possible.

"Hey, hey!" one of the security officers said, hurrying forward, but he ignored the man.

"Thank you," the redhead whispered as he shifted her free of the corpse and she managed to get back on her feet. For a moment, though, her eyes were on his. Huge. A deep, radiant blue, like a cloudless sky. Those eyes had first met his just a few minutes earlier as she rolled the dice. Now he also noticed that she smelled good, not to mention that she *felt* good against him.

As soon as he saw that she was steady, he delved

into his pocket for his ID, presenting it to the security officer.

"Dillon Wolf, licensed P.I.," he said. "Have the police been called?"

"The 911 has gone in, they'll be here momentarily," the security officer said. Two of the men accompanying him had already begun to form an invisible ring around the craps table; two more were hurrying over to bar the door.

"Oh God, I have to get out of here. I have to get out of here!" a woman cried hysterically.

"Calm down," Dillon said, his voice taking on a deep authoritative pitch. He had long ago learned that people didn't obey high voices in an emergency; they only became more hysterical.

The redhead was silent, but he saw that she was shivering. Something in her eyes told him that she knew she was going to be there for a long time, the center of a murder investigation. She was stunning, absolutely stunning, and something about her intrigued him. Las Vegas was full of gorgeous women, of course—showgirls, waitresses, actresses, singers—but she seemed different somehow.

When he'd first noticed her, those eyes of hers had been . . . haunted. Not as if she was afraid of losing a dream, certainly not as if she was afraid of simply losing . . . money, but as if she was terrified of losing something far more precious. As if the roll of the dice could cost her her very soul.

He gave himself a mental shake. He had other

things to think about here. Not only was there a dead man lying on the craps table, but that dead man was Tanner Green.

A man came striding onto the scene. A big guy with an attitude. Jerry Cheever, Las Vegas homicide. Dillon was pretty sure that Cheever resented him, but Cheever knew the lay of the land. He might despise Dillon on every level, but he'd been told by his bosses that Dillon was to be granted free rein. Cheever liked his paycheck and his position, so he obeyed, but he also liked to take credit for things that went well, and he knew Dillon had a talent for seeing an investigation through, and he wasn't above taking advantage of that fact.

Especially because he simply wasn't the sharpest knife in the drawer.

"No one move!" Cheever bellowed. "And I mean *no one!*"

He took note of the blood seeping into the green felt tabletop and soaking the multicolored chips.

"Wolf," he said curtly, acknowledging Dillon's presence. His eyes settled on the redhead as he asked Dillon, "What happened?"

"I wasn't here. I ran over when I heard the screaming," Dillon said.

Jerry Cheever turned to the redhead.

"What happened?" he demanded curtly.

"I was leaving the table. This man came over and . . . and fell on me," she said.

"Do you know him?" Cheever demanded.

28

"I've never seen him before," she said.

"You're sure?" Cheever pressed.

"Absolutely sure," she said with confidence. She was still trembling slightly. Not surprising, Dillon thought, given that she was wearing the dead man's blood.

"Are you hurt?" he asked her quietly.

She shook her head.

Cheever took in the corpse. "Christ! It's Tanner Green." He glared at Dillon again. "Aren't you two working for—"

"Yes," Dillon said curtly.

"But you weren't together?"

"No."

"Lieutenant Cheever, the M.E. is here," a newly arrived police officer informed him.

"Give him room. No one gets out those doors, do you hear?" Cheever said.

A murmur arose from the crowd, but Cheever wasn't disturbed. "Give your payouts, close your tables," he commanded the casino employees, then turned to his fellow officers. "I want men posted at all the doors. No one leaves here without presenting ID and a valid local address, and not until they've been questioned. Are we understood?"

Another swell of protest emanated from the crowd, but no one moved. Not even the casino employees. "Payouts. Now. I want the tables closed up. I want some order here," Cheever announced.

At last things began to happen. The M.E.—it was Doug Tarleton, a decent guy and an expert in his field, Dillon thought—was sliding his gloved hands over the dead man's face, closing the staring eyes.

"Lord!" Tarleton said, startled. "It's Tanner Green."

"Yes," Dillon said simply.

Cheever turned to the redhead. "And you are . . . ?"

"Jessy Sparhawk," she said quietly.

"Exactly what happened?" he asked.

She arched a brow but answered levelly. "I was leaving the table. I don't know where this man came from. He fell on me and knocked me onto the table. I was trapped under him until he—" she pointed at Dillon "—got me out. And that's all I know."

"So you don't know him?"

"No," she said firmly.

Cheever's officers were good, and the floor had quietly filled with them.

Dillon knew there were men already stationed at the doors, and he knew that the others would soon begin questioning the hundreds of people who had been in the casino. Crime-scene tape was already being stretched around the table.

Cheever suddenly stared at Jessy Sparhawk again. "The surveillance cameras will have picked up everything, you know."

"I told you *exactly* what happened," she said, adding, "And I had nothing to do with it."

"Lieutenant Cheever," Dillon said, taking a step forward, "Miss Sparhawk is a victim here, and undoubtedly pretty damn uncomfortable right now."

"That man is uncomfortable," Cheever said irritably, pointing to Tanner Green.

"No," Dr. Tarleton said. "That man isn't feeling a thing. He's dead. Knife wound to the back, short-hilted, long-bladed weapon, which is why no one noticed it—that, and the fact that they were all staring at the tables."

"You're sure on the weapon?" Cheever asked.

Tarleton cleared his throat and looked daggers at the detective. He wasn't fond of Cheever. "Oh, yeah. I'm sure. It's still sticking out of his back."

"Shouldn't there be a blood trail to show where he was stabbed?" Cheever asked, frowning.

"There might be a few specks somewhere. The knife acted like a cork," Doug explained patiently. "When Tanner fell, the knife was knocked aside and the blood began to gush. That's why Miss Sparhawk is covered in it."

"Bring in the crime unit—I want fingerprints ASAP," Cheever said huffily. He was embarrassed, Dillon knew, that he hadn't figured out that the knife would have kept the blood from flowing. "All right, get everyone cleared out of here, and let the crime unit have the area from the door to the table." He glared at Dillon suspiciously. "You, too,

31

Wolf. Let the crime-scene team get in here, and let Tarleton do his job."

Dillon stuck like glue to Jessy Sparhawk, who didn't protest when he led her away. He gave his own name, credentials and address to one of the officers, and watched as Jessy did the same. He noted that her address was in Henderson, a suburb just outside the city, and her occupation was entertainer. She was working at the newly opened Big Easy—casino. When a uniformed officer came over to interrogate her, she answered his questions calmly, even though she was still trembling.

No wonder. She was still bathed in the dead man's blood.

"Hey! How long are we going to be kept here?" a florid man in a plaid jacket shouted angrily.

"Until the lieutenant says you can go," one of the officers said.

Jessy Sparhawk looked at her watch and bit her lower lip.

"Are you late for work?" Wolf asked her.

She shook her head. "No, it's Timothy. . . . I didn't expect to be away from him this long," she murmured.

"Your . . . son?" he asked. She couldn't possibly have a kid over ten, and she didn't look like the kind who would leave a child at home alone while she went out and gambled.

She shook her head. "Timothy's my grandfather."

"I see. Give me a minute."

He strode across the room, to where Lieutenant Cheever was bullying a couple of the players who had been by the door when Green had entered. "Excuse me, Lieutenant," he said politely.

Cheever stared at him and controlled his hostility. "What?"

"The woman who was caught under the corpse, Jessy Sparhawk. She's miserable. Why not have a heart?" Dillon asked, as if there had never been the least animosity between them. "Let her go home and get cleaned up."

Cheever frowned and pointed at Dillon. "I need to talk to you."

"At your convenience. But let her go home. I can see that you've started releasing people once you've questioned them."

For a moment Cheever appeared to be almost human. He shook his head in frustration. "I'm trying to prevent an all-out riot here and not let a murderer slip through my fingers," he said.

"From what I understand, Green entered the casino, staggered through the crowd and crashed down dead on top of Ms. Sparhawk," Dillon said. "It's probable that he was stabbed outside the casino. Even a bunch of hard-core gamblers would probably notice someone going after someone else with a knife that big."

"So you say. He was a bodyguard for Emil Landon, wasn't he? Just like you."

"I'm not a bodyguard. Landon is convinced that someone is trying to kill him. I'm supposed to be finding out who. I just took the case, and I wasn't pals with Tanner Green. I knew him, yes, but that was it."

"So where the hell were you, if you weren't at the table?"

"I'd been playing at the table, but I had just wandered into the high-stakes area over there," Dillon said, pointing toward the far left.

"Oh?" Cheever said, his eyes narrowing. His tone and his look clearly asked, *What were* you *doing in the high-stakes area?*

"I was checking out what players are in Vegas right now," Dillon said. "Like I said, I just accepted Emil Landon's offer. This morning, in fact. Plus, I was nowhere near the front door. And he was stabbed outside. I'd bet ten years that the crime-scene team will find specks of blood somewhere along the way."

Cheever stared at him, knowing he was right.

"The girl obviously didn't kill him," Dillon said flatly. "And she takes care of her grandfather. You need to let her get home."

"Lieutenant?" an officer said, approaching Cheever quickly through the crowd. "The security tapes are ready."

Cheever started to move.

"Lieutenant?" Dillon said, calling him back.

"All right, take her home. But you—I want you

34

in my office tomorrow morning, eight o'clock sharp."

"I'll be there," Dillon assured him. "Emil Landon will want to know everything possible about this."

"And he will—*when* I have something to share."

"He'll want me to see those tapes."

"I don't like repeating myself, Wolf, so I'll only say this once. I know you know someone who knows the damn governor, but you'll still wait until I've seen those tapes myself. Tomorrow morning, eight sharp."

"Right," Dillon said, turning away. More and more people were being released. Some, Dillon thought, would be heading on to other casinos, irritated that a man's death had ruined their evening. Others were guests at the Sun, and some of them would be heading up to their rooms, shaken by tonight's events.

Tanner Green had been no angel. He was known around Vegas. He had a record. And no matter what Cheever did that night, the killer was long gone. Even Cheever himself had to know that. He was just covering his ass, going through the motions.

Cheever suddenly called his name again. "Wolf!"

Dillon paused and waited.

"I mean it. Eight o'clock."

Dillon tried not to laugh. Cheever always liked

having the last word. It gave him a feeling of control.

Dillon turned again and made his way back around the closed-off gaming tables. Dr. Tarleton was still standing by the body with a member of the forensics unit, looking for trace evidence. Dillon paused for a moment, waiting. Watching.

Feeling the room.

But nothing came to him. He paused for a moment longer, then proceeded to the area where Jessy Sparhawk was waiting. He pulled out his investigator's license again, in case the officers on crowd control didn't know him. "Ms. Sparhawk has been cleared," he said quietly to the one standing with his arms crossed over his chest, blocking the exit.

The man nodded, recognizing Dillon and barely glancing at his ID.

Dillon took Jessy's arm and led her out the door. She didn't protest; she readily hurried along at his side.

Once out the door—where police cars were as thick now as ants on a hill at the grand entryway—she let out a sigh of relief. "Thanks. Thanks so much. A P.I., huh? Well, I'm glad you're friends with that lieutenant."

"Not exactly friends," Dillon murmured.

They kept walking until they reached Las Vegas Boulevard, where another crowd had gathered on the sidewalk, everyone staring at the action and speculating.

When his cell phone started to ring, he wasn't surprised. In fact, he was surprised it hadn't done so earlier.

"Excuse me," he said to Jessy, then answered the phone. "Wolf."

Emil Landon's voice came through clearly, and hard with agitation. "I've just heard Tanner Green is dead. *Dead*. Murdered. Knifed in the back."

"Yes, I was in the casino when it happened."

"Did you see—"

"No. I didn't even know he'd come in."

"You should have known, damn you."

"Excuse me?"

"I need to see you. Now."

"As soon as possible."

"He was a bodyguard on my payroll. And he's dead. I want to see you *now*."

"As soon as possible," Dillon repeated steadily.

"I can fire you, Wolf."

"Feel free."

Immediately Landon backed down. "Just get here as soon as you can. I told you I was in danger."

Dillon closed his phone. Jessy was looking away, courteously pretending she hadn't been privy to his conversation. "I'm sorry. You must be busy, and I have to get home."

"Where's your car, then? I'll walk you to it."

"I didn't drive tonight," she said. She flushed. "I had a business appointment, and I thought I might be stopping somewhere on the way home, so I decided not to drive. I, uh, I don't drink and drive."

"I didn't see you drinking."

"I wasn't, but I might have been. Long story. Anyway, I'm sorry, but I really do have to get home now."

"I'll take you. My car is just down the Strip."

"No, no, really. I'm in a hurry, and it's easier just to hail a cab. But thank you. Thank you so much."

What the hell could he do? Insist? He didn't have the right.

"You could be in danger," he said. What a crock.

She smiled, knowing it was a line.

"Thanks. I'll be okay."

He kept his gaze locked on the crystalline blue of her eyes as he reached into his pocket for his card. "Please, call me if you need anything."

She smiled without glancing at it. "Wolf. Ute?" she asked. "Local tribe? Distant tribe? Hell, Erie? Cherokee? Apache?"

He grinned. "Paiute," he informed her, then offered her an awkward grin. "All right, so . . . Sparhawk? Ute, Apache, Nez Perce—stage name?"

"Lakota Sioux, my great-great-grandfather. I'm a real all-American mix," she replied, sounding amused. They stared at each other for another moment. Then she awkwardly took a step away. "I really have to go. Thank you again." She hesitated. "You knew him?"

He nodded.

"I'm sorry."

"I'm always sorry if a man is dead. But he wasn't a close friend."

"Oh."

He frowned. "You didn't cash in your chips, did you? No time, I guess. I forgot about them in the mass confusion."

She shook her head. "So did I. I have them, though. I can cash them tomorrow."

"Those chips represent a lot of money. You could be mugged," he told her.

She laughed. "A cabdriver isn't going to know about my chips," she assured him. "I'm okay, honestly. I'm a big girl. I grew up out here. I carry pepper spray. I'll be all right. I promise."

He saw a taxi. He wondered about the grandfather she had mentioned. Was he ill and waiting for her?

Dillon stepped out to the curb and whistled, flagging down the approaching cab. He saw her into it and waved goodbye. There was nothing else to do.

He frowned, watching the cab as it pulled away. There was a strange shadow next to her, almost as if there was a second person in the seat beside her.

His muscles knotted with tension. The cab passed under a streetlight, and he could see that there was only one person in the backseat. She was alone.

So why was he still so uneasy? he wondered as he watched the cab disappear down the street.

2

She should have driven herself, but she'd known that she was likely to have a bad time out at the home, and that she might stop to have a few drinks on her way home, try to console herself with a pity party and take a little time figuring out her life.

The cab seemed very slow.

She was tense with anxiety by the time the driver pulled up in front of her home in Henderson, and she nearly fell over her own feet in her hurry to get out and reach the house.

"Sandra?" She was calling her friend's name even as she turned the key in the lock. As the door opened, Sandra heard her and came rushing from the back of the house to meet her at the front door.

She was a pretty woman in her mid-thirties and had once been a showgirl, but now she wrote novels for young adults, having found a way to mine her own youthful angst for profit. She also had a sixteen-year-old daughter, born when she was very young herself, and Reggie gave her an even greater insight into the teenage mind.

Sandra Nelson was a good friend. Many people would have shied away from watching Timothy when he was visiting Jessy and she had to go out. Not Sandra. She considered it an easy gig and said all she had to do was listen to Timothy's stories—and see that he didn't set the house on fire because he was convinced he needed another log for his grandfather's sweat-lodge fire.

Sandra's alarmed stare brought an apologetic smile to Jessy's face. "I'm so sorry, it's just that—"

She didn't finish, because just then a loud gasp came from her right, where the family room abutted a courtyard. "Mom! Mom! It's Jessy—she's on TV! A man was murdered!"

Sandra stared at Jessy, who grimaced and went running past her to reach the family room, where Reggie was draped over the big comfortable sofa, staring at the television. She gasped again when Jessy walked in.

Jessy stared at the television. She'd been so focused on getting home that she hadn't noticed the news cameras out front when she and Dillon Wolf had finally escaped the casino, but there she was. She hadn't realized that she had actually been hanging on his arm.

"You were involved in a murder?" Sandra asked.

"Forget that. Who the hell's the hottie?" Reggie demanded. Tall and slim, she had her mother's green, dark-lashed eyes and a perfect heart-shaped face. Despite her beauty and her age, though, she was basically a nice kid, and Jessy was always pleased when she came over to help Sandra with Timothy.

"Murder?" Sandra repeated.

At that moment, Timothy emerged from his bedroom. He was wearing jeans and a plaid shirt that

41

was on backward. Despite that, he maintained his dignity as he straightened regally and said, "Murder? Yes, it *was* murder. They can bury my heart at Wounded Knee for a fact, because the slaughter of the American Indian remains one of the greatest tragedies and injustices of our nation's history."

"Don't worry. The Native Americans are taking a just revenge. It's called bingo, and it's wonderful. They make money, and no one dies," Sandra said, placating him gently.

Jessy walked over to give him a hug, but he only stared at her. His eyes, light blue and misted like fog at the coming of day, were blank at first. Then they registered that she was in front of him. "Granddaughter. You're home. And you're safe."

She was startled to feel him trembling as he hugged her. She looked over his shoulder, frowning questioningly at Sandra.

"This just came on," Reggie said quietly.

"You were in danger," Timothy said. "They told me so."

"Who told you so?" Jessy asked.

"The ghost riders. Their ghosts came and told me that I needed to be strong, that you were in danger, and that I need to defend you," he said earnestly.

"I'm all right. Honestly," Jessy said, really worried now. *Ghosts?* This was new. "Timothy—"

"I miss my bed," he said.

"Tim, you have a bed here," she told him.

He smiled at her, his eyes misty again. "Yes, and I'm grateful. But it's not my bed. I should be in my own place, where you come to visit me."

"You're going back tomorrow, Timothy. It's going to be fine," she said.

Sandra was staring at her, arching a brow. Her silent look said quite clearly, *It's wrong to lie to him. Where can you get that kind of money?*

"Come on, Timothy, let me get you to bed," Jessy told him, ignoring her friend's silent admonition.

His shoulders straightened, and he was entirely lucid. "I can take myself to bed, Jessy girl." He turned to face Sandra and Reggie. "Thank you, ladies, for the lovely dinner, and for listening to an old man tell even older tales. Good night."

Reggie hurried over to give him a hug, and Sandra gave him a kiss on the cheek. He turned and headed back to his room. Jessy didn't want him to see her checking up on him, so she kept an eye on him from where she was and promised herself that she would look in on him later.

When she turned back to Sandra and Reggie, they were both staring at her, wide-eyed.

"What the hell is going on?" Sandra demanded.

"And I still want to know who that guy is," Reggie added.

"And there's . . . blood all over you," Sandra said, ignoring her daughter. "Are you sure you're okay?"

"I'm fine, I promise, but you'll have to excuse me," Jessy said, wiping at the blood, suddenly desperate for a shower.

She practically ran to her room, where she couldn't get her clothing off quickly enough. She threw it all straight into the trash basket, knowing she would never wear a single piece of it ever again. She hurried into the shower and turned the water on so hot that it was almost scalding, then rubbed her skin practically raw. She massaged shampoo through her hair over and over, until, finished at last, she threw on her terry robe and hurried back into the family room.

Reggie and Sandra spun around to stare at her again, and before Sandra could manage a word, Reggie demanded, "Tell me now. Who is that guy? Have you been holding out on us?"

"No. I never saw him before tonight. His name is Dillon Wolf," Jessy told her.

"Oh, okay. They said his name on TV," Reggie said.

"Oh? Did they say my name?" Jessy asked.

"No, you're just the unidentified redhead," Sandra told her. She looked concerned, and rose from the sofa to bring Jessy a cup of tea.

Jessy thanked her and took a sip, then choked. It was half brandy.

"Sandra—"

"You need it," Sandra told her.

"You might have warned me," Jessy protested.

"Could we get back to what happened?" Sandra asked.

"I was playing craps—"

"What?" Sandra broke in, frowning.

"Not to worry, I wasn't betting the house or anything," she said. *Not quite, anyway.*

"And was the hottie playing craps, too?" Reggie asked.

Jessy laughed. "I don't think he'd like being called a hottie."

"Is he here to complain?" Reggie asked.

"No, but—"

"Let's get off the guy," Sandra said. "We know more about him now than Jessy does, I'm willing to bet."

"What are you talking about?" Jessy asked.

"Oh, they kept announcing his name on TV, like Reggie said," Sandra explained. "He's a P.I. with a hush-hush government agency of some kind."

"I think he's working for Emil Landon," Jessy said, confused. She took another swallow of the brandy-laced tea. Now that she was forewarned, it was delicious.

"I bet he's working undercover," Reggie said, excited. "So how did you get to know him so quickly? When is your next date?"

"We weren't on a date," Jessy said.

"I was playing craps. Dillon Wolf was at the table—I didn't even know his name then. But—I

45

won. I won a lot of money. It was bizarre—as if an invisible hand was literally moving the dice until they landed on a hard ten. Anyway, I was starting to leave, and then the man plowed into me, knocked me onto the table—"

"Dillon Wolf knocked you onto the craps table?" Reggie asked.

"No, the dead man, the murder victim."

"He was dead, but he knocked you down?" Sandra asked, confused.

"He was dying when he knocked me down, and then he died on top of me. And then Dillon Wolf came back and helped me up. Actually, I think he convinced the cops to let me out of there, too," Jessy said.

"Cool," Reggie told her. "So are you going to see him again?"

"I don't know why I would," Jessy said.

"I don't know why you wouldn't," Reggie said.

"He didn't ask me out, for one thing."

"He will," Reggie said confidently.

Jessy smiled and took another sip of the tea. It all seemed distant now, as if it had all happened to someone else. The man, Tanner Green, falling on her . . . dying.

"What a night," Sandra said quietly. "What you told Timothy . . . Before all that happened, you made enough to keep him at the home?"

Jessy smiled falteringly. "It was amazing. It never happened before, and I'm sure it will never

46

happen again, but yes, I made enough to keep Timothy there for the year."

Sandra gasped. "You made that much? You *did* bet your house!"

Jessy shook her head. "No, honestly, I wasn't that crazy. It wasn't my money I was betting. I was rolling well, so other people kept throwing money down for me."

"It's all so unbelievable," Sandra said. "All that money. And then a man dying on you. That is one bizarre night." She looked thoughtful for a moment, then asked, "And no one saw anything?"

"Not that I know of. He plowed into me, and he . . . died," Jessy said.

They all sat in silence for a long moment, and then Sandra said, "All right, we're up and out of here. If you're sure you're okay . . . ?"

Jessy nodded.

"I still feel creeped out." Reggie shivered suddenly. "I mean . . . whoever murdered that guy is still out there, right?"

Jessy felt a chill streak down her spine. Suddenly, as if she were reliving the moment, she could see Tanner Green's face, the lips moving, the eyes going dim, clearly before her. Shaking herself to drive the image out of her mind, she stood to see them out. "I'm fine. We'll all forget it in a couple of days," she lied, knowing she would never forget the events of tonight.

"Call me. Let me know if . . . well, if there's anything I can do," Sandra said.

"Will do," Jessy assured her. She watched as the two women made it into Sandra's car, then carefully closed and locked the door. She suddenly wished she had an alarm system, but until tonight, it would have been wasted money, considering the cost of Timothy's care.

With the door closed and locked, she checked in on Timothy, who had dressed for bed properly and was sleeping soundly.

She went on to her own room, thankful for the house. It had belonged to her parents, who had bought it long before Henderson became a popular spot to live. The courtyard was pebbled, with cacti here and there, along with statuary they had bought through the years. The living room held her mother's old piano, and had glass doors that led out to the small patio and pool area. She had a kitchen, dining room, family room, three bedrooms and an office.

Tonight, however, she wished that she also had an alarm.

She tried to tell herself that it was ridiculous to feel fear. Whoever had killed Tanner Green surely had no interest in her. She hadn't seen anything. She had just been in the wrong place at the wrong time. But since Timothy was going to get to live happily because of the evening, she couldn't really regret it.

As she curled up in her own bed, she found herself thinking about Dillon Wolf. She'd been intrigued by him, attracted to him, when he had just been standing there. That he had reappeared in time to help her up from the table was her own little minor miracle.

Why the hell hadn't she let him drive her home?

Because there would have been no point, she told herself. She didn't even have time to date. She was responsible for Timothy, for one thing, and she didn't mind that. Not at all. He had always been there for her, so it made her happy that now she could be there for him. And now she was so accustomed to working, trying to catch whatever overtime came along, that she barely remembered dating, much less having a relationship, and she wouldn't know how to date anymore, anyway, even if the opportunity presented itself.

It had been nice to touch him, though. To be touched. To feel the fabric of his jacket. To . . .

She closed her eyes.

And allowed herself to dream about the man named Wolf.

But in the middle of the dream, just as Dillon Wolf was smiling at her, things suddenly changed. She was at the table again, and everything seemed to shrink away. She turned, and Tanner Green was stumbling toward her. Straight at her. She could almost feel his crushing weight against her again.

See his eyes staring into hers just before the light of life faded from them for good.

She saw his mouth moving, and once again heard the word he had whispered.

Indigo.

She woke with a start. It was still night, and the darkness seemed to press down on her. She was suddenly certain that something was there with her, hidden in the shadows, that she was being watched.

She leaped out of bed and dived for her light switch. The room jumped into view, and she blinked against the sudden harshness, tense, her body ready to spring.

But there was no one there. The room was empty.

She felt foolish, but she went into her bathroom, took the bloodied, discarded clothing and carried it into the kitchen, where she placed it in a larger trash bag, which she hauled out into the garage. She knew it was silly, but she wanted that reminder of the evening as far away as she could get it. Then she went back to bed, where she turned on her small bedroom TV and didn't turn off the light.

It occurred to her then that no one had asked her if the dying man had said anything.

And so she was the only one who knew that he had spoken that single word.

Indigo.

Emil Landon was a man of an indeterminate age; he might have been a worn thirtysomething, or a fit man in his fifties. Because Adam Harrison—owner and director of Harrison Investigations, the rather unique private investigations firm that was Dillon's actual employer——had contacts with access to just about any record on any human being living in the United States and beyond, he knew that Landon was forty-eight, had married and divorced three wives, had fathered one child who lived in Dublin with his mother, and had inherited millions from a grandfather who had been a Turkish oil baron. Sound real-estate investments had added to those millions. He liked to be a player. He liked the clothing and the cars, and the women who followed the call of big money. But he wasn't a lucky gambler himself, so he'd discovered a way to profit from the propensity of most men to count on luck's eventual appearance, gamble—and lose. He'd opened his own casino and was in the process of negotiations to create more gambling meccas, something of a sore point in the community. On his mother's side, he could provide the proper court-required documents to prove that he was one thirty-second Paiute—in fact, he only needed to be one sixty-fourth—which gave him the right to build casinos on Indian land, where he would no doubt see to it that the proceeds of his venture stayed in his pockets and didn't reach the Indian nation that should benefit from it.

Dillon hadn't followed much of the legal process; he had seen it far too often already. He didn't think much of Emil Landon, and he still wasn't sure why a man as moral as Adam Harrison had wanted him to take the case.

Dillon knew plenty of wealthy people who were also extremely responsible with their money and were courteous to those around them, no matter what their financial or social status.

Emil Landon wasn't one of them.

Now Landon was convinced that someone was trying to kill him, and Dillon figured that the man had been a jerk to enough people during his life that there might easily be several who found the thought of killing him appealing. But that was the thing. Most people *thought* about killing someone but didn't actually take steps to do it. Revenge was frequently savored sweetly in the mind. Most people had a conscience, and even if they didn't, they didn't have the means to commit the perfect murder, and they sure as hell didn't want to get caught and spend the rest of their lives in prison. Of course, with enough money, murder for hire was always a possibility. And if a crack assassin couldn't be found, there was usually some dope addict around, willing to take a life for a few thousand—or a few hits. But dope addicts weren't playing with all their cards, and such an attempt usually ended with a dead dope addict.

Tonight Dillon had been checking out the casinos, seeing who was in town and had the right money and connections to order a hit, along with a real bone to pick with Emil Landon. He still wasn't certain that Landon was even in any real danger. During his first consultation with the man, Landon had told him that he'd been having dreams about being murdered. Gunned down in his own casino, stabbed in his own bed. He was certain he was being followed, though he had no proof of it.

He had hired two of the best-known bodyguards in Las Vegas, Hugo Blythe and Tanner Green. Though now only Hugo Blythe was left, and he lived in a penthouse high atop the Big Easy, where the casino security staff—bonded and put through a screening process that would have done the CIA proud—was always on guard at both the penthouse elevators and the actual door to his suite.

When Dillon arrived, Landon was wearing a designer leopard-print robe and was surrounded by his secretary—a blonde with breast implants the size of Texas—his chief security officer and Hugo Blythe.

And he was in a state.

Pacing, he barely paused to glare at Dillon when he entered, then launched right into a tirade. "I told you I was in danger. I could tell you didn't believe me. But now Tanner Green is dead, and it's a warning to me. A message that the killer can pick off people around me so I don't have anyone to depend on. How the hell was he killed right in front of you?" He paused in his pacing to stare accusingly at Dillon.

Dillon just shook his head disdainfully.

"He wasn't killed right in front of me, he was stabbed outside the casino. And there are dozens of security cameras focused on the area, so hopefully the cops will find something on one of the tapes. My theory is that he was stabbed inside a car, then thrown out at the entry. From there, he staggered inside before dying. I suggest checking his phone records and his movements over the last few days to see who might have gotten him into that car and under what pretense. Of course, there's still the possibility that he was killed for something he did in his past, or just because he pissed off the wrong person."

Landon frowned at him, shaking his head. "I told you, someone is after me."

"Yes, you told me that, but have you told me everything I need to know?" Dillon asked. He wasn't expecting a real answer from Landon. The man had been cagey from the start. There was no doubt that his activities hadn't been totally legit through the years, and he seemed to have a hidden agenda, as well, maybe pertaining to the casino on tribal land. Still, asking him questions, even if Dillon didn't expect real answers, might provide some bit of information he needed.

"What the hell are you talking about?" Landon demanded impatiently. "Someone is trying to kill me. What more do you need to know?"

"I need to know all the possible *whys*," Dillon

said. "I need you to be honest with me, to think really hard about any business deal that might have gone sour, any affair that might have ended badly. I need to know any possible reason why someone with the resources to have you killed might want you dead."

"I *am* being honest with you. Sure, I have enemies." Landon's eyes narrowed. "There are some radical members of certain Indian tribes who don't get the fact that my casinos could provide jobs for a lot of people. Any rich man has enemies. You know that. But this . . . shit! Tanner Green? He was a pro."

The quadruple-D blonde came over to Dillon with a tray of shot glasses filled with assorted liquors. "Drink, Mr. Wolf?"

He shook his head. "Thanks, no."

"Mr. Wolf, I'm going to be on duty twenty-four hours a day now," Hugo Blythe said earnestly. "I'll be following Mr. Landon every step he takes. But we've got to figure out who's trying to kill Mr. Landon, and take care of him."

"I'm not an assassin," Dillon said sharply. "Anyway, the police are on this now."

"The police?" Landon exclaimed derisively, then suggested what the police could do with themselves.

Dillon rose. "I should be seeing those tapes first thing in the morning. I'll call you after I've seen them."

"You've got to do something, and you've got to do it quickly," Landon said.

"I can still use more help from you," Dillon said.

Landon looked as if he wanted to explode at Dillon again, but though he wasn't a genius, he wasn't stupid, either. "I'll think back and come up with whatever I can," he acknowledged.

Dillon left. As he rode down on Landon's private elevator and strode out onto the main casino floor, he appreciated the fact that Landon had found the right business managers and builders. The Big Easy was going to do well. He wasn't too sure that he would choose Vegas for a family vacation himself, but plenty of people did, and Landon had made sure to cater to them as well as the hard-core gamblers. The Big Easy offered an entire floor of arcades, character restaurants, toddler rides and one huge roller coaster. There was a Western show aimed just at kids and a room reserved for "young'uns'" birthday parties.

As he headed over to the elevators to the parking garage, his eye was caught by an advertisement for the party room. It showed two Old West gunslingers with a pretty saloon maid between them. The picture was pure PG, but the face of the woman grabbed his attention and stabbed oddly at his heart.

It was Jessy Sparhawk. Smiling, her beautiful red hair twisted up on her head and topped with a saloon-girl hat. The costume she was wearing was almost prim, and yet he didn't think he'd ever seen a picture of such an arresting woman.

He headed down to the parking lot, his mind still full of Jessy, so lost in thought that it took him a moment to recognize the presence at his side.

"Brilliant, just brilliant," Ringo said, keeping pace with Dillon Wolf's strong and determined walk. The folds of his long railway jacket made a slight rustling sound, but nothing compared to his spurs ringing against the ground.

Every now and then Dillon saw a head turn. Someone out there, someone who couldn't quite see Ringo, was still aware that something, some*one*, was in the area. They heard the sound of his passing on some distant level.

"What?" Dillon asked impatiently.

Ringo cleared his throat. "The most beautiful creature in the world holds court at the craps table, I perform amazing tricks—and you let her get away. Brilliant. I may be deceased, but *you're* the one who's really dead, my friend."

"Excuse me, *my friend*," Dillon said. "But I have work to do. Tanner Green was murdered and Emil Landon is getting restless—and working for the man, I might remind you, is something *you* pushed me into."

Ringo ignored him and stuck with his original topic. "I saw the way you smiled at her. Take a minute to smell the roses or you'll be dead a whole hell of a lot sooner than you think," he said knowingly.

"The way I hear it, you stopped to smell the roses and wound up smelling a dung heap," Dillon said curtly.

"Ouch! Not kind at all," Ringo said. "And may I remind you, I died because I was caught up in someone's grudge against one of *your* ancestors."

"Ringo, I'm sorry, but that was more than a hundred years ago, and there's not a damn thing I can do about it now. I'm sure he appreciated your help."

"Probably. I was good back then. Damn good."

A woman walked by, frowning nervously as she stared at him. He lowered his head, wincing. Usually Ringo refrained from speaking to him when they were in public, because usually he didn't reply. What the hell was up with him tonight? A man had been killed, of course. But it went beyond that. Something felt off. Felt . . .

Felt urgent.

It was as if he was facing the onset of something critical. Something that might end in death.

"You *are* going to ask her out, right?" Ringo said.

"I tried to drive her home. She isn't interested."

"A man had just died on top of her. You need to give it another go."

"Look, Ringo, you and Adam got me into this mess with Emil Landon, so let's deal with that first, huh?" He put aside the fact that Jessy Sparhawk had affected him more deeply than he could possibly have expected, but there had just been something about her. She wasn't some hustler hanging on to the money men, wasn't a wild-eyed party child out to prove the truth of the slogan "What happens in Vegas, stays in Vegas." She was different. She lived here, worked here. She knew the city. Knew the pitfalls to be found in a place where every business in town was out to separate you from your money.

So it was interesting that she had been playing high-stakes craps.

"Are you paying *any* attention to me?" Ringo demanded.

He felt himself flushing, because the fact was, he was completely intrigued by the woman. So why was he embarrassed around Ringo? Maybe precisely because he *was* so fascinated by her. But his life didn't allow for emotional intimacy, at least right now, and business had to come first. "Ringo, I'm looking for a killer. Don't you think I ought to find out what the hell is going on before I drag someone else into my life?"

Ringo didn't have an answer for that. He followed Dillon to his car, seeping through the passenger door, though he could have opened it. He sat silently throughout the ride to Dillon's house, just on the outskirts of the Strip.

Clancy, Dillon's huge Belgian shepherd, was

wagging her tail at the door. She knew Ringo was there. At first she had hated him. She had barked up a storm whenever he was around, and it had all but driven Dillon crazy. But then, to his huge relief, she hadn't just accepted Ringo's ghostly presence, she had decided that she liked him. And when Dillon could get Ringo to stay home, rather than trailing after him, he was great, letting the dog in and out, and playing with her.

"So what now?" Ringo asked. "Shouldn't we be off somewhere, doing something?"

"I don't know what *you're* doing, but *I'm* getting some sleep."

Ringo cursed as Dillon headed for his room. Feeling completely worn-out, he stripped down and slipped between the sheets. They were into the wee hours of the morning, and he wanted a nap, at least, before heading to the police station.

But instead he lay awake. And when he closed his eyes, he could hear the drums of his childhood. He could hear the chants, see the warriors in the circle at the dance. A Paiute chief had been the one to develop the Ghost Dance, which had been picked up by many western tribes. The chief had envisioned casting the white men from the land, leading to a return of tribal power.

It hadn't happened. Not by a long shot.

He'd been to dozens of Ghost Dances as a child, but he'd never seen a single ghost at any of them. It had been at his parents' funeral, when he'd been a bitter young idiot, that he'd first seen the maiden in white.

It was rumored among the Indian nations that she was the guardian of the white buffalo, a mythical heroine who knew the hearts and minds of both the living and the dead. She was beautiful and wise, and she could read a man's soul.

She had never been anything but a myth to him, a beautiful story told by his people.

Until that day at the funeral, when he looked up and she was just . . . there. She couldn't be real, he had told himself. She was a figment of his imagination, dredged up by the pain in his heart, and the fury against God and fate that burned so savagely inside him.

She had stared at him across the open graves. Then, later, when he'd been about to get involved in an idiotic fight at the bar, she had stepped in between him and the man he had intentionally insulted. Apparently he'd wanted to get his face smashed in, had wanted to feel the physical pain to ease the deeper pain that tore at his soul.

But she had stopped him. He had felt her hand on his shoulder, and when he'd turned to face her, her eyes had locked with his and she had whispered, "No, this is not the way. Only time and the true path to peace will ease the bleeding in the soul."

And ever since then . . .

Ever since then he'd seen the dead.

Usually they just passed through his life because

they needed something, and once they got it, they moved on. He'd learned that through Adam Harrison and Harrison Investigations. Adam had taken him and turned him from a rebellious and bitter half-breed to a man with a calling. Adam had taught him about life and death, and how to value himself as a human being.

He owed Adam. Not only that, he liked the man.

So the ghosts came, he helped them . . .

And the ghosts left.

Except for Ringo Murphy. The problem was, Ringo himself didn't know why he was sticking around.

He'd lived by the gun, and then he'd died by it, and there had been nothing in his life or death to indicate why he was still here.

Dillon shifted around, longing for even an hour's sleep.

He closed his eyes tightly.

And then, in that state between wakefulness and sleep, in a netherworld between conscious thought and oblivion, he saw the maiden, felt her gentle hand on his face.

"Yes," she whispered to him. "It is the beginning, the beginning—and the end."

3

"I see them dancing in the sky," Timothy told Jessy.

She was driving him back to the home, and she felt torn. Worried about leaving him alone, she'd had Sandra come over to watch him this morning while she'd returned to the casino to turn her chips into cash—later exchanged for a cashier's check made out to the home—and fill out the IRS forms. She'd never had to fill them out before, because her winnings—the few times she'd played a few dollars for fun—had never been close to enough to report to the government.

She didn't mind. The government was welcome to its share.

She was concerned now because she had to work that afternoon, and even her sizable winnings weren't enough to keep her job from being very important to her ongoing well-being. But Sandra had met her at the door when she'd returned and suggested she might want to talk to someone at the home before she left Timothy there.

"Why?" she'd asked.

"Maybe it's not as bad as I think, but . . ." Sandra hesitated. "He's having conversations with imaginary people. And when I asked him who he was talking to, he gave me a sly look and said they were people in the walls, and that they were his friends and they made him happy, so I shouldn't worry. And maybe, if he's happy . . ."

Now it seemed that his friends were in the sky.

Maybe she was just nervous because she'd woken up in the night, certain that someone was watching her again. That kind of feeling usually vanished with the coming of day, though, and this time it hadn't. . . . This morning, as she'd been brewing coffee and tossing raisin bread into the toaster, she'd paused again, feeling eyes on her before telling herself that you couldn't feel someone watching you. Except that you *could.* Somehow people knew when they were being observed. Maybe it had to do with that huge part of the brain scientists said went unused.

But there hadn't been anyone there. Not last night, and not this morning.

But this morning Timothy had been talking to people in the walls, and now he was seeing dancers in the sky.

Which one of us is actually going crazy here? she asked herself.

The Hawthorne Home was just outside Las Vegas proper. She parked in front of the administration building, and Timothy frowned. She usually parked by Building A, his building, when she was bringing him back from a visit or an outing.

"I have to go in and pay Mr. Hoskins," she told him.

"Pay him?" Timothy asked indignantly.

She patted his hand. "Yeah, that's life, Timothy," she said, and leaned over to kiss his cheek. Once upon a time he'd been the best guardian in the world, and she still loved him so much.

"We all have to pay the rent, you know," she said.

"Not in the day of the ghost dancers," he said.

"Maybe, but that was a long time ago. And there's no such thing as ghosts, anyway," she added.

"But if there *were,*" Timothy said, cracking a dry grin, "they wouldn't have to pay rent, would they? They'd just phase in, and phase out, huh?"

She was pleased by the pleasure Timothy took in his small joke. "I'm not so sure this would have been reservation land," she said, grinning back. She started to tell him to wait in the car while she went inside to pay, then thought better of it. He still knew how to drive. His imaginary friends might suggest that he needed to run over to a convenience store for something.

"Why don't you come in with me," she suggested.

"I suppose that idiot Mr. Hoskins will be there?" he asked tartly.

She almost laughed aloud at his indignation. He was half Lakota, which had given him straight black hair—faded to white now—but those genes hadn't reached his eyes. They were blue. He was still a handsome man, she thought, when he was

65

standing straight and proud, as he was now, his face set in firm lines.

"Yes, I need to see him. And don't say anything rude to him, okay? At least we only have to see him once a month or so. . . ."

"I'll be perfectly courteous," he assured her.

She wasn't at all certain about that. Hoskins was a man who didn't just find himself uncomfortable around the aged, he flat out didn't like them, and he let it show—which made her wonder why he'd taken this job to begin with. Well, like all people, he would get there soon enough, she thought. Or maybe he wouldn't. There was always that alternative. But she hoped he would lead a long life, until one day he needed care himself, only to discover that the younger generation wanted nothing to do with *him*.

They got out of the car, and she linked arms with him as they walked inside together. The receptionist was pretty and young, and she looked at Jessy with surprise. "Miss Sparhawk! Good morning. We thought perhaps you'd decided to keep your grandfather at home with you. We . . . we weren't expecting to see you."

"Oh? Why not? I always enjoy having Timothy at home for a visit—" she turned to smile at him "—but it wouldn't be practical for him to live with me, seeing as I have to work. I've brought the rent for the next few months," she added, giving the other woman a saccharine smile.

"Oh. Well, if you'll just excuse me . . . I'll get Mr. Hoskins," the girl said.

She didn't ring his office, she jumped up and went in. A moment later Hoskins appeared, frowning. "Miss Sparhawk, Mr. Sparhawk. I hadn't expected to see you. I was assuming that you'd be making other arrangements today."

"Well, as you can see, we're not. I'll be taking Timothy back to his room now," she said, handing him a cashier's check.

He stared at her as if she were a ghost herself. "He was paid up through today," Jessy said. "Now he's paid up for the next three months. Everything is in perfect order, contractually speaking."

She didn't know why Hoskins looked so distressed, and she didn't care.

"Good day, Mr. Hoskins," Timothy said, then turned to head out. Jessy said her own rather more triumphant goodbye, and followed him.

As they walked back to the car, Jessy saw a luxury sedan pull up a few spaces away. A young guy got out, then went around to help an elderly man from the passenger side, and the reason for Hoskins's white face became suddenly clear. He'd been all set to rent Timothy's room to someone else. She laughed as she and her grandfather got back into the car, sharing the joke as she drove over to his building.

They checked in downstairs with the young male orderly on desk duty during the day—every building had someone at the entry day and night since they weren't taking any chances with wandering seniors—and headed up to Timothy's room. In the upstairs hallway they ran into another orderly, Jimmy Britin, a tall African-American with a wide smile. "Timothy, Jessy," he said, his surprised pleasure evident.

"Hoskins was about to rent my room right out from right under me," Timothy said. "But he underestimated my granddaughter. And the ghosts, of course."

"Well . . ." Jimmy said, obviously unsurprised by what Timothy had said. He looked at Jessy, a question in eyes. *What did you do? Rob a bank?*

As Timothy headed straight for his room, Jessy smiled ruefully at Jimmy. "I don't know about any ghosts, but someone must have been looking out for me. I won a small fortune at the craps table."

"That's wonderful," Jimmy told her.

"I never gamble, but . . ." She shook her head, as if puzzled by the whole thing.

"You were desperate. And you got lucky," Jimmy said.

"Listen, I've got to get to work," she told him.

"No sweat. I'll get him situated. And stop looking so guilty. You take him home lots of weekends. Meanwhile, I'm here, and Liz Freeze, his favorite nurse, is on today, too. He'll be fine. Now out of here."

"I just wanted to let you know, he's . . ."

"He's what?" Jimmy asked.

"He's hallucinating. A lot. About ghosts. They're in the walls, in the sky. . . . He even talks to them."

"Nothing I haven't seen before. It'll be okay, I promise," he said, giving her a reassuring pat on the shoulder.

"Thanks, Jimmy."

With a grateful smile, she hurried into Timothy's room and gave him a kiss on the cheek. "I'm off to work now, okay?"

He nodded gravely. "Don't worry. The ghosts are busy dancing in the sky. Things are going to be all right."

"Of course they are," she said, then gave him another kiss and hurried out. Glancing at her watch, she realized she was going to be a bit rushed getting into costume, but she would manage. Things will be all right, she told herself. She had the routine down pat.

She hurried back down to her car, but before she unlocked it, she paused and looked around, certain that someone was watching her again, but she couldn't see anybody.

She checked the backseat.

No one.

She looked around one last time, then gave herself a mental shake and told herself to stop being ridiculous. It was a bright, sunny day. If anyone was watching her, it was Hoskins, no doubt ruing the fact that she had made the payment, so he couldn't rent Timothy's room to someone else—probably at a higher rate.

But the sensation of being watched followed her as she wove through traffic and all the way into the casino.

It was almost as if someone were sitting right next to her in the car.

"See? Two cameras, but notice the range," Jerry Cheever told Dillon. "There's Tanner Green, though it's difficult to see him because there were a dozen other cars in the entryway at the same time. It looks as if he got out of a white limo. Can't see the plate, though, and there must be a hundred of those things in town," he said in frustration. "And Green looks like half the other drunks coming out of the woodwork at that time of night. He staggers there—" Cheever pointed at the screen "—but the guy ahead of him just shoves him away. See his look? Probably just thought it was a drunk falling on him. Then watch Green moving through the crowd. Everyone is talking to someone, no one is paying him the least bit of attention. Not even the doorman. He's just holding the door open and watching that brunette with the huge tits, completely oblivious to everything else, even the guy with the knife in his back. Okay, right here he's picked up on a new camera. . . ." Cheever's voice trailed off as he flicked the remote control, shifting to a scene in the casino. "He passed six cameras on his way to the craps table, but all you can see on any of them is him stumbling through the crowd—until he bumps into Miss Sparhawk and they both land on the craps table. And there you are, helping her back up."

Cheever was discouraged; his frustration that so many security tapes could yield so few clues was evident in his voice.

"I'd like to run through them all again, if it's all right," Dillon told him.

"Be my guest. I've been staring at them for the last three hours. I had a video tech in here trying to home in on Green, but it didn't help. Someone's head, an arm, whatever, is blocking part of the view every step he took."

Cheever tossed the remote to Dillon, who studied it for a moment, then hit a button to start the tape over. "It's almost as if someone knew that outer drive was just out of the cameras' useful range," he mused.

"Just like," Cheever agreed. "So what do you think it means?"

"I think it means our killer has to be someone involved with the casino, or who knows someone who is."

"God only knows how many people that could be," Cheever muttered.

Dillon turned in his chair and looked at Cheever, who was perched at the edge of his desk. "What's happening with the knife?"

"The lab has it. But preliminary reports aren't giving us a thing. It's a short-bladed work knife, sold—literally—in the thousands here in town. It's a popular blade for breaking the plastic bands on stacks of money. Every casino in Vegas has a few of them. And of course there's not a hint of a fingerprint on the hilt. The killer probably wore gloves. Green was stabbed with considerable force, and the blade was just long enough to pierce the heart, which caused Green to bleed out. Because it was a short blade, he made it through to the craps table before he died."

"Strange," Dillon said, rewinding the tape. "Any possibility I could get a vid tech in here to look at this with me?" he asked.

Jerry Cheever stared at him, his eyes narrowing, as if his first instinct was to defensively tell him to go right to hell. But then he shrugged. "Sure. If you can find something I didn't, that will be great. I'll go grab someone."

The minute he left the office, Dillon was out of his seat, looking at the files on Cheever's desk. Tanner Green's was right on top. He leafed through it quickly, but Cheever had nothing more than he had said.

A minute later a young woman from the video department came in and introduced herself as Sarah Clay. She had a controller with her that made the remote look like a kiddie toy. Dillon started with the first tape, and they went through it frame by frame, but Cheever had been telling the truth. It wasn't that the security equipment wasn't high quality, because it was the best. But the car from which Tanner Green had been expelled was just far enough out of range, of both the cameras and the neon lights, that making out details was impossible.

A white limo. That much was obvious, and also useless. As Cheever had said, Vegas was thick with the things, especially white ones. Every casino owned limos, the casino bosses owned limos, the rental companies owned limos, even half the high rollers in town had their own.

There was no way to tell the make or model, but even once the tapes were enhanced, there didn't seem to be any markings on it, nothing to indicate where it might have come from, which didn't help him now but might mean something when they moved on to the process of elimination.

They went through the other tapes in order, with Dillon asking the tech to freeze certain frames and enhance them, but once again, Jerry Cheever had been dead-on. The crowd in the casino that night had worked heavily against them. The best video tech in the world couldn't remove a body blocking a body, and even though the different angles caught by the different cameras usually helped with that kind of problem, this time they were shit out of luck.

"Are we through?" Sarah asked him politely, glancing at her watch.

73

He knew she probably had a half-dozen other cases she was supposed to be working on, so he smiled. "Just about, and thank you. The last tape . . . could I see it one more time?"

"Sure," she said, but her voice was faint.

He let the tape run until he got to Green staggering up to the craps table, then had her home in on Tanner Green falling forward, pinning Jessy Sparhawk beneath him. Even caught in a moment of pure surprise and horror, she was striking. He had to wonder about that last name. She was a redhead, with huge blue eyes, and he found himself fascinated with her all over again.

"Mr. Wolf?" Sarah asked politely.

He gave himself a mental shake. "Zoom in on Green's face for me, will you?"

She pushed a button, and in seconds Tanner Green's bulging eyes filled the screen.

Hell, the man was dying.

But his expression was surprised, as if he couldn't believe it. Believe he was dying? Or *how* he was dying? Dillon wondered.

Green's lips moved slightly. Dillon replayed the moment and leaned in, trying to discern what the man had been saying. Nothing, maybe. Or maybe he had been begging for help. Maybe he had found God at the moment of death and was praying.

Dillon had Sarah widen the view and surveyed the immediate area. The air had been filled with a cloud of smoke, despite the casino's expensive air filters. Sometimes it seemed as if even people who didn't smoke decided they needed to in Vegas.

He stared intently at the screen for a minute longer.

Then he sat back. "Thanks very much, Sarah."

She might have been aggravated at the time she'd been asked to give him, but she smiled. She probably didn't often get thanked for what was, after all, just her job.

"Sure. Anytime," she told him.

"I mean it." She reached into her shirt pocket and produced a card. Her name and rank were on it, along with a phone number and an e-mail address. "I've heard about you, about what you do, what you . . . see. They say you're the real deal. I meant what I said. Whatever you need—what*ever*—you can call me."

He took her card, nodding gravely. "Now *that,* I really appreciate." He left her feeling very grateful indeed.

She had pretty much just told him that she would work for him on the q.t. That was priceless.

But right now he had to find Jessy Sparhawk. She was the only one who might know what Tanner Green had said right before he died.

There had been a recent period in Vegas's history when—the tourist board had decided to turn Sin City into a family-friendly resort. The plan hadn't worked, and the city had soon reverted to its old image, but the aftereffects lingered, and some parents still brought their children along when they came to gamble. As a result, a lot of the casinos provided diversions aimed toward the kiddie set, because the problem with Vegas was that parents could be distracted—maybe only momentarily, but still with frightening repercussions—by bright, blinking lights and a sudden insistence that the next dollar shoved into a beckoning slot machine would be the one that hit the jackpot.

At the Big Easy the problem had been solved by offering an afternoon of pirate-themed entertainment, food and drink for the younger crowd.

It was glorified babysitting.

But Jessy had never minded that. She liked kids. Sure, every once in a while they wound up with an obnoxious little twerp who wouldn't stop tugging on beards, dumping the treasure chest or trying to look up the skirts of the pirate "queens" or the servers. But all in all, it wasn't a bad gig. It was actually a lot better than performing at a bachelor party for a bunch of drunks who seemed to think that anyone under thirty and wearing a skimpy costume was for sale.

In contrast, working the babysitting detail was usually fun, and that day it was going very well.

They had almost three hundred kids, some of them there gratis for guests of the casino, others had been enrolled at a steep price tag by parents staying elsewhere, though compared to the hundreds—even thousands—that could be dropped at one of the gaming tables or in slot machines in a matter of minutes, it was still small change.

The audience ranged from age two up to twenty-one. The older kids were usually there because they had younger siblings—and because eighteen-to twenty-one-year-olds still couldn't legally step out onto on the casino floor or drink.

The show itself was mostly improvisational banter punctuated by carefully choreographed dance numbers. The cast played pirates who had somehow wound up stuck on Lake Mead, and they sang traditional pirate songs as they searched for treasure.

It was when the kids were shouting, trying to point out to her rather ditsy pirate queen that the treasure chest was right beneath her nose, and she was spinning around searching, that she saw him.

He was standing just outside the room, leaning against a wall painted with a mural of the high seas and pirate ships flying the Jolly Roger, and he was staring through the glass wall that surrounded the theater space, watching her. He was wearing a suit, and he somehow managed to look both real and not real . . .

He wasn't even a foot away from Grant Willow, one of the four security men—all of them highly skilled but able to relate to the kids without intimidating them—who took turns standing watch in the vestibule, and he seemed totally oblivious to the other man.

She knew the watcher's face. She had stared at that face in the most uncomfortable circumstances imaginable. He couldn't possibly be there—and yet he was.

She blinked.

And then he wasn't.

She must have come to a dead halt, stunned, because Aaron Beaton, playing the role of Captain Gray-specked Blackbeard, started prompting her. "Bonny Anne, Bonny Anne, have ye found it? Have ye found me treasure?"

She stared at him without any idea how to respond as her blood grew cold.

He hadn't been real.

She had simply conjured him up in her mind's eye.

Or he *had* been real, just someone else. Someone who only *looked* like a dead man.

After all, a man had died on top of her last night; she had a right to be traumatized. To be seeing things. There was nothing odd about it at all.

"Bonny Anne?" Aaron said sharply.

"*Your* treasure? *My* treasure!" she insisted, dragging herself back into character.

Her declaration started a mock battle that was really a carefully choreographed dance piece. She battled gamely, whirled and jumped, then looked back to the doorway and almost missed a beat.

He was back.

And he was watching her with huge eyes and an expression filled with both tragedy and remorse.

Since the promo poster Dillon had seen the night before pictured Jessy Sparhawk, it was a reasonable assumption that if he headed to the Big Easy she was likely to be working.

She was.

The pirate party was scheduled daily from one to six, giving the parents a full afternoon of worry-free gambling. Dillon wondered how many of them forgot to come back at closing time, but he assumed the casino had a plan for dealing with that.

The theater was surrounded by glass walls, and the outer vestibule was decorated with pirate paraphernalia and wall paintings. Inside the room, the stage held an impressive pirate ship that seemed to float above shimmering blue water, an effect caused by lighting under a glass stage floor. There were interactive areas for the kids, and each seating section sported a different-colored pirate flag, dividing the kids into teams so they could root for their color-matched "champions" onstage. There were huge treasure chests around the room that held soda, candy and chips, along with healthier soy snacks and natural iced teas. It was a top-quality production, designed to appeal to kids of all ages—along with the occasional adult he saw in the audience. He noted that the smaller children were together in one area, and there seemed to be at least three employees wearing pirate-themed casino uniforms to attend to every nine or ten children.

Onstage, the pirates were going at it.

He recognized Jessy right away, despite her wig and makeup and pirate attire. The kids were shouting to her, laughing, and even the almost adults in the room were having fun and shouting right along with everyone else for her to find the treasure.

Then she froze. Just . . . froze, staring at the doorway.

It was only for the blink of an eye; then she jerked her gaze away and responded to one of the male actors. A sword battle ensued, then somehow turned into a dance.

Then, once again, Jessy Sparhawk froze.

Dillon felt a tap on his shoulder and thought it might be the big security guard who was keeping an eagle eye on the room.

But it wasn't. Ringo was at his side.

"Over there," Ringo said quietly.

Across the lobby, standing near the guard, stood another man. A big man in a suit.

Tanner Green.

Dillon started toward him, moving quickly but casually, keeping his eyes focused on the guard, as if he was just going over to ask him a question about the show.

But Tanner Green sensed him, and he was having none of it. He turned and stared hard at Dillon.

And then he disappeared, fading like mist taken by a sudden wind.

"You scared him!" Ringo said accusingly.

Inwardly, Dillon cursed himself. He should have watched the man a while longer. He should have been patient. But if Tanner Green was walking around in some spiritual limbo, it was imperative for Dillon to reach him. Speak with him.

And he had moved without menace. This was one spooked ghost—no pun intended, he thought with a grin.

The guard looked at him and nodded, mistaking him for a parent. "Kids will be out in a little while, maybe twenty minutes or so. A lot of them hang around to get their pictures taken with the cast."

"Thanks," Dillon said, turning away from the guard and putting his hand up to his face as if rubbing his chin, so he could speak softly to Ringo without being overheard.

"Why was he so frightened of me?" he asked.

"Duh. The man was murdered," Ringo pointed out, as if pointing out the obvious to a three-year-old.

Irritated, Dillon chose not to respond to his ghostly companion's sarcasm. Ringo might be from the Old West, but he had adopted the modern vernacular with enthusiasm, as if that somehow made him more a part of the earthly world.

"Maybe he was afraid of *you,* then," Dillon asked. "You're the one carrying a gun."

"That actually makes sense," Ringo admitted. "He probably hasn't seen many other ghosts, and, if he has . . . well, I guess an old gunslinger might be a bit too much for him to handle. And he probably doesn't want to believe that he's dead, either. Probably hasn't accepted it yet."

Whatever the cause, Tanner Green was scared.

Even so, he had come out in the open to stare at Jessy Sparhawk, the woman he had been lying on top of as he breathed his last.

And she had seen him. Dillon would swear to it.

The play finished and the kids rushed the stage. The performers posed for pictures, laughing, talking, signing miniposters that seemed to come out of nowhere. He watched Jessy pick up a toddler for a photo, then talk to the little girl and sign a poster. She seemed totally at ease—until she glanced back toward the door and an uneasy look crossed her face.

Then she saw Dillon and was visibly startled. After that she looked . . . frightened, rattled, though she continued to smile as she interacted with the kids.

He waved to her at one point, and she waved back.

The security guard with the broad shoulders and pleasant smile walked over to him. "You a friend of Jessy's?" the man asked. "Not just a waiting parent?"

"No," Dillon told him, shaking his head. "And yes, I'm a . . . friend of Jessy's."

"You can go on in if you want," the guard said.

"Thanks," Dillon said and headed toward the stage, Ringo still at his side.

He noticed a woman turn around as they passed, a puzzled look on her face. She drew her sweater more closely around her, as if she had suddenly felt a chill. That was the way it was for most people. They didn't see the dead, couldn't communicate with them, but something inside told them that someone was there.

Dillon smiled at the woman and kept going, hoping Ringo wasn't feeling mischievous and wouldn't tease her with a tap on the shoulder or a tug at her skirt. He moved quickly, because if you weren't looking, Ringo wasn't as prone to act up.

Jessy was still onstage, posing with the last of the kids.

She looked at him over the head of a toddler, and he sensed she wasn't all that pleased to see him. But she was in performance mode, so she forced a smile to her lips.

"Very impressive," he told her, reaching the stage. He saw her fellow cast members glancing his way and whispering to one another. He was being assessed, he knew.

"What a surprise to see you here," she said.

He decided not to mince words. "I need to speak with you."

"Oh? This isn't a great time. I have to get out of costume, check my schedule for the next few days."

"I'll wait."

She glanced away, biting her lip. She might be a good performer, but she was a lousy liar. She didn't have a good excuse for refusing to talk to him, and she wasn't going to invent one.

"I'm not having a great day," she said. "I'm really tired."

"I won't take much of your time. And you have to eat, right? Why not let me take you to the fast-food establishment of your choice, and then I'll leave you alone, I promise."

She let out an uneasy sigh and gave in. "Sure. I need about half an hour."

"Thanks. I really appreciate it," he told her.

She nodded curtly, and he couldn't help thinking that she made a gorgeous pirate. Her costume wasn't risqué, but her breasts rode appealingly in the cotton blouse above the top of a leather corset. Her skirt was long, but slit up one side for dancing. Her stage makeup was heavy and came complete with false eyelashes, but even so, up close, she was stunning.

And she was afraid.

He forced himself to take a step back. She was a bit *too* appealing, and he had to concentrate if he wanted to get to the truth behind Tanner Green's death. And he just knew she wasn't going to be receptive to anything he had to say. Most likely, given that he had been there last night, his very presence was probably anathema to her already.

And things weren't going to get better.

"I'll meet you at Chen's. It's just down the Strip," she said.

"Thanks," he told her again. "I'll see you there."

He watched her head backstage. Right before she left, she looked back—and not at him.

Then she shuddered—as if she'd seen a ghost—and disappeared behind a black velvet drape.

4

There was an incredibly simple answer to what was plaguing her, of course. She was simply seeing someone who looked like Tanner Green. It wasn't as if she actually knew the man and could be sure it was him.

Bull.

She knew his face, and that was all that mattered.

That face was etched in her mind. She would never forget it. She had been looking into his eyes as he died.

Key words. *He had died.*

Maybe she had been listening to Timothy too much, and now she was seeing dead people just as he saw ghost dancers in the sky.

She winced as she sat down at her dressing table. Why on earth had she agreed to see Dillon Wolf?

She didn't want to, and she didn't really understand why. The man was attractive, courteous, charming and, well, *hot*, as Sandra would have put it.

But . . .

He was somehow connected to the extremely odd visions she was having. How or why, she didn't know. Everything was tied up in feelings of fear and unease, and she didn't like feeling this way at all. At least the cops were leaving her alone; they evidently knew that she'd had nothing to do with Tanner Green's death other than being in the wrong place at the wrong time.

She reached for a makeup-remover pad and set to work. With her makeup gone, she looked young. And afraid. Hell, she *was* afraid. And she really hated that.

"Who's the hottie?" April Brandon, one of her fellow pirates, asked, grinning.

"Pardon?"

"Tall, dark and super cool," April said, sliding into her own chair in front of the long mirror.

"Oh, just a friend. No, not a friend. Not really."

"An enemy?" April teased.

"No, no, I mean, I just met him."

"Oh. Well, if you decide not to be his friend, introduce him to me, huh?" April winked at her, pulling her plumed hat from her head.

"You've got a boyfriend, remember?"

"Maybe, but I'm not blind," April said. She

pulled off her earrings, then turned around suddenly to survey the room.

Jessy felt as if a million goose bumps broke out over her body and asked, "What is it?"

"Footsteps on my grave, I guess," April said, shrugging. "Sorry. I just had this creepy feeling. Ice along the spine or something."

Jessy looked around, as well. She didn't see anyone, but she felt uncomfortable even so. She had to get herself under control. How was she ever going to lead a normal life if she was suddenly afraid of invisible danger at every turn?

April gave a shrug and reached for her makeup remover." Anyway, friend to friend? I'd go after him if I were you, if only just for the sex. And I'll be wanting details when you do."

Jessy groaned. "I prefer not to kiss and tell."

"He's an Indian, isn't he?"

"The correct terminology these days is Native American."

April rolled her eyes. "I call you an Indian all the time. People think I'm crazy, cuz you're so light."

"Timothy's half Lakota," Jessy said.

"So there you go. You *are* an Indian. Sorry, Native American."

Jessy shed her boots and put them in the box under the table, then shimmied out of her pirate apparel, and quickly slid into her own sandals and knit sheath. "Gotta go," she told April, giving her friend a pat on the shoulder.

"Take Mr. Creepy with you, okay?"

"What?" Jessy froze, turning around to stare at April.

April laughed. "Just kidding. That feeling of being watched, you know?" She shuddered. "Maybe it's because of the newspaper."

"The newspaper?"

"The front page is all about that guy who was killed last night." She lowered her voice to a whisper. "He worked for our boss, you know. Emil Landon, the guy who owns this place. So in a way, it was a coworker who was killed. He died right on top of some poor woman." She looked more closely at Jessy and gasped. "What's wrong? You're white as a ghost. Hadn't you heard about it?"

"No, I knew about it."

"I'm sure it has nothing to do with us. It was probably someone he used to know before he took up the bodyguard business. Still, I guess none of us should go walking to our cars alone these days. Vegas has never been number one in the low-crime sweepstakes."

"No," Jessy agreed.

"You're not walking to your car alone now, are you?" April asked her, concerned.

"No, I'm meeting—I'm going to the Strip. You have someone to walk you to *your* car, right?"

"I'm going to the Strip, too. Now get out of here. I'll be right behind you!"

Jessy left the dressing room, unnerved. As she closed the door behind her, she guiltily hoped she was shutting "Mr. Creepy" in with April. She hurried past the empty theater, anxious to get to the casino floor, where there would be bells, lights and lots of people.

Dillon wondered if she was really going to show, or if she would find a way to avoid him.

But it was almost exactly half an hour from the time she had left him that she walked through the front door of Chen's.

Vegas was filled with beautiful women. Most of them not only had killer bodies but glorious faces and legs that went on forever. And in this city, where a good showgirl was pretty much guaranteed a high-paying job, most of them came with enhanced breasts, as well.

As he watched Jessy Sparhawk come through the door and pause to look around the restaurant, he tried to analyze her appeal. Long sleek hair cascaded like a sunset down her back. Her eyes were large and expressive. Her figure was perfectly curved, but natural in every way. Her legs seemed long enough to stretch to China, and the symmetry of her features made her look simultaneously elegant, confident—and sweetly vulnerable. Nothing about her had grown hard yet, as so often happened to women out here.

He tried to figure out what made her so special,

but an answer escaped him. It might have been her voice, the way she could speak so quietly yet be heard so clearly.

Hell, it might have been her ears or her kneecaps, for God's sake. It was impossible to fathom what made her so appealing. She just was.

She was casual now. Her face was scrubbed clean of makeup, and she had donned a cobalt-blue dress that echoed the color of her eyes. There was nothing showy about the way it fell to her knees and bared her arms, but when she moved, the outfit became a thing of beauty.

Ringo gave a low whistle.

Ignoring him, Dillon stood as she approached the booth and extended a hand. She accepted and sat, though she was actually perching on the edge of the seat, rather than actually *sitting*.

"Miss Jessy," their waitress said, hurrying over before Dillon could say anything. Evidently Jessy had chosen a place she frequented. Was that a good sign? Or just the first thing that had come to her mind?

"Hi, Mai," Jessy said, smiling broadly at the pretty, young Chinese woman. "How are you?"

"Good, good, I bring Michael on Saturday?" Mai asked anxiously.

"Please do. I promise we'll see that he has a great time," Jessy assured her.

"Thank you. I pour your tea," Mai told her, suiting her action to her words and picking up the

90

pot of tea in front of Dillon. He'd been pleased to discover that they brewed some of the most delicious green tea he'd ever tasted.

"So our waitress is Mai and she has a son?" Dillon said after Mai left them to decide on their order.

"She and her husband own the restaurant," Jessy said. "And they have a four-year-old. He's the cutest little thing I've ever seen."

"If the food is as good as the tea, this is going to be a great dinner."

She cocked her head toward him and almost smiled. Apparently she appreciated a man who knew good tea, he thought.

But not that much, he added silently as she spoke.

"I don't understand what you want. I don't understand what you think I can tell you. You were there last night. I never saw that man before he died on top of me," she said, cutting to the chase.

"I just thought that, if we spent a little time talking, something might occur to you," he said, watching her eyes.

She stared across the table at him and shook her head. "You work for Emil Landon."

"Actually, you've worked for him longer than I have. I've only just been hired by the man."

"Because he thinks he's in danger," Jessy said flatly.

"Yes."

"What do *you* think?"

"I don't know what to think yet," Dillon told her truthfully. "I'm trying to find out more about the man. There are a lot of rumors, but if you go through public documents and legal records, you can get a feel for someone. He's rich. He owns a casino. Whether he's really played it rough and created a few financial corpses along the way, or gotten in with the wrong connections, who knows? He doesn't trust anyone."

"It doesn't sound as if you like him much."

"Do you?" he asked her.

She shook her head. "I don't know him. I've seen him on the news, but I've never actually seen him in person. It's unlikely I would have any cause to meet him, unless he suddenly decided to bring in a pack of little kids."

He sipped his tea, not wanting her to see him smile at the thought of how well she dealt with children. It was nice. Although, admittedly, he found himself so entranced by her that she might have said that lap dances were her thing and he would have found a way to find *that* nice, too.

Mai returned to the table, and to Dillon's pleased surprise, Jessy looked at him hesitantly and asked if it would be all right if she and Mai decided on their order. He grinned and told her to go right ahead.

Jessy seemed to be relaxing. She was at least sitting all the way back in the booth now.

"It must be difficult for you," she mused, sipping her tea after Mai had left again. "Emil Landon certainly has a past, maybe a lot of enemies. And Tanner Green—from what I saw on the news, he had a past, as well. It does seem strange that a man as big as he was went down without a fight. You have to get close to use a knife."

She looked thoughtful as she spoke. Dillon wondered if she was disturbed or just stating facts.

"It suggests that he was with someone he trusted," Dillon said. "Also, in a place as densely populated as a casino, it's easy to get close to someone without them noticing. But he might have been stabbed before he even got to the casino. Not enough evidence yet to be certain of much."

She gave a little shudder and offered him a rueful smile. "I feel guilty saying this, but it's reassuring to think that someone wanted Tanner Green dead. It's better than thinking there's a killer out there, seeking victims at random."

"It's more comforting, yes," Dillon agreed.

The meal arrived, and Dillon thought he had passed muster, because Jessy introduced him to Mai as a friend. Jessy had ordered two dishes, one chicken and one beef dish, one Cantonese and one Mandarin, and both were delicious. There were a few precious moments when the food first arrived that felt almost like being on a regular date. But she hadn't agreed to go on a date with him; she'd agreed—reluctantly—to see him because he needed to talk to her. She didn't dislike him, he was pretty sure, but she seemed determined to create a wall between them, and she apparently hoped that he would stopped banging on the gate.

But they couldn't talk about food forever, and finally he brought the subject back to Green's death.

"I don't know what you think I can tell you," she said, staring at him while he chewed a piece of beef.

"I think that there's something. Maybe in your subconscious. Something you don't think is important or even realize you know, but it might just be the clue that changes everything."

She set down her fork and leaned toward him. "I can't help you. A man I had never seen before stumbled through the crowd, fell on me and died on top of a craps table. You know I didn't know him, that it happened just the way I've described it, and just that quickly."

"He spoke to you," Dillon said quietly.

Her instant frown of surprise and confusion was definitely real. Had she forgotten? Was the information he needed actually buried in her subconscious? She sat back, thinking. "We didn't carry on a conversation," she told him.

"I saw the security tapes. His lips moved."

"He might have whispered something," she said. "I'm sorry. I don't know. He was dying. He could have said anything. I don't remember. All I remember is the feeling of being trapped, the horror of realizing that he was bleeding to death on top of me. And those are images I would just as soon forget."

He couldn't let it go at that, even though he sensed that this wasn't the time to push her. She knew what Tanner Green had said, either consciously or subconsciously, but for now, he had lost her. Time to change the subject.

"How was your grandfather last night? Everything okay?"

"Yes, thank you very much." She stared at him. "Timothy is . . . slipping," she said, as if she thought the idea might frighten him away.

"I'm sorry. Is it Alzheimer's?"

"He's just slipping . . . that's all. He's fine, he takes care of himself, he just . . . he just needs to be watched. He has his moments. He's functioning. He knows me, and he knows the people who care for him." She hesitated. "He actually lives in a home, but he loves it because he has a wonderful doctor, and the people there are terrific." Once again she hesitated, as if saying more than she wanted, but spilling it out anyway. Maybe it was still an involuntary attempt to scare him away. "My folks died when I was young. Timothy raised me. I love him to death, but I can't work and keep him at home. He forgets things on the stove, and he talks to friends in the walls and in the sky."

"As long as they're friends, it sounds as if it's all right to me," Dillon said lightly.

"I have friends who can help me out when he's home," she said, toying with the food on her plate.

"You were gambling last night to pay for his home, weren't you?"

Her gaze shot over to him, and she shrugged. "It's extremely expensive to get old in this country, you know."

"I do know. I've seen it many times. I'm glad the numbers came in for you. I didn't get the impression that you gamble that often."

She laughed. "I pretty much *never* do. I grew up here, went to school here, and now I work here. Timothy is the only family I have left. I have friends, of course, and I love working with kids. There you have it. My life. Let's hear about yours. Rumor has it you're a secret agent of some sort. So what's the truth?"

"Hardly a secret agent," he said, hiding his surprise that she'd been talking to someone about him. "It's certainly no secret that I've been hired by Emil Landon."

"But that's not what you usually do," she said flatly.

"I'm basically a free agent—licensed, of course," he said. "These days I work for a business called Harrison Investigations, headed by a man named Adam Harrison who hires people from around the country—around the world, actually. My roots are here, though. My folks are gone, but I have family who live not too far away. The case came up, Adam suggested I take it, so here I am."

"Why?"

Dillon hesitated. *Why? Because the ghost who hangs around with me wanted me to take it, and Adam thinks if a ghost has a feeling about something, it needs to be looked into.*

"I'm not exactly sure," he said. That much, at least, was honest.

"Does your family live on reservation land?"

"Some of them, and some on private."

"Why is your employer so secretive, and what are all the jobs he supposedly does for the government?" she asked.

"Adam's been called in over the years to investigate various crimes, some of them federal, and he's cultivated a lot of contacts in the various law enforcement agencies around the country. I don't know everything about him, or even about my fellow agents or the cases they've worked. Sometimes a few of us work a case together, and sometimes things are handled on a smaller and more personal scale, and they're settled. There's nothing undercover about us, though Adam doesn't seek publicity. And he chooses our cases carefully, or sometimes a particular investigator chooses a case, that's all."

"But Adam Harrison suggested you take Emil Landon's case. And I think that's interesting," she said. "Why do you suppose he chose the case of a powerful man who has lots of money but, from what I hear, few scruples?" The question was a challenge, he thought. She sounded as if she wanted to find out that there was something not quite legit about him.

"I don't know yet. Hopefully, by the time I get to the bottom of things, I will. So far, I've met Emil Landon and his retinue, and now one of his body-guards is dead—a death you were involved in through no fault of your own. That's why I can use all the help I can get." He watched her eyes, her face, hoping for a sign of trust. The slightest possibility that she might admit to seeing a ghost.

Nothing.

Instead, she stood suddenly. "Forgive me, but I'm exhausted right now. I'll think about it. I'll try to remember if he said anything, but as I said . . . I never saw the man before. Technically I work for Emil Landon, too, but I've never met *him,* either. I'm sorry."

She started to walk away, then returned, blushing. "I forgot. The check—"

"Please. I asked you to meet me." She blushed harder, as if she didn't want him to get the impression they were on a date. "Consider it a business expense. Our mutual boss will pay it."

He watched her go, torn. He wanted to follow her through to the garage and make sure she got into her car okay. Whether she knew it or not, she was being followed by Tanner Green, and though Dillon was certain the specter had no intention of doing her harm, someone *had* murdered the man, she had been there when he died, and that meant she could be in danger, too.

"I'm on it, sagebrush," Ringo said.

Dillon had actually forgotten about the ghost's presence. But now Ringo followed Jessy Sparhawk from the restaurant, the barely perceptible jingle of his spurs and the slight breeze of his passing causing frowns of confusion as he passed.

Jessy walked quickly through the bustling casino toward the garage elevators. The place was full of activity, even though things wouldn't really be in full swing until later. Still, bells were ringing, people were laughing and talking loudly to be heard over the machines, and hawkers were advertising certain games.

She stepped into the elevator along with a musician in Mexican attire carrying an acoustic guitar, a couple who clung to one another and giggled constantly and a man from a pizza-delivery company. The door started to shut, then opened again, as if a latecomer had triggered the sensor.

Except no one was there.

"Ghosts in the machine," the deliveryman offered with a laugh.

The giggling couple giggled louder, and even the musician smiled. The door slid closed again, and Jessy felt as if a cold draft was wafting around her.

She had to get a grip, she told herself. Every little shift in the air around her made her feel as if she was being watched, followed, and it was ridiculous. She had to stop being so paranoid or she wouldn't be any good to anyone.

She was glad when the musician got off on her level, and glad that he wasn't far away as she headed toward her car. She deactivated the alarm, slid into the driver's seat and immediately locked the doors. Then she turned around to investigate the backseat, assuring herself that she was alone in the car, even while ridiculing herself for having seen too many movies where the killer waited in the back of a car to attack his unwary victim.

But she was alone.

She turned on the stereo—loudly. Music was a good way to drown out any sounds she might not want to hear. But it was Seventies Night on the local station, and the minute the DJ introduced Blue Oyster Cult's "Don't Fear the Reaper" she switched the frequency. She drove out the back way, avoiding the Strip, and headed for Henderson, all the while reminding herself that she was safe. She had locked the doors. She had checked the back.

And still she felt as if she wasn't alone. As if someone she couldn't see had followed her. Was right there with her.

But she reached home without incident, then forced herself to walk at a normal pace up the front walk. She quickly closed and locked the door behind her, then reset the newly installed alarm.

But even inside, she couldn't escape the uncomfortable sensation of being watched, of not being alone.

She went first to the kitchen and picked up her heaviest frying pan. She wished that she golfed—a nice strong golf club would have made an excellent weapon, though she was sure that, if need be, she could wield a mean frying pan.

But a walk through her house convinced her that she was entirely alone. She was also desperately in need of sleep, and she thought about taking a nighttime painkiller, but they left her feeling drowsy in the morning, so she poured herself a large Baileys instead. She was standing in the kitchen, glass in hand, when the phone rang and she jumped a foot off the floor. Laughing at her own foolishness, she picked up the receiver.

"Hey, how's it going?" came Sandra's cheerful voice in her ear.

"Fine," Jessy said, realizing she didn't sound entirely convincing.

"So everything's all right with Timothy?"

"It was great, actually. Hoskins was so sure I couldn't come up with the money that he promised Timothy's room to someone else. I'm sure they weren't very happy to find out they couldn't move in after all, but Hoskins is a jerk and deserves to get reamed out. But Timothy's just fine."

"I'm glad to hear that. And how about you?" Sandra asked.

"I'm fine, too."

"I guess you haven't seen the news, huh?"

"Why? What's happened?"

"Oh, nothing more actually *happened*. But you're famous."

"What?"

Sandra laughed. "They're calling you 'the mystery woman.' Hang on—Reggie wants to talk to you."

"It's so cool," Reggie said. "No one has used your name, but they all say he fell down and died on top of a mystery woman. A *beautiful* mystery woman. I'd like to be a mystery woman someday," Reggie finished with a dramatic sigh.

"I'd like to forget it ever happened," Jessy told her.

Sandra came back on the line. "It's okay. It will all die down in time. I'm sure the cops will figure it out. It probably had something to do with drugs or revenge or some such thing. Or maybe it was mob related. I'm glad I'm not a cop. I don't know how they sort through it all. Anyway, I just wanted to check on you."

"I'm fine. I've got a show tomorrow, so I'm going to bed. I'll check in on Timothy in the morning, then head to work—and hope no one there has heard about the mystery woman," Jessy told her. "They'll never stop teasing me if they have."

They said good night, with Sandra telling her to

call if she needed anything. Jessy hung up, half her glass of Baileys gone, resolved that she was going to get some sleep. As she stood, she thought that she heard a jingling sound but decided it was just the phone giving a little hiccup.

She quickly drank the rest of the Baileys and headed to her room.

She got ready for bed quickly, then surprised herself by pausing before she lay down.

"I'm really tired, and I'm begging you to leave me alone," she said loudly to the empty room.

Naturally, there was no response.

A few minutes later—and contrary to her own expectations—she was asleep.

Dillon was tempted to call Jessy just to reassure himself that she had made it home safely, but he refrained. Anyway, it was ridiculous to think she was in any real danger. She'd happened to be there when a man had died, but she had no connection to him. Okay, the man's ghost was following her for some reason, but that didn't mean she was in any real danger.

Besides, Ringo had followed her, and he had over a hundred years' experience learning to deal with life after death and the rules of spectral existence. He was a real pro, as ghosts went. He could move things—like those dice—even knock them over, if necessary. He could probably even manage to call 911 if necessary.

To keep himself from thinking about Jessy, he decided to head over to the Sun and interview some of the workers there, especially the bellmen and valet-parking attendants, who might have seen something the night Green was stabbed.

It was Thursday night. The crime-scene tape had been taken down and the casino reopened sometime that morning, which had been an invitation for the place to go wild. It was hugely busy, but Dillon was good at getting people to talk—in this case, that consisted of handing out a lot of tips. The manager of the valet service had been inside his glass box and hadn't seen anything. Three of the bellmen had been inside at the time, and none of them had seen anything useful. The parking attendants were no help, either.

"The thing is," one of them told him, "we're so used to seeing people wander in drunk that if someone was staggering, we wouldn't have paid any attention. We've all been questioned by the police, and I wish we could help. It feels almost ridiculous that we can't, but you know how it is. Dozens of limos come through here every night."

"Still," Dillon persisted, "*this* limo managed to be just out of range of the cameras. As if someone knew where security cameras could reach and where they couldn't."

"Yeah, in the far lane, the cops said. Check with Rudy Yorba—I remember seeing him out there that night, waiting to park the next car in line."

Dillon tracked down the young man named Rudy Yorba and found a tall, thin thirty-five-year-old with a lot of nervous energy.

Rudy was pleased to accept a tip for his time and gave Dillon his full attention. "I'm not sure what I saw, to tell you the truth," he told Dillon. "That homicide guy was such a jerk, I was kind of afraid to talk to him. He said he wanted facts, not theories, that he didn't want to know what anyone *thought* they saw, only what they really *did* see, and I couldn't give him any facts. Said he didn't want to be chasing his tail following up a bunch of false leads."

"He's a cop, I'm an investigator, and I don't mind chasing my tail," Dillon assured him. "Nothing else for me to do right now anyway, right?"

Rudy looked at him and nodded. "Okay, well, here's what I think. I think that guy came out of a white stretch Caddy. I'd looked up cuz I was waiting for a guy to get out and hand over his car, and I saw someone getting out of the Caddy, but I don't know who. But the next thing I know, there's this huge hulk of a guy blundering through the crowd. He looked rude, like he was pushing people around. Then I looked down to say something to my guy, and by the time I looked back up, the big guy was gone. So, like I said, I *think* he came out of that Caddy, but I don't know it for a fact. I *can* tell you for a fact that it came in fast, and it went out fast. I mean, it's hard for a Caddy that big to burn rubber, but if you ask me, that limo did just that."

"Thanks, Rudy, thanks very much," Dillon told him, and handed the younger man one of his cards. "If you think of anything else, let me know."

"Sure thing," Rudy said, and shook his head. "You'd'a thought someone would have noticed the knife." He shrugged. "But, hey, this is Vegas. What gets stabbed in Vegas, stays in Vegas, right?" He laughed weakly at his own grim joke.

"Sad but true," Dillon said.

Privately, Dillon was certain Rudy was right about the Caddy, which meant whoever had killed Green had plenty of money, enough to hire a pricey limo, and was savvy enough to know just where the security cameras' reach ended.

Dillon headed back home at that point and turned on his computer, putting the Internet to use to figure out which casinos were currently making use of which limo services. There were six that touted the availability of limos for a price, or gratis for their high rollers.

There were also three agencies that specialized in limo rentals.

He was mulling over the information he had garnered when his cell phone rang. "Wolf here."

"Mr. Wolf? It's Rudy Yorba."

"Hello. Did you think of something else?"

"Yeah, I did. I know the year of that limo. I just remembered it, cuz you got me thinking."

"Oh?"

"It's this year's model. I know because of the design of the mirrors. After you left, some of us guys were talking about how things don't really change much, that sometimes you can't tell one year from the other, and then I thought about the mirrors. Maybe it's nothing, but I thought you should know."

"It's definitely something. Thanks, Rudy, thanks a lot."

He hung up and turned back to his computer. None of the rental agencies advertised the latest model, but two casinos did: the Sun, and the newest entry on the Strip—the Big Easy.

5

Rudy Yorba left work at two in the morning. Most of the time, things at the casino began to wind down around then. The partiers were drunk enough that, whether they thought it was time to go to bed or not, their eyes were closing as their alcohol-infused bodies longed for a bed.

Rock stars and their retinues had a tendency to come in late, of course, but there hadn't been any rock stars that night. So though he often hung around until three or four in hopes of picking up a job, he was off that night by two.

He said goodbye to his friends and coworkers, and headed to the parking lot. Employees had to use the open-air top floor, but that was no big deal.

He just took the service elevator and rode up to where his little Bug was waiting. He loved his car. In a world where gas prices kept skyrocketing, he could go forever on a single tank.

He paused and looked out at the night, the moon and stars hidden by thick cloud cover. Good God, it was black. He imagined that, out in the desert, beyond the neon lights, it would be darker than eternity. Dark as hell. And cold, too. Freezing. That was the desert for you. Hotter than hell by day, cold as a witch's tit by night. And Vegas itself nothing but a pile of neon and money in the middle of that desert.

He hit the remote and heard the alarm chirp cheerfully. Friends made fun of him for his car, but he loved her. He called her Mary. Mary for both his mom and his daughter. His mother had been gone for years, and he pretty much never saw his daughter. She lived in New Hampshire with his ex. He got out there once a year if he was lucky, and Mary was allowed to spend two weeks with him in summer. He didn't hate his ex-wife for that, and he didn't resent her new husband, either.

When Mary had been born, he'd thought he was a hotshot. He'd been working on Wall Street, making big money, and he'd driven a Hummer.

Then he'd gotten hooked on cocaine and gone through everything he'd ever made—and nearly dropped Mary off the balcony of his high-priced condo when he was high out of his mind one night.

Now he didn't touch drugs or so much as a drop of alcohol, and he was making his way back to humanity. He knew he had to prove himself to his daughter, and he wasn't sure that she loved him as much as she loved her stepfather or ever would, but he didn't blame her.

As he headed toward the car, he saw someone heading away from it, making their way through the lot. He didn't think anything of it. Employees came and went all night.

Then he heard footsteps behind him and swung around, inexplicably edgy.

"Hey, Rudy!" The woman who called out to him was Amber Olsen, a cocktail waitress.

"Hey, Amber. Quiet night, huh?"

"Yeah, too quiet. Nothing like a man dying to drive away business," she told him.

"Hey, don't sweat it. Maybe they'll put us on the ghost tour."

"Hope so," Amber said, and waved as she headed down another aisle to her car.

Rudy reached his Bug and got inside, then thought to look in the backseat. He grinned ruefully to himself. It was empty. Of course.

It wasn't until he was out on the highway and felt the first little *chug* of his engine that he frowned and looked at his instrument panel.

What the . . . ? He was out of gas—which was impossible. He had filled the tank just that morning.

A moment's uncertainty filled him. Had he had

one of his little blackouts and only *thought* he'd filled his tank? No, he never blacked out in the car. Never. It only happened when he was standing around doing nothing while he was waiting for his turn to park a car or go retrieve one. He wouldn't drive if he had any fear of blacking out when he was actually concentrating. He was trying to rebuild his life, not kill someone.

But that didn't change the fact that he was out of gas. He knew he should have invested in an AAA membership, but it was one of those things he hadn't gotten around to yet.

Swearing, he pulled over to the side of the road before the engine sputtered out completely. Luckily, he was only a couple of miles from the next exit and a gas station.

Dumb. Dumb, dumb, dumb. He swore at himself as he got out of the car, careful to lock the door behind himself. He loved his Mary, and he didn't want anyone stealing her.

He thought about hitchhiking, then decided he might as well just walk, seeing as there weren't many other cars on the highway anyway. A quiet night all around, he supposed.

He walked for half a mile, humming to himself to keep from cursing aloud at his own stupidity.

There were lights behind him, but hell, this *was* a highway. He paused and turned, thinking about trying to flag down the driver and bum a ride after all.

He knew he was still on the shoulder, but it seemed as if the car was coming straight toward him. He raised his hands against the blinding glare, wondering what kind of idiot was driving.

The lights grew brighter as the car drew closer. It must have been doing at least eighty.

And it was coming right at him.

He never screamed.

And he never suffered.

He didn't even have time for a dying thought.

Morning.

Light seeping into her bedroom woke Jessy, and she opened her eyes slowly, afraid of what she might see.

The clock ticked away time on the bedside table. The dream catcher that Timothy had bought her when she was a child, beautifully crafted and dotted with beads and crystals, hung from the dressing-table mirror, just catching the first glints of day.

She was alone.

And still . . .

It was eerie, waking up with the sensation of being observed.

"You are not being watched," she told herself firmly. "You *are* in danger of becoming paranoid."

She'd been dreaming, she knew, though she couldn't remember the specifics. She did know that people had been watching her in the dream.

No, not people.

Tanner Green.

She needed to get a life and quit obsessing, she told herself. *Sex.* That was what Sandra would tell her she needed. A red-hot relationship with a real-life man. She actually laughed as she got out of bed, wondering if a bout of good old-fashioned sex could make her stop seeing a ghost.

If so, she might have to jump the first stranger she ran into on the street.

God, no, her situation wasn't that bad, was it?

She was, she admitted, actually attracted, both physically and mentally, to Dillon Wolf. Maybe if she . . .

No, she would *not* go there. Eyes straight ahead, that was the ticket. No thoughts of Dillon Wolf—and no ghosts, either.

She got ready early and left the house, suddenly anxious to be around other people. Her first stop, as it almost always was, would be breakfast with Timothy.

He greeted her as if he was totally in control of all his faculties, which in fact he was at times. The news was on, and the anchor was talking about the murder at the Sun, then cut away to an interview with a couple who had been in the casino at the time. Jessy was surprised to see her favorite gambler on camera, Coot Calhoun, accompanied by his silver-haired wife, Minnie.

"It was like nothing I ever saw before," Coot

said, his Texas accent as broad as always. "Feller just plowed in out of nowhere and fell flat on the table, taking that pretty young thing down with him."

"And you didn't see where he came from?" the interviewer asked.

"No, ma'am. Nothing at all. Feller just plowed through the crowd and died right there on top of that poor girl."

"Was she a friend of his? Maybe a girlfriend?" the interviewer pressed.

"Not that I know about," Coot said.

"So you know the woman?"

Jessy felt her muscles tense, fear clamping around her throat. But Coot was a gentleman, to the bone.

"No, ma'am, I never met her before that night. I just told you how it happened, and that's that. Came after one of the longest runs I've ever seen at a craps table, though."

The interview ended there, and the anchor announced that she would return after the commercial break.

"Darnedest thing I ever did hear," Timothy said, a teasing light entering his bright blue eyes. "I've heard of casinos sending in new folks, hoping to turn the tide when a winning streak goes on too long, but I can't think of a casino out there that would stoop to killing a man just to stop the game."

113

Jessy gasped. "That's horrible. And the winning streak had already ended when it happened."

Timothy's eyes narrowed. "And how would you know that, young lady?"

She didn't want him knowing that she had been desperately playing the last of her reserves to keep him here in the home. She pointed to the television. "That's what *he* said. The man being interviewed."

"It's still odd as hell. A man with a knife in his back stumbles through a casino—and no one sees where he came from, not even the cameras. Like an inside job of some kind," he said.

"Or coincidence," Jessy suggested.

"Coincidence?" Timothy shook his head. "Somehow, it was all rigged. How or why, I don't know."

"The police will find the killer," Jessy said with far more conviction than she felt. "Anyway, you're looking great, Timothy."

He smiled, pleased. "I feel great. We'll go on an adventure soon, huh?"

She gave him a big hug, thrilled with how fully in control of his thoughts he was.

"Sure. A day trip. We'll plan something fun."

Suddenly he frowned and wagged a finger at her. "You be careful."

"What? Why?" she asked, frowning back at him.

"The ghosts," he said seriously. "The ghost *dancers.*"

114

She stared at him, unnerved. "Timothy, I don't think any ghost dancers can hurt me, I really don't."

Timothy shook his head. "They don't want to hurt you, they want to help you. The ghost dancers saw their ancestors and spoke with the dead because the dead brought important messages, to those who listened."

She sighed. "Timothy, listen to me. You know I have tremendous respect for your father's people and their traditions, but the ghost dancers are a thing of the past, so I wouldn't suggest putting a lot of faith in them now."

She was surprised when he smiled patiently at her, as if she were a child again. "Faith is the most important thing in the world, Jessy. Faith in one-self, faith in the world, in God, in the Great Spirit. We don't see everything that happens, but the ghost dancers do."

She walked over and kissed him on the forehead, trying not to let him see how much he was upsetting her. "Believe me, I'm grateful for my heritage and very proud of it. For now, though, I have to live in the real world and get to work. I love you, and if I get any messages, I know you'll help me understand them."

He looked up at her, his expression grave. "There's danger when the ghost dancers speak, granddaughter, that's why you have to listen."

"Of course, Timothy, of course," she assured him.

And then she fled.

• • •

Dillon arrived at the executive penthouse at the Big Easy at ten, after calling to make an appointment with Emil Landon. He never slept late, but today, for some inexplicable reason, he had. He'd barely had time to feed the dog and let her out before he had to leave the house.

And he didn't know where the hell Ringo was, other than nowhere nearby, because Ringo definitely would have woken him up.

He'd been having strange dreams of the maiden again, and he wasn't sure why. Long ago, when he had first seen her, he'd been convinced that she had come to save his life. He'd been so bitter in those days. Ready for any fight that came along, aching at the loss of his parents—a jailbird about to happen.

He had no idea what she was trying to tell him now. His dreams were just bits and pieces of confusion, adding up to nothing. Traditionally, the maiden appeared when the tribe had need of her, or when a Native American was in trouble. But Tanner Green had been a Euro-mutt, without a trace of Indian blood.

Whatever the cause—assuming there even was one—his restless night had imbued the morning with a strange groggy fog of hurrying. He never turned on the television, didn't even check his e-mail, before he left the house.

When he was shown into the office promptly at

116

ten, he told Landon he wanted to speak with him alone, then waited patiently while the man made a show of protesting, then gave in and asked his retinue of leggy beauties, along with Hugo Blythe, to wait outside.

"I think you have a big problem, and I think it's someone close to you," Dillon told him bluntly when they were alone at last. There were undoubtedly hidden cameras in the room, and for all he knew it was bugged, as well, but that was a risk he had to take. The cameras were Landon's choice, and if the man didn't sweep for bugs . . . well, there was only so far he could go in getting information to the man.

"What the hell are you talking about?" Landon demanded. It was ten o'clock, but he was still in a dressing gown—cheetah-print silk. He was fit and tanned, a man who had a gym in his penthouse, along with the time to sit out in the sun just the right amount of time to acquire just the right amount of color. His hair was dark—aided by an expensive dye job, Dillon thought—but his face, despite expensive work, was showing signs of wear and tear. He could don the aura of a rich and attractive man, but time and stress were taking their toll.

"I've been questioning the valets, and I've interviewed the bellmen and anyone else I could find who was outside when it happened. I'll start on the inside staff next. Meanwhile, I've ID'd the car as a current model white Cadillac limo, and there are only two casinos that use those right now—yours and the Sun. None of the rental companies in the area have one. That suggests to me that you need to watch your associates and employees," Dillon told him.

Landon stared at him. "That's it? For what I'm paying you, you come back to me with something like that? A fifty percent possibility *at best?*"

"As I said before, feel free to stop paying for my services at any time," Dillon told him.

"I need results. I need to know what the hell got Tanner Green killed. Especially if he found out something about who's after me. Hell, I need to know anything. Someone out there knows something, and I want you to find out what it is," Landon said angrily.

"Be careful in your own house, that's what I've got for you so far. What you do with that is your concern," Dillon told him, standing. "If you want more, then you damn well need to give me more."

"What the hell more can I give you? Someone is after me. I know it. I don't know who, but I know I've been followed. And now Green is dead. That's what I've got, and if I had more, I'd damn well give it to you, because this is my life I'm trying to preserve," Emil Landon growled. "Find out what happened to Tanner Green and why, then maybe we'll know where to look and what the hell is happening. Now get out of here and go do something useful."

"Fine," Dillon snapped. "I'd like to get your limo to the crime lab."

"My limo!" Emil Landon exploded. "You're working for me, remember? Go to the Sun. Check out *their* fucking limo!"

"I find that very curious, Mr. Landon. I'd think you'd want to know what was happening in your own backyard," Dillon commented dryly.

"You know what? You're fired. Your sorry ass is fired," Landon screeched. "Get out! Get out of my office *now!*"

"As you wish," Dillon told him, and turned to leave.

"Wait!" Landon called to him.

Dillon turned.

"Just check out their damn limo first, will you?" Landon demanded. "Then . . . come back to me."

"I'll need a warrant for that."

"Get one."

"I'm not a cop. I'm a P.I."

"Hell, you can get whatever you want, and you damn well know it." Landon waved a hand in the air in dismissal.

Had Landon hired him with a hidden agenda? To help him in setting up someone else?

Dillon walked over to the desk and leaned on it, staring Landon in the eyes. For a moment the casino owner looked afraid. "I'll do my best,"

Dillon said. "But don't let me find out that you're jerking me around. Because when—not if—I find out the truth, if you're guilty in any way, I'll make sure you pay the price."

He left before Emil Landon could respond to his threat.

Jessy loved kids. They were so quick to suspend disbelief, and they were delighted with simple things, like chocolates wrapped in gold foil. The pirate show was probably her favorite of all the shows she'd ever done. It never felt old or routine to her.

But today, while she was once again in the midst of a battle of words, she found herself looking out and seeing the man. Tanner Green.

Staring at her through the glass.

She turned away, insisting to herself that he wasn't there. He couldn't be there. Tanner Green was *dead*.

She focused on her lines and on her fellow actors. She avoided looking past the audience to where she had seen him.

But she could still *feel* him watching her.

She tried hard not to look, but in the end she couldn't stop herself. Being careful not to lose a beat, she turned to look and was relieved to see that he was gone. So maybe that was the answer. Ignore him. Pretend that she didn't see him, because, of course, she *couldn't* be seeing him.

Ghosts weren't real. And if they weren't real, they couldn't walk around in human form, staring through glass with a melancholy expression.

Anyone who thought they saw ghosts was crazy.

And she was completely and totally sane.

Completely.

And totally.

She forced herself to concentrate on the children's reactions, on the story she and the rest of the cast were telling, and on the ad-libbing that was so much a part of the show.

And she didn't look toward the glass.

A little girl in the front row held a foil-wrapped chocolate coin, one of the "pieces of eight" the cast gave out. Now Jessy strode toward the girl, saying, "I see treasure, and there's more to be had!"

The little girl offered her the chocolate. "Ah, no, lassie! That's your treasure. I be wanting me own!" The kids all laughed, and Jessy smiled and returned to the stage, determined to keep her eyes on the kids and nowhere else.

"Hey, how's it going?" Jim Martin asked, sliding into the booth across from Dillon at the coffee shop just off Paiute land. Like Dillon, he had Paiute in his background; in fact, his brother was an officer with the local tribal police.

"Good, thanks, and thanks for coming."

"Not a problem. I don't work today. Actually, I had to drag myself out of bed to get here."

121

"Sorry."

"No, it's okay. I needed to get moving. And I'm happy to help out—if I can."

"You were working, overseeing the croupiers, when Tanner Green died," Dillon said.

"Yeah, I was." Jim shook his head. "I was there, and I didn't see a damn thing."

"Nothing at all?"

"I probably should have seen him stumbling through the crowd. It was weird, though. I mean, wouldn't you think he'd have been trying to get help? I don't know why he didn't grab someone outside, or in the crowd. But he made it all the way over to the table. The thing is, I had just come on."

"What?"

"I had just come on duty. Darrell Frye was on before me. He went on break, and I came on just as things were going down, and I didn't notice because I was busy getting a feel for what was going on. There's huge money out there on those tables, you know. And we're responsible for making sure everything runs smoothly."

"Well, thanks for coming to talk to me," Dillon told him a few minutes later, after they'd run through the events of Green's death again, just to be sure they hadn't missed something. "I appreciate it. I'll find Darrell Frye and see if he can remember anything about what happened before you got there."

"Sure. You'd think someone would have noticed

something. Green sure took one hell of a long walk with a knife in his back. Maybe he was stoned or something and didn't even know he'd been stabbed."

"Maybe he was," Dillon said. Not only would that explain why he had stumbled through the crowd, half-dead, without stopping someone and begging for help, it could explain his confusion and fear as a ghost.

The minute James left, Dillon put in a call to Cheever, cursing the fact that he needed to go through the proper channels if he wanted to remain in the loop.

He was given the runaround for several minutes, but if there was one stereotype he rather liked, it had to do with the belief that men of Indian blood were stoic. Determined. He kept that thought in mind as he waited, and eventually Jerry Cheever came on the line.

"What?" the cop asked, and Dillon wasn't sure if the question held annoyance or curiosity.

"I was anxious to see if the autopsy report was in on Tanner Green."

"Autopsy report? You were there—the man had a knife in his back," Cheever said sarcastically.

"Right," Dillon said with an edge. "And a man with a knife in his back would want it out, I imagine. Wouldn't you think he'd approach the nearest person and ask for help? Unless he was dis-oriented."

"A knife in his back would make him disoriented—wouldn't *you* think?"

"He stumbled like a drunk man. Or someone who had been drugged," Dillon said.

"I'll get back to you. I'm sure the morgue ran a basic tox screen. If not, I'll see that they do," Cheever said.

"Thanks. I appreciate it."

Dillon was pretty sure Cheever muttered something as he hung up. Whether he was irritated for not having figured out himself that Green might have been drugged, or if he was just annoyed that his superiors had told him he had to work with a private investigator, Dillon couldn't tell. And he didn't really care, as long as the man followed through.

There had been other witnesses that night, of course, and it would be interesting to find out what they had to say. Especially Darrell Frye, the pit boss who had been in charge, only to disappear just when Tanner Green had stumbled in. Not that there was necessarily anything suspicious about that. People went on break all the time.

But it was possible that the limo had belonged to the Sun, and that might make Frye's whereabouts relevant. He took a stroll over to the casino, and was told that Darrell Frye wasn't working, that in fact he was taking some vacation time.

Back out front, Dillon asked for Rudy Yorba.

He was startled when the woman at valet parking

sucked in her breath and stared at him in horror. "I'm so sorry. I guess you haven't heard."

"Heard what?"

"Rudy's dead."

"What?" Dillon said, incredulous.

"He's dead. Hit-and-run last night. It's so terrible! It's been all over the news the last few hours. He was walking along the shoulder of the highway when he was hit and thrown down an embankment. . . . No one even found the body until a few hours ago."

Dillon winced inwardly. He always listened to the news, but he'd woken up so late this morning that he hadn't even turned on the TV. And Cheever might have heard about it, but he wouldn't have thought about saying anything because he wouldn't have seen the connection.

"My God. No, I'm sorry. I haven't seen the news today."

The woman shook her head sadly. "He was killed not five miles from his home. It's just so sad. They think he was struck on his way home last night. A guy driving out to Lake Mead saw the vultures, so he went to see what they were so interested in, found the body and called the police out. It's just so awful, everything that's going on around here. First that bodyguard, and now Rudy . . . it's just tragic."

Dillon thanked her and turned away.

It wasn't just tragic. It was criminal.

6

Backstage, before she even got out of her costume and makeup, Jessy called Sandra and arranged to go to the movies. Anything to take her mind off what was going on. Not only that, she didn't want to drive, because she was afraid of what she would do if she looked out the window and saw Tanner Green. Luckily Sandra had no objection to picking her up, and she sang to herself all the way home, thinking that might keep any ghosts at bay. Whatever the reason, she made it home without incident.

She and Sandra pulled up at almost the same moment.

"You look like hell," Sandra told her with the comfortable bluntness that came from years of close friendship.

"I know. I didn't sleep well," Jessy told her.

"Are you frightened?"

"Frightened? Of what?" Jessy asked warily.

"Well, of whoever killed Tanner Green thinking you could recognize him and coming after you, too."

"Of course not," Jessy responded immediately, glad the possibility hadn't occurred to her earlier. "I mean, if I knew anything, I would have told the police, and the person would already have been arrested. Right?"

"Of course. If the police could figure out who he was from your description."

Jessy stared at her. "You know, you're not helping."

"Sorry," Sandra said, then forced a reassuring smile and asked, "Hey, what happened to tall, dark and very handsome?"

"Who?" Jessy asked.

"You know exactly who I mean."

"Oh, Dillon."

"Yes, Mr. Oh-Dillon. What's up? What happened to him?"

"What do you mean, what happened to him? To the best of my knowledge, he's fine."

"You haven't talked to him again?" Sandra sounded dismayed.

"Actually, I have. He took me to dinner last night after the show."

Sandra stared at her in total exasperation. "Honestly, Jessy, if for no reason other than self-preservation, you should be hanging with that hunk of lean, mean security right now."

"Sandra, I am not going to hang with a guy just for protection."

"People have done worse," Sandra said with a shrug. "Wait, I have it."

"Have what?"

"The reason you're steering clear of him. Of all men. Because I know you're attracted to him," Sandra accused. "The thing is, you're chicken, and you have been for as long as I've known you. You're afraid of being hurt, so you push guys away."

"I have responsibilities," Jessy told her.

"Don't make excuses. You have a grandfather who loves you. He suffers from being old, but so do lots of people. The whole human race comes with baggage, Jessy, but if you let yourself be scared of every guy out there because you're defensive about Timothy, you're turning him into a brick around your neck, which he's not—and I know you don't really think he is, either. You're afraid someone else wouldn't love him the way you do, and that's not fair to Mr. Oh-Dillon or anyone else, or to Timothy himself. So start trusting someone, or else you're actually hurting Timothy yourself."

To Sandra's credit, Jessy saw the truth in her friend's words and was appalled at herself. "It's not Timothy. I know he's a gift in my life. And it isn't a lack of trust in humanity, or not only that. It's also a lack of time. Only it isn't any of those things with Dillon Wolf."

"But you do think he's hot," Sandra said, grinning.

"He's an attractive man," Jessy said evasively.

"Yes, so . . . ?"

"All right, honestly? First off, he hasn't asked me on a date. He wants information, that's all. Second, I'm still not sure about his job and who he works for. It seems as if he answers me honestly, that he likes and respects the man he works for, and that everything's on the up-and-up, but . . . I still don't understand exactly what he does, what he has done, why he's here. . . . I mean, Dillon claims there's nothing shady about what's going on, but what is Harrison Investigations, exactly? How is that no one seems to know anything about it even though he says it's all out in the open, but somehow he has access to cops who don't really want him butting in? I don't get it. Who *are* these people?"

"You're sounding panicky," Sandra said.

"I'm not panicky, I'm concerned. I just want to know who he really is and understand what's going on. So . . . what are they? Do you know?"

"Ghost hunters. Real ones," Sandra said soberly.

"What?" Jessy demanded. "Ghost hunters?"

"Okay, that's not what they call themselves. But it's what they do."

"And you know this because . . . ?"

"Because I read," Sandra said.

Jessy frowned. "Hey, I read all the time."

Sandra laughed. "I'm not casting aspersions. I read *People* cover to cover, too. But I did some research when the whole Harrison Investigations thing was first mentioned, and what I found was pretty interesting. Adam Harrison declines interviews, and says he and his people are just like any other investigators. But . . . hang on. I had a feeling you'd be interested, so I brought a few things with me." Sandra reached into her huge tote and pulled out several magazines. "Read these."

The first magazine was a sensationalist rag. The headline read, *Elvis never died. He was just recalled to his ship!*

Jessy stared at Sandra, arching a brow.

"Oh, ignore that," Sandra said. "Go to page four."

Jessy flipped through to an article about a ghost in the D.C. house of one of North Dakota's state senators. Harrison Investigations had been called in, only to report that the "eerie noises" and weird happenings in the historic home were being caused by a nest of squirrels—and an unhappy constituent who had managed to get a job as a housekeeper for the senator. The reporter claimed to know, however, that the house had been haunted by a man shot in a quarrel after the Lincoln assassination for insisting that Dr. Samuel Mudd had treated John Wilkes Booth's leg as he would have any patient's, unaware that Booth had just killed the president. The reporter was certain that a member of Harrison Investigations had assured the ghost that Mudd—and he—had been vindicated, and the ghost had moved on.

Jessy stared at Sandra. "You've got to be kidding."

"Check this one out, then."

She handed Jessy another magazine, a respected

news weekly, which carried an article about the same incident and mentioned several others, finishing by saying, *Whatever the problem—wildlife, pranksters or even revenants with a grudge—Harrison Investigations seems capable of solving the problem, quietly and without fanfare.*

"So they investigate squirrels," Jessy said irritably.

"They're ghost busters," Sandra said firmly.

"If that's true, it just proves my point exactly. Do I really want to get involved with a whack job who thinks investigating ghosts is the way to solve a crime?"

"You're hopeless," Sandra said. "Don't get involved with him, then. Have sex. Maybe even let him be a friend—with benefits. But stop spending your life in a funk, doing nothing but working, eating a TV dinner, going to bed—"

"I never eat TV dinners," Jessy protested.

Sandra ignored her. "And visiting Timothy. And frankly, hanging out with a nice strong guy would be a pretty good idea, if you ask me, because I think you *should* be afraid. That guy didn't die from having too much fun. He was murdered. Knifed in the back. And like it or not, you're connected to his death. The more I think about it, the scarier I think it is."

"What the hell is the matter with you, trying to scare me like this?" Jessy demanded.

"I'm looking out for your welfare," Sandra told her.

"By scaring me to death?"

"You're not dead, so apparently my evil plan didn't work. But I still think you're in danger," Sandra said, nodding to show how serious she was.

"So you want me to get . . . involved with a man who might be crazy," Jessy accused.

"It's what you want, and you know it," Sandra said.

Jessy groaned and changed the subject. "Are we seeing a movie or not?"

"There's a new horror—" Sandra began.

"Very funny," Jessy said.

"Sorry," Sandra teased. "How about that new cops film?"

They agreed, then moved on to wrangling over what restaurant to go to as they left.

Dillon arrived at the crime lab just as the shift was changing, was hoping to find an old friend, Wally Valdez.

The first thing he had done after hearing about Rudy Yorba's death to was call Jerry Cheever and suggest it was too much of a coincidence not to be connected, even revealing the fact that he had talked to Rudy shortly before he was killed. Cheever told him that they had already checked out Rudy's car, which had been found parked on the side of the highway. It had been out of gas, plain and simple. Some cowardly drunk was probably busy, even now, praying that he wasn't somehow traced.

"You got anything to go on?" Dillon had demanded.

Cheever had grown impatient at that point, stressing that it wasn't his case and was being handled as accidental vehicular homicide. His own hackles had been raised by Cheever's attitude, keeping him from being totally forthcoming when Cheever demanded to know what Yorba had told him.

As soon as they'd hung up, he'd come here.

As he was asking after Wally, Sarah Clay, the woman who had helped him with the video the day before, appeared in the reception area.

"What are you doing here?" she asked him.

"Just looking for a friend, Wally Valdez. Do you know him?"

"I do."

He frowned. "Actually, what are *you* doing here? I thought you worked over at the station."

Sarah smiled. "Actually, I'm usually here. I was just called in to work with the casino tapes. Anyway, Wally is off tonight, but he'll be back tomorrow." She paused and looked thoughtful.

"Wally says you're one of the good guys."

"Glad to hear it."

She smiled. "If I can help you . . . ?"

"Thanks for the offer. It's nothing to do with the casino tapes, actually. I'm here because of the hit-and-run last night."

"The Rudy Yorba case," she said somberly.

"Right. It just seems odd to me that Rudy Yorba, who happened to be parking cars at the Sun when Green was killed, managed to run out of gas and end up struck by a hit-and-run driver in the middle of the night. Even in Vegas, that's a quiet time."

"There are always lots of drunks behind the wheel in this town, though," Sarah told him.

"Still, it's quite a coincidence, don't you think? Two dead in two days, and both deaths connected to the same casino?"

"I wish I could say our non-natural death rate was so low that that seemed weird to me," Sarah told him gravely, "but it's not. One murder, one accident. A pretty normal ratio around here, really."

"Still . . . I questioned Rudy about what had happened the night Green died just hours before he was killed. Have the investigators come up with anything yet? Any clue at all?"

She studied him gravely for a moment. "I don't know anything yet, and it's not my case. But I can try to find out what's going on, and I'll be able to give you what we get on paint evidence, if nothing else. I think they were able to find a few chips on the body," she said. "I'll call you when I have something. Just give me a number. I did hear that the cop on the case has been calling body shops, and no one has come in with a damaged car."

"Thanks. I appreciate it." He gave her one of his cards, then turned to leave.

"He was struck really hard," she said softly.

He turned back to look at her. She had large brown eyes and a heart-shaped faced, and, despite the scrubs she was now wearing over her uniform, she was a beautiful young woman, one who right now looked not just sad but worried.

"As if there was something personal? As if he was struck on purpose?" he asked.

"In my mind, yes," she said decisively. "How do you hit a man hard enough to break just about every bone in his body—and not crash into the guardrail or go over the embankment yourself? Especially if you're a drunk, so your reflexes are slow?" She shook her head. "I'm not high enough in the force for anyone to want my opinion, but that's my take on the situation. If you want it."

"Definitely. And thank you again."

"Call me. Anytime."

He was pretty sure she was actually flirting with him then. And she was certainly attractive, bright and intriguing.

He was working, he reminded himself.

But that wasn't what caused him to ignore the signals and courteously extend his thanks one last time, then walk away.

It was the memory of a woman with deep cobalt eyes and a mane of sunset hair.

Sandra was quiet as they drove back to Jessy's house after their night out.

"What's the matter?" Jessy asked her.

"Want to come and stay with me?" Sandra asked.

Yes, I do, Jessy thought, surprising herself.

But she wasn't going to abandon her home. If she did, she might never have the nerve to go back.

"Thank you, but I'm fine." She frowned. Sandra was actually looking worried.

"What is it?"

"I admit I was trying to get to you before. But now . . . I think I've managed to actually scare myself over you."

"I have an alarm," Jessy reminded her. "And if someone was really afraid I knew something, they'd have to know I'd have spilled it by now, right? Haven't we already figured all that out?"

"All right. But if you need anything, call me." Sandra paused, then added, "Hell, if you're really scared, dial 911. Fast."

"You know I will," Jessy assured her.

"I'll go in with you," Sandra volunteered.

They walked through the house together, Sandra brandishing one of her spiked heels like a weapon, just in case they surprised an intruder.

But the house was empty. Not that Jessy had ever thought there was actually someone there.

Not a *living* someone, anyway.

She told Sandra good-night, then silently repeated her new mantra. *Look straight ahead. No peripheral vision allowed. Do not make eye contact.*

She hummed loudly, and blasted her television as she made a cup of tea and got ready for bed.

Even in bed, she kept humming.

Like any private detective, Dillon had picked up a few tricks in his day.

And since Cheever had informed him that he didn't have enough to go to the ADA and ask for a search warrant, Dillon had decided that he had to take matters into his own hands. In fact, Cheever had said, "It's nuts. Cops have to follow certain rules and the public doesn't. Some things just suck."

Dillon had taken that to mean that Cheever was all for him doing a few things that skirted the wrong side of the law.

Limos were often sitting just outside the entrances of the various hotels and casinos, awaiting the pleasure of some newly flush high roller.

But a walk along the Strip showed him that neither the Sun nor the Big Easy currently had its latest-model white super-stretch out front. A few casual questions to the right people elicited the information that both limos were at a garage for maintenance. Interesting coincidence, that.

A few more questions gave him the name of the garage each casino used. The same name both times. Another interesting coincidence.

The garage wasn't open when he swung by, not

that he had expected it to be. It was surrounded by a high fence with a barbed-wire coil along the top, but it wasn't electrified.

Two Dobermans guarded the premises instead.

After a quick stop at a nearby supermarket, he headed back to the garage. He opted to park on the road that ran behind the property, then dodged the traffic and crossed the median to reach the rear of the establishment. There, he waited for the dogs to appear. It wasn't a long wait. He spoke to them as they approached, concentrating on the tone of his voice as he lured them over for the meat he'd purchased. He hadn't drugged it; he was counting on his ability to befriend the dogs. He was patient, feeding them, talking to them. He slipped his hand through the wire, touching them, still reassuring them. Finally, he climbed the fence, crossing carefully over the barbed wire. One of the dogs started to snarl, but he spoke to it firmly, and the snarl became a whine. He patted both dogs as he walked slowly through the lot toward the garage itself, encouraging the animals to accompany him.

There was no alarm on the door to the garage itself, and the lock was easy to pick. The owners apparently had a lot of faith in their dogs. Then again, a garage wasn't usually a prime target for thieves.

It took a while for his eyes to adjust to the dim light, but after that it was easy to find the two super-stretches. He was dismayed to see that both had just received new paint jobs. It was easy enough to identify which limo went to which casino, though, thanks to the vanity plates. *Sun 1* and *Big E* were pretty damn obvious.

He wore thin plastic gloves, to keep his own prints out of the equation, just in case the limos become part of an investigation.

Neither one appeared to have been involved in the kind of accident that would have killed someone. The paint was fresh, but neither vehicle appeared to have had any bodywork done, not that he thought the murderer would have been sloppy enough to use the same vehicle twice.

A thorough inspection of the Sun's limo yielded nothing. He was sure no obvious blood spill would have been left behind for the cops or anyone else to find, but he'd come prepared. A spray of Luminol and a small black light showed no signs of bloodshed, either.

It was possible, though, that the knife itself would have temporarily sealed the wound, but he searched thoroughly anyway. In the end, he found nothing, not only no blood, but no sign of bleaching to remove blood, either.

Lots of semen, though.

He moved on to the limo from the Big Easy.

Once again, both his first inspection and then a spray of Luminol showed nothing. Not a speck of blood, and no hint of bleaching. But as he ran his fingers along the upholstery next to the right-hand passenger door, he found something else, maybe something just as good.

It looked like a button from a designer shirt. He studied it in the narrow beam of his small flashlight and wondered if Tanner Green had been missing a button when he died. That would be easy enough to ascertain. He pulled out his phone and took a quick picture of the button, then returned it to where he had found it.

One of the Dobermans was starting to whine.

Dillon quickly flicked off his light, then quietly stepped out of the limo and closed the door softly behind himself, as both dogs raced toward the door, which he had left slightly ajar.

Someone was coming in. He cursed himself for not having heard signs of movement earlier, but it seemed that whoever was arriving had come in as stealthily as he had himself.

He rolled under the BMW parked beside the limo, and did his best to look and sound like a slab of cement floor.

"Idiots left the door open," a man noted irritably. "Fat lot of good you friggin' dogs were doing, sleeping in here."

Hugo Blythe, Emil Landon's surviving bodyguard. Dillon rolled again, moving from car to car, making his way toward the door—which, luckily, Blythe had also left open—as the other man made his way straight to the limo Dillon had just exited.

The dogs, thankfully, were following Blythe,

140

tails tucked as they whined nervously. Apparently they knew the man. Maybe Emil Landon did business with the garage that went beyond having his vehicles serviced here. The dogs knew Hugo Blythe. And they didn't love him, they feared him.

Mulling over the possible meanings of that knowledge, Dillon slipped under the car parked closest to the rear door and watched as Blythe entered the limo.

Then he made his escape.

He raced for the fence, scaled it quickly and had just leaped free of the barbed wire and landed hard, rolling to mitigate the impact, when he heard the first shot.

It was followed quickly by a second.

Blythe was running in his direction as he fired again.

Dillon sprang to a crouch and ran.

Luckily Blythe was lumbering and slow. Dillon made it to the road and crossed the flow of traffic. He was in his own car and rejoining the stream of traffic before Blythe ever made it to the fence.

Jessy became aware that she was dreaming somewhere in the middle of her dream.

She was back at the Sun, which was as crowded as always, and she was being chased. She was weaving through the crowd and between the tables, craps tables, poker tables, roulette tables. She was inside, but there was a low ground fog,

141

which she knew was ridiculous. Fog didn't rise inside. Fog was for outside.

Suddenly she—and the fog—were outside. Now she was being chased around a cemetery. But it wasn't an ordinary cemetery. It was like Boot Hill. Old West cemeteries didn't have fine marble markers. The crosses were wooden and primitively made, the graves surrounded by stones.

Sagebrush danced by in a breeze she couldn't feel. The dust of the desert seemed to choke her, then die away in a fog that couldn't—shouldn't—be in such a dry place.

And from the distance, she could hear the buzzers and bells of the casino. She could see a poker table. . . .

There were men around it, but something wasn't right about them. They weren't real. They were part of the fog. And they were dressed in old railway frock coats and dusty old hats. She could hear the faint sound of a tinkly old-time piano.

She needed to stay away from the poker players; somehow she knew that. So she veered away, and then, though she was still in a cemetery, it wasn't the one she had just run through but a Native American burial ground, where the dead had been placed high above the ground on wooden platforms, wrapped in their best furs, with their spears, arrows, quivers and buffalo-skin shields left to hang at their sides. The rows of scaffolds that marked the graves seemed to stretch on forever, but she was sure it was better to run between them than toward the poker players.

The mist rose around her, but it was thin enough that she could peer through it and see Dillon Wolf standing there, wearing a long black frock coat and somehow seeming to be one with the burial ground, the dead and the past.

She shook her head, because she didn't want to be part of that world.

But she *did* want to touch him. She wanted to reach out and touch him, see the heated gaze of his eyes and feel the slow stroke of his hands on her skin. Despite the situation, the location, he wasn't afraid, and she sensed that if she could find the courage to run to him, she wouldn't be afraid, either. She would find security and more, because the light in his eyes was like a promise. Even then, even in a dream and surrounded by mist, she wanted to join him, to know his touch. She almost literally burned to move closer.

Yet something in her was still afraid. She didn't quite have the courage to breach the chasm—of age, experience, *power*—that lay between them.

He was one with the mist, knew the souls that rested there.

And she was still being pursued.

She could hear men behind her, their voices growing louder as they drew closer, and though she didn't know what they were saying, she knew that they represented a real and imminent danger.

They wanted her dead.

She turned away, too afraid to go forward, and angled to the west. She had to escape both the promise and the fear.

She heard a jingling, like spurs. . . .

But when she looked back, the men coming after her were wearing suits and could have stepped off the floor of any of the casinos, except that their faces were shrouded by the eerie fog that continued to rise and thickened strangely to hide their features. . . .

She turned in absolute terror to run again.

And then Timothy was standing right in front of her. "Trust in the ghost dancers!" he cried. His arms were open, as if to catch her in his safe embrace, and he looked as young and strong as he had been for so much of her life. He was a bastion of safety against the danger that was nipping at her heels. "The ghost dancers speak with the dead, and the dead will give them the answers they need. They see what was, and they can help stop what must never come to pass."

"Timothy, there are no ghost dancers anymore," she told him. "They failed. The words they heard weren't true, and they died as they tried to restore tribal control to their former lands."

"You must listen, and listen well," he went on, ignoring her outburst. "You must let yourself hear the truth. We must all hear what they are saying, not drown them out because of what we want to hear."

She woke up abruptly.

Or did she?

Was she really awake? Or was she still trapped in her nightmare?

For there, sitting at the end of her bed, was a man.

A dead man.

Tanner Green.

She drew a gasping breath . . . and screamed.

7

"It's all right; I got rid of him."

Startled awake, Dillon blinked into the first pink stages of early-morning sunlight to see Ringo standing over him.

Dillon jerked to a sitting position. "Where the hell have you been? And . . . got rid of whom? What happened?"

Ringo perched at the foot of the bed, dusting off his hat on his knee and shaking his head in disgust. "Tanner Green. Was that guy really supposed to be some kind of scary bodyguard? Because he's a pussy, a wuss, as you guys say these days. All I have to do is jingle my spurs and he's gone."

"I don't want him to go away—I want to talk to him."

"Oh yeah? Before or after he gives Jessy Sparhawk a heart attack?"

"Oh, hell. What happened, exactly?"

"He's following her like some lovesick calf. He was just sitting in her room, and when she woke up and saw him, I thought she might have a coronary on the spot. So I stepped up. He disappeared. She blinked. Got up, made coffee, and sat in the living room staring at the television, only the television wasn't on. After a while, the sun started coming up, and it seemed like she was all right, so I came back over here to tell you what was going on. Hey, did you hear about the guy who was killed in a hit-and-run? He worked at the Sun."

"I know. And I know where the car Tanner Green *might* have been pushed out of *might* have come from *because* of the guy who was killed in that hit-and-run."

Ringo swore softly. "So he was murdered?"

"I'd say so."

"He told you about the car—and then he was killed."

"Yes."

"I'm sorry. And I know you. It's eating you alive, right?"

Dillon nodded. "Yeah," he admitted. "But I don't know whether the fact that he spoke to me had anything to do with it, or whether the killer already suspected he had seen something and might mention it to someone." He sighed deeply and repeated, "I just don't know."

"But he gave you a clue on the car? At least there's a start."

"It was a limo. And I'm pretty sure I've been in it."

"Well, you still seem to be all in one piece," Ringo commented. "So—who killed Tanner Green?"

"I still don't know, but it might have been someone from the Big Easy. I need to find out more before I bring the cops in, or the evidence will be gone, and I won't have enough so someone can be charged with a crime and hauled in."

"So you found blood?" Ringo asked.

"No, but I found a button."

"A button. Wow," Ringo said sarcastically.

"My point exactly—I need more. And you need to get back over to Jessy's place," Dillon said, frowning. He wanted to get to the crime lab and find out if Tanner Green had been missing a button from his shirt.

"I'm a ghost," Ringo reminded him.

"Yes, and . . . ?" Dillon said dryly, returning the sarcasm.

"*You* need to get over to Jessy's place."

"Ringo, I'm worried about her, but I can't go where I'm not wanted," Dillon said. "Or at least not invited."

"You've got to get that woman to talk to you," Ringo said, looking at him seriously. "She's . . . she could wind up in trouble. She could wind up being hurt."

She could wind up being dead.

The thought rose silently between them.

A strong sense of unease swept through Dillon. "She didn't know Tanner Green. She has nothing to do with what's going on. And there would have been no reason for her to know Rudy Yorba, either."

"Yes, but you're convinced that Tanner Green said something to her before he died."

"I know he did. I saw the tape."

"Other people have seen that tape," Ringo pointed out.

"Other people? *Cops.* Jerry Cheever can be a jerk, but I'd swear he's an honest cop."

"Maybe he is. But it's a big police force. Someone else could be on the take. And there's big money floating around this town. Most men have a price they're willing to do just about anything for."

Dillon was feeling worried enough about Jessy. He didn't need Ringo giving him this guilt trip, especially when there wasn't a damn thing he could do. He couldn't force Jessy Sparhawk to see him. She'd only agreed to talk to him the first time to be polite. If he was too persistent, he might never get close to her.

"Call her," Ringo said.

"Ringo, it isn't 7:00 a.m. yet."

"That would practically be lunchtime out on a ranch," Ringo said.

"Well, this isn't a ranch, this is Vegas, and I need you to get back over to her place. Now. Watch over her, Ringo. Somehow—today—I'll find a way to see her. To make her trust me."

"I'll do my best," Ringo said. "But . . ."

"But what?"

"I'm a dead man. She's going to need flesh and blood to help her against the danger that's out there now."

Jessy sat in front of the television, shivering. She was even too afraid to go and take a shower.

She turned on the news, but she hardly paid any attention to the national news.

She was too busy wondering if she could somehow manage to get dressed, or if she would see another ghostly image and end up fleeing out the front door in her nightshirt and bare feet.

The local news drew her attention, though, when the picture of a gaunt young man filled the screen. She didn't recognize him, but according to the newscaster his name was Rudy Yorba, and he was dead, the victim of a hit-and-run after he had left work two nights ago.

The news anchor went on to say that this particular crime was particularly troubling because the victim had been working for the Sun, the casino that had been the site of the murder of Tanner Green just one night earlier. The police were asking anyone with information that might pertain to the accident to call their local precinct.

There were no ghosts on the screen, just an

anchorman. And there didn't seem to be any ghosts hanging around the house, either. Even so, she wanted to scream and go running from the house.

She stood up decisively. She had to get ready and get out. Get close to people. Lots of them.

She kept her eyes straight ahead as she hurried into her bedroom, gathered her clothing and locked herself in the bathroom. She soaped and rinsed in record time, then dried herself off furiously, brushed her hair and teeth, and managed a minimum of makeup.

Then she left the house in a rush.

She burst into Timothy's building, then stopped to give herself a firm mental shake. Maybe she should have gone for therapy after what had happened. Maybe she was suffering from some kind of civilian post-traumatic stress disorder and that was why she kept seeing the dead man.

"You're here early," Jimmy, the orderly, said, smiling, looking normal and reassuring in his scrubs. Seeing him, Jessy instantly felt as if the world was returning to normal.

"Yeah, I woke up early," she said, "so I thought I'd have breakfast with Timothy."

"Go on ahead. He's in the breakfast room, sitting with Mrs. Teasdale." Jimmy winked playfully.

She had to laugh. Her grandfather was quite the ladies' man when he chose. "Thanks, I'll go up."

The television was on in the breakfast room, and the 8:00 a.m. news was on. She saw Rudy Yorba's face on the screen again, with the anchor repeating the police request for anyone with information to call them.

Timothy saw Jessy as she approached the table and rose with a surprised smile. "Granddaughter. So early. It's a delight to see you. You know Mrs. Teasdale, of course?"

"Of course. How are you, Mrs. Teasdale?" she asked.

Mrs. Teasdale had suffered a stroke, followed by a heart attack, but she'd worked like a trouper to walk and talk again, and she had done very well. She was immensely wealthy, but her family lived on the East Coast. They had tried to get her to move East to be nearer to them, but she had decided that she was never leaving the home. She and Timothy were great friends, and Jessy was pretty sure that "friendship" was behind the older woman's decision.

"I'm fine, dear, but the news is just so distressing these days. That gangster or bodyguard, the other night . . . that was one thing. Live by the sword, die by the sword." She waved a jeweled hand toward the TV. "But now this poor young fellow . . . He lived by parking cars, and he died after being hit by a car. It's not a totally accurate analogy, I suppose, but still, it's awfully ironic. And sad."

"It's very sad," Jessy agreed. "The police try very hard to crack down on drunk driving, but they can't catch everyone."

"People don't listen," Timothy said. "They don't listen to the wind. There are signs, but no one pays attention."

Jessy almost groaned aloud. If there was one day when she didn't want to hear Timothy talk about ghost dancers or people in the walls or talking in the wind, it was today.

It would be better if her ghost *were* in the wall or drifting in the wind. But no, *her* ghost had to sit at the foot of her bed.

"Let's not dwell on sad thoughts," Mrs. Teasdale said. "How are you, Jessy? How's that pirate show of yours going? Did Timothy ever tell you? I was a showgirl once."

"Yes, Timothy told me," Jessy said.

"I had a twin sister back then," Mrs. Teasdale said wistfully, a sad smile curving her lips. "Serena. We were identical, but, oh, what fire she had! I went on to marry Roger—though, sadly, we had no children. Serena burned up the Strip all by her lonesome for another decade, then went on to marry and have four boys. I'm blessed, though. With Roger gone, the boys are very good to me."

That was it! Jessy thought suddenly. Tanner Green had been a twin. She had seen his twin walking around town, and maybe the twin had even been drawn to keep an eye on her because of her involvement with his brother's death. Stranger things had happened. Twins had a special bond, or so she had always heard.

Of course the twin hadn't been in her house. *That* had been a trick of her mind.

"I have Jessy. And the ghost dancers, of course," Timothy said. "Jessy, one of these days, I want to go out to Mallaluca and see the family. Maybe we could go out for a festival, and show Sally here the Ghost Dance?" Timothy said.

"Of course," Jessy said. Mallaluca, the town where some of his distant relatives still lived, was only a few hours away. "That would be lovely. I'll look into some dates." She stood, her intention of staying for breakfast forgotten now, suddenly anxious to drive down to the police station and find someone who could tell her more about Tanner Green. She kissed Timothy on the cheek and offered Mrs. Teasdale a broad smile. "You two have a nice day. Timothy, I'll see you tomorrow. Call me if you need anything."

She barely said goodbye to Jimmy, she was so anxious to leave. And yet, even as she drove, she felt her heart sinking.

Surely if Tanner Green had a twin someone would have mentioned it. She had to know for sure, though. Because if Tanner Green *did* have a twin, then maybe she could begin to be . . .

Sane.

Dressed and ready to leave the house, Dillon paused when the newscaster started talking about Rudy Yorba.

He tried to tell himself that the younger man's

153

death was nothing but coincidence. Even after more than twenty-four hours, the police still had no leads, and they were asking the public to notify them if they saw a newly damaged vehicle or had any other information that might aid the investigation into the accident in any way.

Accident, hell. He'd been questioning Rudy, and now he was dead. The victim of a mysterious hit-and-run. That was no coincidence.

He left his house and headed to the police station, where he found Jerry Cheever in his office. The detective seemed both disturbed and surprised when Dillon started asking what was going on with the Rudy Yorba case.

"We went through this yesterday," Cheever reminded him.

"It wasn't an accident."

Jerry groaned. "Either way, it's not my case," Jerry told him. "I know you have a bug up your ass about this case, but it makes no sense. What could his death have to do with Tanner Green?"

"Jerry, I questioned Rudy Yorba about Green right before he was killed," Dillon told him. He had no intention of telling Cheever yet that he'd also broken into a garage based on the information Rudy had given him, even if Cheever had basically suggested it.

"Come on, Jerry, what would the man have been doing walking along the highway that late?"

"He ran out of gas, sweet and simple. He was

probably walking to the off-ramp, looking for a gas station," Jerry explained.

"No AAA?" Dillon demanded.

"No, not in his wallet, anyway. There's just no mystery here."

"Really? I think there is. These days, everyone has a cell phone, and cars come with roadside assistance."

"He drove an old car. And without AAA, who was he going to call? A drunk hit him, got scared and drove away. Come on, Dillon, not everything is a conspiracy." Jerry ran his fingers through his hair, shaking his head. "Don't I wish this *was* all related, that somewhere there's a clue that would give me some answers."

"Don't you have *any*thing?" Dillon demanded.

"It's not my case. I've told you that. Go check with vehicular homicide."

"Cheever, what the hell kind of a cop are you?" Dillon demanded.

For a moment Jerry Cheever seemed about to explode in turn, but then he looked down, gritted his teeth, then looked up again. "It's departmental organization, and that's just the way it is. But go and talk to Len Durso. He and his partner got the call. They're top-notch, and so are the crime-scene team, who've inspected the body, his clothing, the road, you name it. If there *is* a connection, I sure as hell pray they—*we*—find it."

Dillon realized that Cheever was looking past

155

him, frowning slightly as he peered through the glass windows of his office.

Dillon swung around and groaned softly. Jessy Sparhawk was standing just outside. Her eyes widened as she saw him, and for a moment he thought she was going to turn around and leave. But she didn't. Blue eyes wide and captivatingly innocent, she stood her ground. Dillon felt his heart surge and silently cursed himself, wondering again just what it was about this woman that he found so compelling.

He stood as Jerry strode across the room and opened the door.

"Sorry. I don't mean to intrude."

"Dillon was just leaving," Jerry said.

Dillon thought about finding a way to stay, then opted not to. She was going to have to decide that she needed to open up to him. She was going to have to trust him.

Besides, if she wanted to speak privately to Cheever, well . . .

Ringo could listen in and tell him if there was anything he needed to know.

"Jessy," he acknowledged politely, and left, deciding he might as well make good use of the time. He headed down the hall to ask the desk sergeant where he could find Detective Durso.

"Sit down, sit down, how can I help you?" Jerry Cheever asked.

Jessy took the chair in front of the desk, while he perched on the edge of it.

"Have you discovered anything more about the murder of Tanner Green?" she asked him without preamble.

He arched a brow and answered slowly. "You know, investigations take time. Unfortunately, we don't usually solve things as easily as the crime shows would have you believe."

"I know that. I was just anxious, I guess," she told him.

"We're investigating several leads, though," he told her. "We're doing our best, and, I'm certain, in the end, that we *will* discover the truth. Have you thought of anything that might help with the case?" he asked her.

"No. Actually . . . I'm just curious about Mr. Green himself," Jessy told him.

"Oh? Why?" Cheever asked.

"I wanted to know if he had a twin, or maybe a brother who looks a lot like him," she said.

Cheever seemed surprised, but he stood and walked around behind his desk, hit a few keys on his computer, then met her eyes. "Nope. No siblings. He was the only child of Mathew and Virginia Green, both deceased many years ago."

"Oh," she said with a noticeable lack of enthusiasm. Great. She had asked, the question had been just as ridiculous as she'd feared, and now

Cheever was staring at her as if he was about to grill her once again.

She stood quickly. "I'm sorry. I shouldn't have taken your time."

"Why the concern about siblings?" Cheever asked, getting up to see her out.

"I just thought that . . . well, I haven't seen anything in the paper about a funeral," she said, amazed that the lie came to her tongue so easily, even though it wouldn't stand up to close investigation.

"The body is still being held in the morgue. But there's a note here that Emil Landon called to say that he'll handle the arrangements once it's released."

"That's nice to hear," she said.

"Keep your eye on the papers. I'm sure there'll be a notice when the time comes," Jerry suggested.

"Yes, of course. And thank you." She started out of the office, then hesitated. "It's kind of strange, isn't it? That poor guy who worked for the Sun is dead, too."

"Don't worry. We intend to find out who was responsible."

She nodded and left at last.

Dillon hadn't met Len Durso before, but the cop seemed to be a decent guy. He was a big-enough man that he could have been intimidating, but his response was open and friendly when Dillon introduced himself and presented his card, with the Harrison Investigations logo on it, then explained why he'd come.

"We've just started investigating," Durso said, shaking Dillon's hand and studying him from under heavy lids, as if he'd heard about him and was intrigued.

"I don't believe it was an accident," Dillon said flatly.

"It was a hard impact, killing the guy instantly, I can tell you that. The body is at the morgue—probably in autopsy right now. The M.E. hasn't signed off yet, but she's already told me that whoever hit him was going a good sixty miles an hour. There are no tire marks on the highway, so the driver didn't try to stop," Durso told him. "We'll know more when we get the full forensic and autopsy reports."

"Can you call me to let me know what you learn?" Dillon pointed to the card in Durso's hand.

"I'm curious," Durso told him. "What's your interest in this?"

Durso was being honest with him, more forthcoming than Dillon had any right to expect, so he replied in kind. "I think it was murder. I think Yorba might have been able to ID whoever killed Tanner Green, and that's why he's dead now." "You working for Emil Landon?" Durso demanded, seeming to retreat slightly.

"My boss's call," Dillon told him. "Landon thinks he's a target."

"Yeah? Well, Landon is walking around just fine, and if you're right, two other men have died in his stead," Durso said. Dillon decided he'd made the right call, telling the cop that he'd been instructed to take the case.

Dillon said, "I'm thinking it might be some kind of an inside job, with someone from the Big Easy working with somebody from the Sun. Because if it's not, the Tanner Green murder is the most coincidence-filled case I've ever seen."

Durso studied him gravely. "I'll look into anything you give me. I met Adam Harrison when he was here on a case a few years back. No one ever talked about the details, but he's clearly an amazing guy, so anything I can do . . . For now, tell me how you think this might have gone down. What makes you think it was an inside job?"

"The limo that dropped Tanner Green off at the casino was just out of range of several security cameras. That's almost impossible to accomplish—unless you know the exact range and angle of view of those cameras," Dillon explained.

"A tech guru might be able to figure it out."

"That would be very tough and not very likely," Dillon said. "And like I said, the reason I think the two deaths are connected is that Rudy was parking cars at the Sun that night, and I think *he* got a look at what the cameras missed. So thanks. I appreciate the offer of help."

"I'll appreciate yours, too, if you get anything," Durso told him.

The two men shook hands goodbye, and as Dillon walked slowly back toward the exit, he keyed in the phone number Sarah had given him the night before.

"Hey there," she said, once he identified himself.

"Hey yourself. I have a question for you. Do you know anything about what Tanner Green was wearing the night he died?"

"Top of the line," she told him. "Designer all the way. His shoes must have cost more than I make in a week."

"Was there any damage to his clothing?"

"Well, there was the hole made by the knife," she said. "And the bloodstains."

"Anything else?"

"Wait a minute." He could hear her rustling papers.

"Yeah, his shirt was missing two buttons," she read off a report.

"Thanks," he said. *"Thanks."*

"What have you got?"

"As soon as I'm closer to really knowing something, I'll let you know."

Passing the squad room on her way out, Jessy looked over at the sea of desks and the officers who were hurrying from place to place, almost as if they were ants busying themselves around their hill.

She still felt tense, and she didn't know why. Looking around again, she found herself half expecting Tanner Green to be seated at one of the desks, staring at her. But he was nowhere in sight, a fact that should have filled her with more relief than it did.

One piece of information sat dully in her mind. Tanner Green had been an only child.

She was also curious about the fact that Dillon Wolf had been in with Cheever. She supposed it was because they were both investigating Green's death, so they undoubtedly needed to work with one another, even if they didn't necessarily like one another.

And why hadn't she told Cheever what she hadn't been willing to tell Dillon, either: that just before dying, Tanner Green had whispered a single word to her?

Indigo.

"Jessy?"

The sound of her own name startled her, and she jumped. Dillon Wolf was walking down the hall toward her.

"I'm sorry. I didn't mean to startle you," he said.

He was tall, solid. Certainly attractive. And it wasn't just his looks, either. It was the confident way he moved. The way he spoke. Even in a dream, she had felt the attraction, the longing to be with him. The need to be held. And touched. Was this strange attraction all because she was seeing a

162

ghost, or was she genuinely attracted to him? She was very much afraid it was the latter.

She was edgy around him, and she wasn't sure why. She wasn't afraid of him, exactly, it was more that she was afraid of . . . how much he seemed to know about her, the way he saw through to the vulnerability she longed to deny.

"Are you all right?" he asked, looking at her skeptically.

"Fine, thank you." Oh, God, she was such a liar. And he could see it, of course. He didn't ask another question, he just studied her with his dark, intense eyes, and she found herself babbling. "I just came in to see what was going on with the investigation."

"Sure." He glanced at his watch. "You working today?"

"Yes."

"The same show?" When she nodded, he asked, "Does that mean you have time for a late breakfast or an early lunch . . . or just a cup of coffee?"

She wanted to say no. She wanted to run away.

Which was just crazy. And seriously, did she want to be alone right now?

"Please?" he added.

Why couldn't he be so obnoxious that she would have a good reason to say no?

"I guess brunch would be a good thing," she said.

"Great," he told her, then laid his hand against

the base of her back to usher her from the station. Outside, he suggested that they take his car, offering to drive her back afterward for hers, and she reluctantly agreed.

He drove a small hybrid. Vegas might be a city of extravagance, but thinking about the man, she decided she wasn't surprised.

He chose a charming mom-and-pop place she'd never been to before. At first she was surprised by that, and then she realized that Las Vegas was filled with restaurants, many of which came and went in the blink of an eye, so perhaps it wasn't so strange after all.

The restaurant was sparkling clean; the little vases of flowers on the table were fresh. The room itself was sunny and airy, but despite that, as they sat down, she looked around, afraid she was going to see the mournful eyes of Tanner Green staring at her. Pleading with her. But for what?

"The eggs Benedict are excellent," he suggested. "And the soups are homemade."

She wasn't really interested in the food. "Eggs Benedict sounds fine," she told him.

The waitress turned out to be one of the owners. Dillon chatted pleasantly with her for a few minutes as he ordered.

Once cups of steaming coffee had been set before them, he looked at her and smiled. "Why have you been avoiding me?" he asked her.

"I—I'm not," she protested.

"The thing is, I think you need me," he told her soberly.

It wasn't a line, and she knew it. Still, she tossed back a lock of hair and said, "Well, that's a new come-on," she said.

He didn't reply, didn't even crack a smile.

"I think your life might be in danger," he said flatly.

Her fingers trembled as she held her coffee cup; she decided not to try to take a sip. "Why?" she breathed.

He leaned toward her. "Tanner Green spoke to you before he died. I saw it on the tapes."

"But . . . only the cops have those tapes, right?" she asked him. "Are you trying to tell me that the police department is crooked?"

"I don't know how many copies of those tapes are out there. As for the police . . . it's a huge department. I'm sure not everyone is crooked, but that doesn't mean *some*one can't be. And the casino has the tapes, too. Look, you heard about the guy who was killed in that hit-and-run—un, right?"

"Yes. It's very sad."

"No, it's more than sad. I'm almost positive he was killed because he spoke with me," he told her seriously.

"Oh, great—and now *I'm* speaking with you."

"Jessy, you know something, and sooner or later the killer's going to figure that out," he said.

Eggs Benedict, aromatic and enticing, were set before her. She picked up her fork and cut a bite, then couldn't bring the fork to her lips.

Tell him, she thought. *Just spit out that one word and it will be all over.*

She stared down at her coffee cup, but when she looked up again, about to speak, she went silent in stunned terror instead.

Tanner Green was sitting at the table behind Dillon Wolf, staring at her morosely.

Worse. At the table behind *him*—not with him, just behind him—was another specter.

She'd never met the man in life, but she'd seen his picture on the news, and she couldn't mistake the face.

Rudy Yorba.

Dillon Wolf saw her expression and swung around to see what she was staring at.

As Dillon turned, Tanner Green leaped to his feet, jostling the table in the process. The salt and pepper shakers rattled.

And then he was gone, with Rudy Yorba disappearing seemingly into thin air right along with him.

Several other diners looked around, aware of something, but seeing nothing.

Not Dillon Wolf. He leaned toward her and said flatly, "You saw them." It wasn't a question.

She stared at him, blinked, and tried to deny it.

"I didn't see anything."

166

He had seen them, too, she suddenly realized.

She wanted to scream.

A part of her heard chatter, laughter, the clink of cups and the sounds of forks on plates. She heard music playing in the background, something country, pleasant and soft.

She jumped up, forgetting all about her food.

"You have to stay away from me," she told Dillon.

He had risen when she did. He grimly dropped money on the table, and when she turned to flee the restaurant, he was right behind her.

In the parking lot, she remembered that they had come in his car.

She winced, but didn't jump, when she felt his hand on her arm. When she turned, she saw the light of empathy and concern in his eyes, and she was torn between wanting to laugh and wanting to cry, right there in the parking lot. She was tempted to throw herself into his arms, wishing she could forget all of this—the murder, the ghost—and suggest that she screw work and, well, hell, screw him, as well.

But that wasn't her. No matter what was going on in her life or how attracted to him she felt.

"You're seeing Tanner Green," he said without inflection.

"No. Tanner Green is dead," she said.

"He's a ghost, and he's out there," Dillon assured her. His hand was still on her arm, and she found herself feeling inexplicably grateful. Her knees had gone to water, and her mind kept insisting that none of this could be real, not even the man before her.

She stared at him, the misery suddenly rising uncontrollably. "Why? Why is he doing this to me? Why the hell is he haunting me?" Dillon leaned toward her, eyes intent. "Short and simple. He needs you."

8

It was time to find the treasure. And, as amazing as it seemed, with her going through the entire performance on autopilot, she was managing to do a decent job. Somehow she'd compartmentalized the part of her that was in shock and terror, so she could make the show everything it should be for the kids.

She didn't remember saying much as they'd driven to the casino. She still didn't have her car. Dillon had suggested that she would be better off not driving, and she had agreed with him. He had hung around in the hall while she got dressed, and her coworkers had teased her about her handsome admirer. He spent a few minutes talking to the guard, and when the show began, he watched from the audience. He was sitting with a bunch of what looked like six-year-olds, and he seemed to be having a good time. He seemed so austere at times, and yet he could also unbend and have fun, and easily elicit trust from those around him.

Everything was going to be all right, she insisted to herself.

She was careful not to look toward the back of the room. It was bad enough seeing Tanner Green. It was adding insult to injury, being haunted by Rudy Yorba, a man she'd never even met. Not that she'd ever been formally introduced to Tanner Green, of course.

She made it through the show.

And when it was all over, when the pictures had been taken and the last gold-covered chocolate coin had been given away, Dillon was still there, waiting for her.

In the dressing room, she scrubbed her face, managed some casual conversation with a few other cast members and changed back into her street clothes. Dillon was in the hall, and when she joined him, she once again resisted the temptation to reach out for him, bury her head against his shoulder and cry. Or maybe just scream. She tried not to look like a doe caught in the headlights as she said, "Thanks for waiting."

She was surprised to see the admiration in his eyes. "You were terrific."

"You think?"

"Hey, not many people have to admit that not one, but two, ghosts are following them around, then go out onstage."

He should have been joking, she thought, because the words were just that crazy. Instead, he was dead serious.

"I think you need some company, and I know for sure you need some food," he said. "How would you feel about seeing my place? I have a house, a yard, the whole bit, and best of all, it's not far away. You didn't eat, and I'm not a great cook, but I can manage a mean frozen lasagna with a fresh salad."

"Your house will be fine," she said. She didn't care where they went—as long as he didn't leave her alone.

It took only a few minutes to reach his raised ranch–style house, which wasn't far from the Strip. There was an adobe wall around the yard, which was handsomely landscaped with cacti and stone-bordered gardens. Inside, they were immediately greeted by a huge dog.

"Clancy, be polite. This is Jessy Sparhawk. I know she looks like she should be Swedish, but she's actually part Lakota. Clancy is Belgian," he informed Jessy.

"She's beautiful," Jessy told him awkwardly. It was true; the dog *was* beautiful—and very friendly. She didn't jump up or slobber, but she was happy to be petted, though it was apparent that she adored her master.

"Come on in and have a seat," Dillon offered.

"Thanks," she said.

She heard a slight jingling sound and looked around nervously, but she couldn't see anything. At least neither Tanner Green nor Rudy Yorba seemed to have followed her.

Dillon was studying her as if he was about to say something, but apparently he thought better of it, because he turned and headed through the stone-paved entryway into the living room. Native American art decorated the room, representing a number of different tribes. She recognized some of the pieces as local Paiute art, and some she recognized because they were similar to pieces in Timothy's collection. Lakota dolls sat on the mantel, several dreamcatchers hung in the windows, and she recognized a Seminole shirt on one wall, ringed by small Inuit pieces.

There was a high-def television set opposite a leather sofa and matching chairs, and a cypress coffee table. Steps led up to a counter separating the kitchen from the living room, and beyond that, she could see a family room and French doors that led out to a small pool and patio, with the yard enclosed by an extension of the adobe wall, which was higher there in the back.

"Would you like something to drink?" he asked her.

"Yes, thank you."

"What?"

"I don't care, as long as it has alcohol in it," she said, sinking down onto the sofa. It was definitely a masculine room. She saw no sign that any female—other than Clancy—shared the space.

"Beer or bourbon, those are your choices—well, other than glass or bottle?"

"You can probably just hand me the bottle of bourbon," she joked, then said, "No, I didn't mean that. A beer will be fine."

He came out with two, then returned to the kitchen. She sat back with her beer, letting herself appreciate the art and artifacts that gave the room its character. It felt good to be sitting there in silence—and safe.

He returned in a couple of minutes with a platter holding cheese, sliced pepperoni, fruit and chips. "I hope you're not a vegetarian or a health-food addict," he said.

"No," she told him, and suddenly she was starving. She reached for a piece of cheese, which was delicious, and then another. She forced herself to slow down. He had taken one of the nearby chairs, and she smiled over at him. "Thanks. This really hits the spot."

"Sure. You must be starving by now."

Clancy came and lay down between them. The dog didn't beg, even when Dillon reached down and stroked her head.

"You still doing okay?" he asked.

Jessy nodded. Then she stared at him, taking a long swallow of beer. "Harrison Investigations is a . . . a ghost-busting organization, isn't it?" she asked.

He smiled. "The truth? Sometimes, yes. Other times we go in and find out that there's a natural explanation for a 'haunting' or whatever is supposedly going on."

"But . . . you saw them," she whispered. "You saw Tanner Green and Rudy Yorba, the same as I did." She couldn't believe she was admitting out loud that she'd seen a ghost. Two ghosts.

"I saw them, but too briefly to find out anything," he said regretfully.

She tried not to let her voice rise to a squeak. "You *want* to see them?"

"Of course."

"Oh." She took another long swallow of her beer. "Well, I don't."

"They're only here because they have something to say, something to ask. They need help clearing up the mystery surrounding their own deaths," Dillon explained.

"Then they should be following *you* around," she whispered. "*You're* the investigator."

"Yeah, I agree, and I admit to being perplexed about that myself. I mean, I understand Tanner Green. You were his last contact. But I was one of the last people to speak to Rudy, and you never even met him. I think he's too green, too new, and that he can't figure it out."

"Figure what out?" she asked.

"Sometimes the body dies but the soul, or whatever you want to call it, remains, because it's looking for justice. For closure, to use the trendy term. But sometimes it takes the soul, the ghost, a while to even figure out what's happened to him, much less how he can get the help he needs. Neither I, nor anyone I know, has all the answers. What's clear so far is that Tanner Green seems to be afraid."

"Afraid?" Jessy repeated skeptically.

Dillon smiled. "Yes. Afraid to accept death. But he seems to trust you and no one else."

"How can I tell him that I'm not trustworthy?" Jessy asked.

Dillon laughed at that. Jessy didn't.

"You can't," Dillon said. "But you can help me make contact with him, and when that happens, I can try to help him. And once he's gotten the help he needs, then he won't haunt you anymore."

"I'm supposed to introduce you to a ghost?" she asked incredulously.

He offered her a rueful smile. "Something like that, but not so easy, I'm afraid. You'll have to let him get close, and let him see that you trust me. Eventually he'll trust me, too, and let me know how I can help."

"Eventually?" she said with dismay.

"He's not trying to hurt you, you know," Dillon told her.

"Maybe not," she said. "but what if I'm driving and he suddenly pops up? Doesn't he realize I might run into a wall or take a few pedestrians out with me?"

"People don't always think rationally, and ghosts don't, either," he said, then changed the subject.

"Would you like another?" he asked, indicating her empty beer bottle.

She nodded.

This time, when he headed toward the kitchen, she rose and followed him. Clancy pattered along, as well, sitting at her feet when she took a stool at the counter.

"Have you always seen ghosts?" she asked him.

He smiled and shook his head. "I grew up on one of the Paiute reservations near here, and I was a wiseass kid. My mom was a nurse who was working for the government, vaccinating kids. She met my dad, and they fell in love. They were a couple of dreamers, in love with the whole world. I was an only child, and when they moved onto a government military base—my dad joined the army, and we were sent to North Carolina—I suddenly became an oddity. Kids can be brutal. Not so much when they're really young. At that point they don't know Chinese from Indian, black man from Inuit. They see skin color the way most men see the color of someone's hair, but when they get older . . . Anyway, I started getting into scrapes when I hit my teens. Nothing really bad, mostly because my parents would have been so disappointed. Then they were killed together in a small-plane crash. I turned into a real asshole then. After their funeral—they were buried back here, in

Nevada, because they both loved it here—I was at a bar, drinking pretty heavily, and I picked a fight with a big white burly guy just because he was blond." His smile twisted into a grim slash. "You're Lakota, right? Our tribes share a lot of the same myths and beliefs. You've heard the stories about the maiden who wears white, and the great white buffalo, and the magic that comes when they're seen? Well, I saw the maiden. She was at the funeral. At first I chalked it up to the trauma of my parents' deaths. Then, at the bar—right when I'd started the fight and the guy was about to rearrange my face—she stepped between us. She spoke to me. I can still hear her words. 'No. It's not the way. You must grow strong. Pain must never cause pain. You must find your peace—for them, for yourself.' I think some friends dragged me away and apologized for me, told the guy my folks had just died. Anyway, after that day . . . I started seeing . . . people. Ghosts. Then I met Adam."

"Adam Harrison," she said softly.

He nodded. "Adam had a son, Josh, and Adam adored him. He died, but he still hung around Adam, trying to help, even though Adam couldn't actually see him. Adam started putting together a team of people to look into cases with a para-normal angle because he always recognized the ability to see ghosts, to talk to them, in others, even though he didn't have it himself for many years. He's still not really able to see ghosts the way

176

some of us can, but he's learned to sense their presence, sometimes even get a sense of what they want. In my family, the ability—which I thought for a long time was just me being crazy—is called nightwalking. It's being able to see what exists in a slightly different dimension, I guess. But it's not an evil ability. It's just frightening to some people, at first. When you think about it, though, the whole thing is actually kind of reassuring."

"It's reassuring to think I might end up seeing *more* ghosts?" she asked. She realized that at some point he had come over to the counter, leaned across it and taken her hands. She liked the feeling. It was almost as if his warmth and vitality was passing into her, as if he was giving her strength.

He gave her hands a quick final squeeze, then released them, turning back to open the oven. He grabbed pot holders and drew out a foil pan of lasagna, which he set on a trivet on the counter. Then he looked at her. "I was glad to become a nightwalker," he said, "because it meant there was another place, another world after this one. That there was a supreme being and the essence of a person lived on." He smiled and shrugged. "My mom was a Catholic, so my spiritual ethic has a lot of elements mixed into it. In my mind, there's one big power, and it doesn't matter how you recognize it or what you call it. I think a person's time on earth is best spent learning how to be decent to others. If there is a heaven or a great white prairie

177

in the sky, I know my parents have earned their place there. And that's something I find reassuring."

She stared back at him. It was a wonderful thing, belief, she had to admit.

"Want to set the table?" he asked her.

"Uh, sure."

He was already reaching into the refrigerator for the salad makings. She slipped off the stool and started retrieving plates from the cabinet he indicated, then found silverware, napkins and glasses, and set them out in the family room, on a table that looked out over the patio.

"This is a very nice house," she told him.

"Thanks. I like it."

"I guess you make a decent living as a ghost buster," she said, hoping her tone was light enough, then thinking maybe she shouldn't have spoken at all. "Sorry, that was nosy and none of my business."

"It's all right. We're paid pretty much the same rates as any investigators, but we do all right. Adam negotiates the contracts and gives us our assignments. We can turn down any case we don't feel comfortable with, though."

"Emil Landon just doesn't seem like the kind of guy you'd work for," she said, and then realized the rudeness of her comment.

He laughed. "Honestly? I loathe the bastard."

"So why did you accept the assignment?"

He shrugged. "I just figured that if Adam wanted me to, there had to be a reason somewhere. Now, even if Landon fires me, I'll stay on it. I barely knew Tanner Green, and I knew Rudy Yorba even less, but they deserve justice. I won't let Yorba's death go down as an accident. Not when he was murdered."

"You can't blame yourself for his death," she told him.

A slight heightening of his color told her that she had touched a nerve, and she was suddenly sorry she'd said anything.

"He might have been targeted already. I just don't know. And that's why solving this is so important."

He finished fixing the salad and poured iced tea for them to drink with dinner. While they ate, the conversation flowed easily. She asked questions, he answered them, and then he asked her about her life. He was a comfortable man to be with, she thought as she found herself telling him about the other cast members and about Timothy—even about old Mrs. Teasdale and the other people at the home who made it such a nice place for Timothy to live.

The frozen lasagna was actually very good, which she hadn't expected, and the salad was fresh and delicious. Best of all, she was starting to feel as if she had known Dillon Wolf forever.

She didn't want to leave.

But when the dishes were washed, Clancy fed, and they'd even had coffee out back by the pool, she decided it was time to say something before she overstayed her welcome.

"I should go home."

"Do you have a pet?" he asked her.

She shook her head. "Huh? No."

"Then why are you worried about leaving?" he asked.

"Well, my car is still at the police station, for one thing," she told him.

"I have friends there. Nothing will happen to it," he told her. "Look, you've been scared—nearly frightened to death—tonight. Stay here. There's a guest room. And a computer—anything you might need."

"I shouldn't stay. It wouldn't be right."

"What's really right and what's wrong?" he asked her. "Are you worried about what people might think? Are you worried about your grandfather?"

"No, no, Timothy's fine. He stays at the home most of the time. I take him out for weekends, sometimes, and I had him the other night because I was afraid they were going to force him out. I don't usually play a lot of money at the craps table. Not that I'm anti-gambling or anything. It can be fun, if you don't get carried away. But—" She broke off, looking at him. "I'm babbling, I think."

"Babble all you want. I still think you should stay."

180

"Are you using me as bait?" she asked him. "Are you trying to lure a ghost in?"

"Aren't you trying to get rid of a ghost?"

She laughed.

He stood. "Come on. I'll show you the guest room."

He was serious, she realized. Apparently he really wasn't after her body, and she had to admit, she was somewhat disappointed. He led her to the guest room, which was done in mauve and a sand shade that complemented the desert tones of the house and yard. The guest room even had its own bath.

And a new wide-screen television.

He offered her a T-shirt and baggy sweatpants to sleep in, and she thanked him, realizing that this was the first time in what seemed like forever that she hadn't been afraid.

That she was even ready to see a ghost.

He left her, excusing himself to go work on the computer. She showered and changed, and was some what dismayed to realize that she liked wearing his clothes, as if they were a touch of the man himself.

Her cell phone rang, startling her. She made a dive for her purse and answered it quickly. Sandra's voice came over the line. "Are you all right? Why haven't you called me? I've been waiting for you to call," she chided.

"I'm fine. Did I say I was going to call?"

"No. But I'm worried sick about you. Is everything all right?"

"Everything is fine. And thanks for caring and checking up, Sandra."

"So you're home and you're all locked in?"

"Everything is fine," Jessy repeated, then hesitated before adding, "I'm at Dillon Wolf's house."

Sandra's shriek was so loud that Jessy winced. "You're *what?*"

"Calm down. It's not a date or anything," Jessy said quickly. "I'm not even with him anymore."

"You're at his house without him?"

"No, he's here. He's in the other room, on his computer."

"I'm going to want details. I hope you know that." Jessy heard Reggie saying something in the background, followed by an excited explosion that matched her mother's.

"What's going on?" Jessy demanded.

"Reggie wants details, too. I told her no, but that doesn't mean *I* don't get them."

"There *are* no details," Jessy insisted. "And I'm going now. But, Sandra?"

"What?"

"Thanks for calling me."

"You bet, kid. I'm going to *keep* calling, too."

With a smile, Jessy closed her phone. It wasn't such a bad world. She had really good friends. And she didn't have to be afraid, at least not tonight, because Dillon Wolf was just beyond the door.

• • •

It was probably a little late to be calling anyone, but Dillon had known Dr. Doug Tarleton, one of Las Vegas's top medical examiners, for many years. Doug either answered his phone or he didn't. If he saw the caller ID and wasn't interested, he wouldn't answer. If he was sleeping, the only number that would ring through was his emergency number.

Doug answered the phone on the second ring.

"Dillon Wolf," he said, without even a hello. "I was wondering when the hell I'd be hearing from you."

"Well, I was trying to go through proper channels," Dillon said.

Doug laughed. "You mean Jerry Cheever? He's a decent cop. He's just got a chip on his shoulder. And, frankly, he's not as enamored of Harrison Investigations as a lot of folks are."

"He just acts like he's got a stick up his ass, is all," Dillon agreed. "Maybe it's not his fault. Maybe a bully stole his Froot Loops when he was a kid. Anyway, I've been trying to keep the channels of communication going through him, but it seemed past time to start going straight to the source. Where did I catch you?"

"I'm still at the morgue."

"You are?"

"Yeah. I was just finishing up when the report on that young guy came in—the hit-and-run

183

victim. Man, dead is dead, I know, but the injuries that guy had . . . hell. Thank God the impact broke his neck—along with crushing his rib cage, and every bone in his chest and pelvis. Anyway, I had just finished reading that—damn thing was as long as a book—when the tox reports on Tanner Green came in. Get this. The guy was tripping."

"Tripping? You mean acid?"

"Yup, LSD. Some bodyguard—he must have been higher than a kite."

"Well, he wasn't on duty," Dillon mused. "You got anything else?"

"He'd have been dead before fifty, I can tell you that. His liver was going, and judging by his cholesterol, he must have dined on red meat for breakfast, lunch and dinner. Plus, he was overweight. But the cause of death was a punctured lung. He drowned in his own blood."

There had been no sign of blood in either limo, Dillon thought.

"Would the injury have caused any spatter?"

"Well, it was one hard strike. From the back, missing the bone, straight into the lung. The outer blood loss was a slow leak down his back that increased once the knife was jarred by his fall—his shirt was drenched, and the craps table took some of it. I'm assuming the woman he died on would have been covered in blood, too. But he might not have left any kind of a trail, because, until he fell, it was collecting mostly in his lungs. The knife actually worked like a cork at first, keeping seepage to a minimum."

"Thanks, Doug. I appreciate the help."

"Not a problem. It's my job. But this case is pretty bizarre, huh? And there's no way to avoid the fact that Tanner Green was no angel. I'm glad you're on it, because it's not as if they'll be sending out an army to find his killer." Doug was quiet for a minute. "You're involved because you think his death connects to something bigger, don't you?"

"I do. I think the two deaths are connected," Dillon said.

"A murder and a hit-and-run?" Doug asked.

"A murder and a murder," Dillon told him, then thanked his friend and hung up. Tomorrow, he decided, he would take a trip down to the morgue.

Jessy didn't fall asleep easily, but for the first time since the incident, it wasn't because she was afraid. She was giddy because she *wasn't* afraid.

The room was comfortable.

Dillon was nearby.

She stayed awake with the television on, flipping through a magazine and reading about different politicians' plans to improve the state of the country.

Eventually she fell asleep.

And dreamed.

But tonight wasn't a repeat of the nightmares that had plagued her. There were no visions of dead men, no graveyards, no people who looked like they'd lived long ago. Tonight's dreams were so erotic that she could feel herself blushing, but they were also so sweet that she had no desire to wake up, even though she knew she was dreaming. Dillon played a starring role, and there was no awkwardness between them. She didn't know where they were, or who had initiated the encounter, only that their bodies were entangled, his copper-hued flesh strong and vibrant. She could hear their whispers, their laughter and the gasp of her own breath, matched by his. She felt as if they had been together forever, as if she had known him for years. She could feel the force of his kiss, the seductive journey of his lips and tongue along her flesh. She could see his face and feel his body straddling hers, bathing her in liquid fire. . . .

Suddenly she jolted into wakefulness, seized by inward panic. But when she sat up and looked around, she was alone, no sign of Tanner Green.

There was a tap on her door, soft, hesitant.

"Yes?" she said quickly, fighting the fear that threatened to swamp her.

The door opened and Dillon was there, silhouetted against the light from the hall.

"Are you all right?" he asked her.

Embarrassment swept through her as she thought about what an honest answer would sound like.

Yes, I'm fine, I was just dreaming about having wild sex with you, but don't worry. It's just the pathetic longings of a woman with no sex life.

"I'm fine," she said, and left it at that.

"You cried out," he told her.

"I did?"

"Yes."

"Lord, I'm sorry. I'm fine. Honestly. I haven't been so fine in . . . a while. I didn't mean to wake you."

"It's all right. I sleep lightly. Good night," he said, and started to close the door.

"Wait!"

He hesitated.

And then she did, too, suddenly unable to go on.

It was as if the air itself grew heavy with anticipation, with anxiety, as if fate itself hung on what would happen next. She half rose, thinking that she could suggest they make some tea. Talk. Head to the living room, the kitchen, or just take the dog for a walk. . . .

"Please, don't leave," she told him.

He paused in the doorway, then walked slowly into the room. He had thrown on a robe, and she knew—without knowing how she knew—that he had nothing on beneath it. His eyes were sober, and his voice was low and even when he told her, "You have nothing to fear here, you know. I'm right across the hall. Just yell and I'll be right here."

187

"I know that," she told him. "I'm not afraid."

He reached out, the most fascinating man she'd ever encountered, and smoothed a strand of her hair.

"Really," he said, with one of the smiles that so charmed her.

"Really," she echoed.

"We could watch a movie," he suggested.

"We could. But that's not what I had in mind," she told him.

His smile broadened, and when he touched her, the jolt was palpable, as if a circuit had been completed. She nearly gasped in awe as what had been a dream became real, because the truth of his hands on her was far more exciting than anything her subconscious could conjure. He slid into bed beside her, fingers twining into her hair, his mouth sure, firm, seductive, and an explosion of arousal followed his first touch. She felt as if they were fused together, and it was easy to overcome the hesitancy of a lifetime and slip her arms around him, to relish the solidity of his muscles and the smooth hot skin beneath the robe. There was urgency in every touch, and yet they both seemed filled with a determination to take their time, to savor the process of getting to know one another.

The first kiss seemed to go on for aeons, but aeons filled with wonder, where every deep thrust led to a new burst of exploding fire and arousal in which their bodies shifted again, touching anew, hands roving and discovering more and more. His robe was easily dispensed with, and his naked flesh against hers further kindled the frantic rise of heat within her. She had known that he was muscle and sinew wrapped in sleek copper, and now the feel of him against her was as powerful as burning metal. His hands were exactly like the man himself, sure, confident, with a strength that elicited trust and wonder, and swiftly simmering excitement. Their limbs tangled and locked as his fingers brushed her face, stroked her neck and throat. His lips burned through the cotton material of the shirt she had borrowed, and she would never know exactly when or even who removed it at last, so that his tongue could blaze like sunlight across her breasts and abdomen.

She savored the magic of his embrace, the vibrant bonds of flesh and muscle, and found herself insatiable in her longing to touch and taste in return, to run her fingers into his hair, over his shoulders, down the length of his body. Her lips, too, strayed to his torso, a courtesy of introduction before exploring ever intimately, until she lifted her head their lips locked once more.

At last she was on her back, staring up into his eyes, ink dark and paradoxically filled with both an ancient wisdom and buoyant youth, as well as vitality, humor and passion. She gasped as he moved between her thighs, slow and sure, and filling the world, *her* world, with his presence as he took her to a physical extreme she had never known existed. She was caught in an inferno, a massive bonfire burning in the darkness of a desert night. She clung to him, writhed against him, arched to meet every thrust and shift, and relished each gasp and rising thrill as she was tossed in a tempest of need and desire. She raked his shoulders with her nails and was aware of his hands gripping her buttocks as he drove her upward toward the explosion of climax. But then he drew back from the precipice and slowed the pace, before sending her soaring once more. Again and again, accelerating, then braking, until she was frantic, her fingers dancing down his back in a frenzy, her lips against his throat, demanding and voracious. She climaxed at last, the moment violent in its intensity and wild abandon, shaking in his hold, jerking against him again and again, her flesh wet and slick and trembling against him as the world shook and receded and reality finally, slowly, returned.

Because this was no dream. Everything about him was real and solid.

He held her, the aftereffects of his own release still rippling through him, his embrace firm. He was a careful lover, easing the weight of his body from hers, yet never releasing her, never allowing her to think for one moment that she was anything less than precious and coveted. Still gasping for breath, she lay spooned against him, the moonlight playing across their bodies, and the shyness that assailed her so often when she wasn't on a stage returned. She knew that they would have to move eventually, that there would have to be words. Sex was sex; they had done nothing new, nothing that changed the world, no matter how it had felt at the time. Even so, for her, the night hadn't been casual, and she could only hope that he hadn't made love to her only to ease her fears or because of a momentary urge.

He didn't speak at first, only kissed the nape of her neck as her heart kept thundering. And then at last he whispered, "Shall I stay? I don't want to leave."

She wound her fingers through his, where they rested on her abdomen, and was both sorry that she couldn't see the ebony depths of his eyes, yet glad he couldn't see her own slightly panicked expression.

"Please," she managed to say, regretting her own lack of eloquence. She'd sounded as if she were agreeing to sugar in her coffee.

But he didn't seem put off, because his arms tightened around her, and she felt the brush of his kiss against her nape again.

And in a while, after she had dozed, roused and moved against him, she felt the force of his body and they once more made love. The first had been a duel of passion and resistance; this was sleepy and slower, yet still possessed of that sensation of desperate and passionate urgency.

She never wanted to move. Never.

With his arms around her, she slept at last.

Even so, she was plagued by dreams.

She was running through the old cemetery again, with its crosses of wood and graves encircled with stones. The wind was light and warm, and at first there was sun but then there wasn't. Always, though, there were people behind her. Chasing her.

Hunting her.

They were coming to kill her, and so she ran, tripping over the stones, running against the sagebrush that blew at her as if a tempest was coming. Just as she heard the footsteps coming closer and closer, she saw a light ahead of her, and a man framed in that light.

It was Dillon.

As she neared him, the sun came out again and her pursuers vanished, fading to nothing but empty darkness behind her, because in him she found the anger and strength and desire to fight back.

She opened her eyes slowly. It was morning, a soft glow filtering through the drapes.

She wasn't alone. And for once she was glad of that.

Dillon lay beside her, just holding her, though she saw that he, too, was awake. When she turned to face him, she saw in his eyes the humor, the kindness and the strength she had expected—along with something more that made her heart leap. There was an intimacy there that made her blood heat, and when he smiled slowly, she felt a little tremor ripple through her as she realized that she wanted him—that look, his touch, everything about him—in her life for much longer than just one night. She had been wary of relationships for so long, like a kid with a chip on her shoulder. She had felt that she needed to defend Timothy from anyone who might pity him or mock her for her devotion to him, but no more. She knew without question that Dillon would understand Timothy's condition, would honor an elder, and would never expect anything from her but loyalty to the grandfather who had raised her.

"Good morning," he said softly. "Did you sleep well?"

She nodded.

"No nightmares?"

"Only one, but you were there," she told him gravely.

"Great," he murmured dryly.

She laughed. "No, you were there in a good way," she assured him. "I was running away from these people I knew wanted to kill me, but then I saw you."

"I hoped I rescued you," he said.

"You did even more."

"Oh?"

"You gave me strength, and when they knew

they couldn't scare me anymore, they disappeared."

"Well, I'm glad of that," he told her, then sat up suddenly, frowning. "Fear can be a good thing sometimes, though. Fear can keep you safe."

"I've been afraid of a ghost," she said softly. "A ghost who *you* said needs help."

"But someone made Tanner Green into a ghost," he said. "And someone killed Rudy Yorba. That person is alive, and it's wise to be afraid of him and what he can do."

She stared at him, her mind suddenly embracing the true importance of what they had shared, and what had—and hadn't—been said.

"Indigo," she told him.

She was startled by his reaction. It was a color, just a color, and when Tanner Green had whispered the word with his dying breath, it hadn't meant anything to her, hadn't struck her as anything that could possibly be important.

"What?" he said sharply.

"Indigo. That's what Tanner Green said right before he died. I'm sorry. I trust you, and I would tell you if he'd said anything more, but that was it. One word. Indigo. Just a color."

He rose, lean muscle and sinew, his back to her, tall and straight in the early-morning light.

"It's more than a color," he said tightly, his back still toward her.

"Oh?"

"It's a place. Indigo, Nevada."

"I've never heard of it. What kind of a place?"

He turned to face her, his dark eyes grim and worried. "A ghost town."

9

Dillon was preparing coffee when Ringo made his first appearance of the day.

Death, apparently, didn't quell a man's sense of humor.

"You look like hell, my friend, and here I was, thinking *I* was the dead man."

"Funny. Now sit down, will you? I'm pretty sure she hears your spurs. And you sure as hell better not have been hanging around here last night."

"I'm deeply wounded!" Ringo protested. "And I was *not* hanging around," he added indignantly. "But aren't you going to introduce us?"

"I was trying to get her accustomed to the ghosts already haunting her. I thought she needed to get a handle on that before realizing that sometimes someone might be . . . *gifted* . . . with an unearthly presence for quite some time."

"Hey, I'm fun and I'm helpful. It's thanks to me that her grandfather is a happy man in that hoity-toity place he likes. I'm anxious to get to know the lady."

"Just don't freak her out when the time comes, okay, Ringo?"

"Stop panicking." Ringo was quiet for a moment. "You took this job with that creep Emil Landon because of me."

"Adam asked, too—though there didn't seem to be a supernatural angle at the time, but I guess he knew something somehow—so . . ." Dillon trailed off with a shrug. "Get out of here for now, though, huh?"

"Hey, that was my room you guys were hogging last night."

"I gave you my room, so quit complaining."

Ringo laughed. "Hey, doesn't much matter to me. Anything is better than being out in the cold. Oh, wait. I don't feel the cold. Still, it's a nice feeling, being in the house and all. Even the damn dog finally likes me."

"Clancy is a good old girl," Dillon said. She was standing next to him and he scratched her ears. "Ringo, listen, I'm going with Jessy to have breakfast with her grandfather. Then you and I are going to take a drive."

"Where?"

"Out to Indigo," Dillon said.

"Indigo?" Ringo said, stunned and anything but pleased. "But that's where—"

"It's where you died. Yeah, I know. And where you hooked yourself with my ancestors. I know that, too. It's also the word that Tanner Green whispered to Jessy before he died."

"Hell and damnation. You're serious?" Ringo demanded.

"Dead serious."

"Excuse me?" Ringo said irritably.

"Bad choice of words. Sorry."

"What are we looking for?" Ringo asked.

"I don't know. But why the hell would a dying man say 'Indigo' unless he had a damn good reason?" He frowned. "When you wanted me to take the Emil Landon assignment, did you know anything about this?" Dillon asked him.

Ringo shook his head with what looked like honesty. "Like I told you then, even for Vegas, that guy is one strange player. I figured there had to be something going on, and the job paid big bucks. I figured it would get you in good with the cops to save one of the local money men." Ringo shrugged. "Okay, I'm outta here right. I'm going to see if I can find out where Tanner Green hangs out when he's not haunting Jessy. And I'll see if I can find Rudy Yorba, too. Maybe I'll even do some spying on Emil Landon."

"You do that. The spying part could be useful. I'll be heading to Indigo about one."

"Doesn't Jessy have to be at work by noon?" Ringo asked him.

"Yeah, I want to run by the morgue after I drop her off. You can meet me there."

"The morgue?" Ringo said with distaste.

"What's the matter? Don't tell me you're squeamish."

"I'll be waiting outside. Just don't hang around

in there too long. You never know what you might pick up. Or who," Ringo warned.

"I'll, uh, be careful," Dillon promised.

"Aren't you worried about leaving Jessy alone? I thought she wanted you around, even when she was working," Ringo said.

"She's going to be all right. She isn't terrified of seeing Tanner Green anymore. She knows now that she's . . . sane," Dillon said.

Ringo nodded, and with a little jingle of spurs, he was gone.

A few minutes later Jessy made her appearance. She had showered but had been forced to put on her outfit from the night before.

She could have worn cardboard for all Dillon cared. The woman was beautiful. With makeup or without. Whatever made her magic was in the way she spoke, in her eyes, in the way she moved, in the sound of her laughter. In her soul. He saw beautiful women all the time, but what made Jessy unique went beyond looks. The phrase was so overused that it had become a joke, but she really *was* beautiful inside and out.

"Ooh, coffee," she said, looking around the room. She was still wary, but she had lost the panic he had seen in her eyes when she had spotted Tanner Green—and then Rudy Yorba—in the café yesterday. "There's no one here, is there?" she asked him.

He shook his head. "No."

She jumped up on one of the bar stools at the counter. "Good." She hesitated. "How do you know when . . . when someone is around?"

"You just . . . see them," he told her. "And it's unusual to be hounded the way you've been, but for some reason Tanner Green's desperate, and he's decided that he trusts you. Soon we've actually got to try to talk to him. But for right now, we'll have coffee, get your car and drop it off at your place, and then we'll go have breakfast with your grandfather, and afterward I'll drop you at the casino."

"How will I get home?" she asked.

"Not alone," he said firmly. "Stay with other people—or call Sandra. Hang with her."

"I need to change," she said, indicating her outfit.

"There's plenty of time," he assured her.

They had coffee, he fed Clancy, and then they left. He opted to wait in the living room at her house, afraid that neither one of them would be able to resist temptation if he went into the bedroom while she changed, and they didn't have that kind of time.

At the home, she directed him straight to Timothy's building.

Timothy was waiting for them in the breakfast room, sipping coffee and nibbling on a piece of toast as he read the paper.

"Good morning," Jessy said, dipping down to

plant a kiss on his head before taking the chair next to him and gesturing toward Dillon. "I've brought a friend to meet you."

Timothy stared at Dillon with interest, smiling slowly and reaching out a hand.

"I knew you would be coming to see me."

"This is Dillon, Timothy. You're meeting him for the first time," Jessy explained.

"Oh. Well, sit down and join us. The buffet here is simple but good," Timothy said politely.

Jessy had gotten her incredible blue eyes from Timothy, Dillon thought, though the older man's were fading a bit now. His Indian heritage was visible in his angled cheekbones, he still sported a full head of white hair, and his posture was ramrod straight.

"Thank you," Dillon told him, surprised at the strength of the old man's grip.

"I'll get us some coffee," Jessy said to Dillon. "What else would you like? Toast? Croissant? Bagel?"

"Toast, thanks," Dillon said.

Timothy hadn't taken his eyes off Dillon. "Ute?" he asked. "Sioux? No, you're Paiute, aren't you?"

"I am," Dillon agreed.

Jessy returned to the table balancing plates of buttered whole wheat toast and packets of jelly on one arm, and carefully holding two coffee mugs by their handles in the other hand. Dillon rose quickly and took one, thanking her.

Timothy was still eyeing him, now with what seemed to be approval, Dillon thought. Good. It was important for this man to like him.

"It was a Paiute shaman, Wovoka, who first spoke of the ghost dancers. He founded the movement," Timothy said.

It was apparent from the look on her face that Jessy was unhappy with her grandfather's preoccupation with the ghost dancers, and her words only confirmed that impression. "Timothy, I know you want me to be proud of your father's people, and I am, but—"

"She doesn't like it that I see the dancers," Timothy explained to Dillon.

"I just don't understand why you're so pleased to see them, as if you think they mean something good. Think about it." She turned to Dillon as if asking for support. "I suppose you know all about them. How they danced themselves into a frenzy and made people believe they could wear special shirts that would protect them from bullets. Wovoka said that he saw his dead ancestors, and that they told him they could wipe the white man from the land. And you know what came of that? Sitting Bull's death and the massacre at Wounded Knee." She looked pleadingly at Timothy again. "The ghost dancers were a resistance movement— a *failed* resistance movement—and it was a long time . . . ago."

"Time means nothing," Timothy said, waving a

hand dismissively. "You're missing the point, my dearest granddaughter." He nodded at Dillon, as if convinced that he understood. "What was important was that the western tribes learned to speak to those who had gone before. A new tradition was begun. The Ghost Dance was a gift. In any society there are those who believe and those who don't. To this day, our people do the Ghost Dance."

"For tourist dollars," Jessy said.

Timothy laughed. "But it's all right to dress up like a pirate for those same tourist dollars?"

Jessy flushed. "It's just a show."

"And to some the Ghost Dance is just a show. But to others it's as real now as it was in Wovoka's day. I only wish that you would see, that you would understand. That you would *believe*."

Jessy hesitated. "Timothy, you see a different world than I do."

Timothy shook his head and addressed Dillon again. "The dancers in the wall told me that you would come. That you're here because Jessy is in danger."

"Timothy . . ." Jessy protested.

But Timothy was looking at Dillon, who smiled slowly. Timothy *had* known. Whether he had a sixth sense that informed him of danger or really *had* spoken to men in the walls, somehow he had known, and he seemed as sane a man as any as he spoke to. "She will find her strength, but she will need you, too."

Suddenly he looked away, frowning, as if distracted.

After a moment he looked up at Jessy. "Granddaughter, will you get me more coffee?"

She cast a speaking glance at Dillon, but she took Timothy's mug and headed for the buffet.

As soon as she left the table, Timothy turned to Dillon. He was more than distracted. He was upset. "They know. They know she was there."

"Who? Who knows she was there?" Dillon asked him.

"I don't know their names. I don't know what they look like. But Billie Tiger just spoke to me. He was here with Wovoka, then lost his life at Wounded Knee."

Dillon hesitated, worried that Timothy had lost touch with reality after all.

Then the old man's hand fell over Dillon's, and his grip was steely. "They know that she can see spirits, and they will come after her. You are her guardian now. You must take care of her."

Jessy heard the last as she approached the table, and she tossed her hair behind her shoulder as a cross look rose to her face. She sat down and took Timothy's hands, forcing him to look at her.

"Timothy, no one has to look out for me. I'm always careful."

Timothy shook his head. "They are assembling. And once they are all together, they will recreate what happened long ago."

"Timothy, here's your coffee," Jessy said.

The look in her eyes was distressed, and Dillon knew she was worried that Timothy's mind was going. He wasn't so sure.

He offered her a small smile, hoping she would realize he was telling her not to worry.

"Timothy, *who* is assembling?" Dillon asked.

"I don't know who they are, but Billie Tiger said they were there before the Ghost Dance. The civil war was over, and the white men were looking to the West, to the territories. Many were desperate. Others were getting rich on the backs of others."

Jessy touched his cheek soothingly. "It's all right, Timothy. The world hasn't exactly been fixed, but it's a whole lot better. And a lot of people say the Indian casinos are the tribes' way of getting revenge on the white men."

Timothy shook his head to dismiss her words, then stared at his coffee. "There's no cream," he said.

"Oh, sorry," Jessy said, and got up again.

"Timothy, you were saying?" Dillon prompted as soon as she was gone.

Timothy stared at him blankly. "I said there was no cream."

"No, before that. What were you saying about the ghost dancers and Billie Tiger and things happening again?"

"Oh, the ghost dancers. Sometimes they're in the walls. Sometimes, if you look hard, you can see them in the sky. I really need cream in my coffee," he said, sighing.

Dillon sat back. Whatever Timothy might have had to say, it was lost now, and it was impossible to tell whether he really had some kind of an occult connection or if disease was destroying his mind.

Jessy returned and Timothy smiled broadly as he poured the cream into his coffee, then waved to an attractive older woman across the room. She joined them, and he introduced her as Mrs. Teasdale. The conversation was light and casual after that. Apparently Jessy had promised to take the older couple on an outing, and Mrs. Teasdale was glad—she simply did not go out alone, not even to the mall, not with "the way things are these days."

A little while later Jessy said that they needed to leave so she could get to the casino and start getting ready to go onstage. She was silent in the car, and when he glanced her way, she flashed him a troubled smile, then turned away to look out the window.

"He wasn't well today," she said sadly, still looking out at the scenery.

"Actually, I thought he seemed pretty lucid. Believe me, I've seen a lot worse."

She turned and met his eyes. "I'm sorry. Do you have relatives who . . . are elderly?"

"Not really. I've just been around," he told her. "I've dealt with the elderly in my investigations," he explained. He decided this wasn't the time to tell her that sometimes, when people thought the elderly were crazy, they were just closer to the door that separated one world from the next.

"He's okay," he told her, reaching out to pat her knee. "Honestly."

"You know, I *was* scared—okay, terrified—when I kept seeing Tanner Green, and I'm very grateful to you for helping me understand what's going on, but no one has to watch out for me. It's very strange. Now that I know I'm not crazy. I'm not terrified of seeing Tanner Green again. In fact, I'm going to tell him—if he gets close enough—that I will try to help him." She was silent for a long moment. "And Rudy, too. Though I never met him, so why he's appearing to me, I have no clue. Oh, Lord. I sound crazy, don't I? Maybe I shouldn't be so worried about Timothy."

"It's all going to be all right," he assured her. "So will you still be okay if I drop you off at the casino and then do a few things on my own today?" he asked her.

"I'll be fine," she assured him, flashing a smile. "I swear. I don't plan to ruin your life."

He looked straight out the window. "Trust me. You aren't ruining my life."

She was silent for a moment. "Do you want to stay at my house tonight? Tanner Green might show up."

He tried not to smile too broadly. "Sure. Sounds

good to me. Hey, if I wind up getting back into town late tonight and can't—"

"I'll call my friend Sandra to pick me up. She won't mind."

Tanner Green was staring at her through the glass again.

The minute Jessy had come out onstage, she'd noticed him, his face pressed against the glass. He still looked so sad—and so afraid.

She offered him a smile, to assure him that she didn't mind him being there, but he didn't respond.

She had no choice but to turn her attention to the show, but every once in a while she looked toward the window.

And he was always there.

An assistant met Dillon in reception and took him back to autopsy room number 3 to see Doug Tarleton, who met him at the door wearing green scrubs and a matching green mask that hid everything but his eyes, which were a bright hazel, clear and intelligent, behind flip-up magnifying lenses.

"I've had Tanner Green brought back out," he told Dillon, his words clear despite the mask. "Though my report is so complete that I'm not sure what—if anything—else I'll find. But since Emil Landon is making burial arrangements and doesn't seem to be in much of a hurry—no one has called yet to ask when we're releasing the body—I figure there's time to take one last look."

"Thanks. I appreciate it."

"It's no problem. I never mind looking for something hinky. I had an old guy come through this morning who'd died of what looked like a heart attack."

"It wasn't?" Dillon asked.

Tarleton shook his head. "This can be a dangerous city."

"So what *did* he die of?"

"He hit the jackpot a little over a year ago. He was already one of those nuts who hobble in with a walker and an oxygen tank, but apparently someone—my guess is his son—couldn't wait for natural causes to free up all that money. He had enough morphine in his system to kill a rhino. Thing is, he would have died of cancer soon enough."

"Maybe it was a mercy killing. A morphine OD's a hell of a lot easier than a slow death from cancer," Dillon commented.

"That will be for the cops and the courts to sort out. I just report what the body tells me. Now grab some scrubs or else you'll be smelling like chemicals and death all day."

Dillon did as directed, then followed Tarleton into the autopsy room and toward a sheet-draped form lying on a stainless-steel autopsy table.

Tarleton pulled down the sheet. Tanner Green, in

his dead and bloated nakedness, was not a pretty picture. The man had been heavily muscled, but he'd also been just plain big. In life, he'd liked food and alcohol, predilections that were very apparent as he lay on the table.

Other than the Y incision made during the initial autopsy, his torso looked unblemished, and his sex lay limp and tiny between the giant slabs of his thighs. Tanner Green, if he could have seen that, would not have been happy at all.

But if Tanner Green was hanging around the morgue, Dillon didn't see him. Maybe he had more sense than that, or maybe he hadn't accepted his own death yet, so he was still hanging around the same places he'd frequented in life.

"Burton!" Tarleton called, and an assistant, otherwise known as a dernier, materialized in the doorway. "Come over here and lend me a hand, please."

As soon as Burton was by his side, Tarleton resumed talking.

"As you can see, there's no sign of violence or struggle, and when we turn Mr. Tanner over—" he and Burton suited action to words "—there's your wound. One strike, swift, sure and hard. The blade went in all the way to the hilt, which was short and explains why none of the drunken idiots milling around the entrance or the tables noticed that the man plowing past had a knife in his back."

Someone had either been damn lucky or they had

known exactly what they were doing, Dillon mused silently. The knife had penetrated cleanly into the lung, missing the ribs. Only someone with either combat or medical training would have been capable of that kind of precision. A jilted girlfriend or angry coworker was unlikely to have managed it.

"All right, we can roll him back over now," Tarleton told Burton. They were both good-size men, but Tanner Green had been built like the proverbial brick shit house, and moving his dead weight was no easy task.

Burton gave them a nod after Dillon thanked him, then left to resume whatever he'd been doing before Tarleton summoned him.

"So the tests came back positive for LSD?" Dillon said.

"That's what I told you, and that's the way it was. He was tripping his ass off," Tarleton said.

"Do you know how the drug got into his system?"

"Ingested. It usually comes in tablet form."

Dillon shook his head. "I just don't see it. I can't say I knew him well, but . . . LSD? I just don't see it," he repeated. "Hell, it's such an old-fashioned drug."

"Doesn't mean it isn't on the streets, right along with the new designer stuff," Tarleton told him.

"I can't see him taking it on purpose. Someone must have slipped it to him."

"He'd had a martini or two," Tarleton said. "Could someone have slipped the LSD into him that way? Sure."

"He must have been with someone he trusted."

"Maybe. Or maybe he was tripping, then stumbled into his killer."

"I don't think so. I think he was drugged, then killed, and that everything was perpetrated by someone who knew exactly what he was doing," Dillon said. "What about food? Where did he have his last meal?"

"Do I look like an entertainment directory? I don't know where, only what. He had steak and mashed potatoes. Not a single vegetable passed his palate, not in the last twenty-four hours, at any rate. Steak and potatoes, at least three hours before his death, for whatever help that will give you."

"Thanks." Dillon wasn't sure that the menu helped, but the martinis . . . they had been mixed somewhere. As far as he knew, though, none of the bartenders in town had contacted the cops to say they had seen Tanner Green in the hours before his death.

Not that that meant anything. This was Vegas. No one had noticed the knife in his back, for God's sake.

But now that his face had shown up in the newspapers and on television, someone should have remembered seeing the man. Unless he'd been drinking in private somewhere. In someone's room.

In a penthouse, maybe? Emil Landon's penthouse?

"Do you want to see the other man?" Tarleton asked him.

"Rudy Yorba?"

Tarleton nodded.

Inwardly, Dillon winced. He couldn't help feeling responsible for Rudy's death. He nodded back.

"This way. He's in a drawer right now. His ex-wife is having the body shipped back East. She wants a proper funeral. They had a kid."

"Great," Dillon said beneath his breath. They left the autopsy room and walked down a hallway to the room Tarleton referred to as "the coolers."

There, he glanced over the wall of human-content drawers, selected one and opened it.

Rudy Yorba was virtually unrecognizable. His face was mottled, cut and scraped in a dozen places, and appeared to have been squeezed between the hands of a yeti.

The body was in no better shape. He was so bruised and broken that it was difficult to see where the Y incision had been made at autopsy.

A low whistle escaped Dillon's lungs.

Tarleton shook his head regretfully. "The vehicle impact took him in the legs. Speed and force crushed his thighs and threw him backward, against the windshield. His face and upper body took a beating, and his neck was broken—which was the specific cause of death, by the way—all in a few seconds, I'd guess. That action created an equal *re*action, and the body was thrown over the embankment, where it bounced and rolled, hitting boulders, sand and the usual roadside crap before coming to a stop. Thank God the poor bastard was already dead at that point. That's the only plus I can see here. No drugs in his system, not even a whiff of alcohol. His heart was sound, organs were normal—well, had been normal, before the ripping and tearing. No way he could have survived, even if his neck hadn't been broken. His spleen, pancreas and liver were all ripped to shreds, and he would have bled to death internally in minutes. His last meal was spaghetti, barely digested, probably consumed at the employee cafeteria. He had a heart like a lion. Probably had fifty good years left. He'd been a junkie at one point, but he'd cleaned himself up. He was lily white the night he died."

Dillon stared at the corpse. He had seldom seen the human body turned into such a ruin.

Sorry, buddy, he said silently. *I am so damn sorry.*

"I can't believe I talked to him not long before it happened," he said to Tarleton. "I can't help but feel responsible."

"Prove they were related, then. Prove this conspiracy theory of yours. I'd love to see someone locked up for life for this one," Tarleton said. "Actually, I'd love to see the killer tarred and feathered and then disemboweled, but unfortunately that's against the law. Anyway, I'd just like to see you bring someone to justice on this."

"I'll do my best," Dillon told him. "I swear."

"Keep in touch," Tarleton said. "And if I can help, just say the word."

"All right, and thanks." Dillon paused as Tarleton closed the drawer. "You might want to suggest to the ex that she request a closed-coffin service."

"I was going to suggest cremation, actually. But I'm trying to hold on to both bodies a little while longer. Just in case, you know?"

Dillon nodded and left, depositing his scrubs in a laundry bin on the way out. When he stepped from the building, he looked around, wondering if Tanner or Rudy might have shown up. But the only ghost he saw was Ringo, who was sitting on a bench at a nearby bus stop, one leg crossed over the other, his hat pulled down low over his eyes to shade them from the Vegas sun. He looked up at Dillon.

"I guess you got it right," Ringo said, "Tanner Green was watching your girl, and Miss Sparhawk saw him. Confusing? I spent some time up in the penthouse first, watching Emil Landon."

"And?"

"I watched him stare at a stack of papers. I watched Hugo Blythe sit outside his office, reading magazines. Then I decided your girl needed my maybe-not-so-helpful presence more and left. That's when I saw her and Tanner Green watching each other. No sign of Rudy Yorba. And Miss Sparhawk looked like she was managing just fine. Does that mean you can introduce us now?"

"You're sure?" Dillon asked, ignoring Ringo's question. "She saw him and she wasn't freaked out?"

"She was fine," Ringo said with assurance. "She's got a backbone. She just had to get over the it's-really-a-ghost thing."

"How can you be so certain?"

Ringo gave him a dry stare, then sighed. "I've been watching people for over a hundred years now. How's that for a reason?"

"Yeah, okay. You probably know what you're talking about."

Ringo sniffed. "So when do we let her know about me? The time will come when I might be able to help on this thing, you know."

"Soon, okay?"

"All right. So how was the. . . ." Ringo paused and shuddered. "The morgue? Hell, when I died, they just threw me into a hole in the ground."

"In Indigo?" Dillon said.

"Hell, yes, in Indigo," Ringo agreed.

"Well, it's time. Let's go," Dillon told him, and Ringo rose and followed him to the car, along with the ever-present jingling of his spurs.

Tanner Green didn't stay for the entire show, and

Jessy actually forgot about the ghost for a while because there were so many children and parents who lingered that day. She signed autographs and posed for a seemingly endless succession of pictures.

After saying goodbye to a pretty, young woman who had accompanied two five-year-olds, she looked up and realized she was the only one left on set.

She got up and headed backstage, and was just approaching the curtain that separated the set from the dressing rooms when she heard a sudden whooshing sound. She turned just in time to see one of the giant sails, rigged to fall apart when a fake cannon boomed, swinging toward her. She let out a yelp and fell flat on the floor, rolling away more quickly than she would have thought possible.

She heard the mast crash as it fell, which it did during every performance, but all the players were safely on the deck of the ship when it happened.

She scrambled to her feet and shouted up into the rigging, "Hey! Idiot! I'm still here! Quit messing with the set until I'm in the clear."

There was no answer, though she thought she heard a scrambling in the rigging, and her heart started to pound. Had she heard human footsteps . . . ?

Or a ghost?

She walked back to the women's dressing room to find April just slipping into her dress.

"What took you so long?" the other woman asked. "Good show today, huh?"

"Yeah—until the sail just almost fell on me," Jessy said.

"You're kidding!" April said. "Better tell the stage manager."

"I will, thanks."

"Okay, I'm outta here, then. Hey, where's tall, dark and to-die-for today?"

"He had to work," Jessy said.

April grinned. "Bummer. Well, you take care, sweetie. See you tomorrow."

Before changing, Jessy found the stage manager, Ron Pearl, and told him what had happened. He was perplexed and concerned, though she had a feeling he was more worried about the legal repercussions of someone getting hurt than how she herself was actually feeling. But he swore he would find out what had happened, so she left him to it and headed back to the dressing room.

She was alone there as she cleaned her face and changed into her street clothes, and though she felt edgy, her senses heightened, as far as she could tell there were no ghosts in sight.

As soon as she was dressed, she called Sandra, who was delighted with the idea of meeting her for dinner on the Strip.

It wasn't until Jessy had left the casino and was waiting out front for Sandra to show up that she once again had the sense of *someone* watching her, raising goose pimples on her flesh.

She paused, looking around. There were people everywhere, some just strolling along sightseeing, others hurrying toward some unknown destination. Some were alone and quiet, while others talked and laughed as they passed in groups. And some of them were weaving as if they were already drunk.

None of them was Tanner Green or Rudy Yorba.

Despite her inability to spot anyone, she was sure she was being followed. The thing of it was, she didn't think her shadow was a ghost.

She was being stalked.

By someone who was very much alive.

10

Indigo.

It was a ghost town now, and Dillon parked in the dust alongside what passed for a road, then got out and leaned against the hood, looking around. He knew without even glancing over that Ringo was next to him, just checking out the place, the same as he was doing.

It might have been a movie set. The facades of the buildings were faded but still mostly intact, facing the barren and godforsaken stretch of road that had once lived up to the name of Main Street. Sand and dust coated everything with a film that only added to the surreal effect. The road itself remained dirt, as it had always been. Time and the elements had left it a rutted mess.

The remains of the sidewalks that fronted the buildings were wooden, the boards, cracked and broken, at least where they weren't missing altogether. Peeling, faded paint still proclaimed the names of various buildings: Leif's Livery, Miners' Bank of Nevada, even—decipherable despite the missing letters—Martin's Harness, N w and Repa red. A freestanding house advertised itself as the office of Dr. Benjamin Sully, M.D.

"There's the jail," Ringo pointed out, and Dillon looked over and made out the words *Sheriff's Office, Town of Indigo, Nevada.*

Dillon had been to Indigo twice before. The second time was after his grandfather had died and Ringo had come to stay. Dillon had learned his story and come here to see the town through Ringo's eyes. He'd been here once before that because his ancestor John Wolf, a legend to his tribe, had associations with the town. John Wolf had given his own life so that a white girl, a Paiute adoptee, could live, in the process protecting the tribe's claim to the land beneath the town, as well as a nearby claim. Though the claim hadn't yielded the riches the tribe had dreamed of, this was still Indian land. A man named Varny—a con artist with a nasty streak—had ruled the town until he and John had shot each other in the same gunfight that had killed Ringo. With Varny's death, the brothel sandbars he ran closed, and that—

combined with the fact that the rest of the claim hadn't yielded the hoped-for gold—had completed the demise of Indigo. Roads and the railroad had gone elsewhere, and the town had become nothing more than a proud but ultimately worthless symbol of one man's victory over injustice.

Ringo had attached himself to Dillon because he was a descendant of John Wolf, and he had admired John during their brief acquaintance. The white girl, Mariah, had been Dillon's many-times great-grandmother. Mariah had been pregnant with John's child when he'd died. Ensuing years of inter-racial marriage had created his own mix of white and Indian blood.

Indigo didn't look any different now than since he'd been here the first time, much less since the last. A few years back, some Hollywood execs had paid the tribe to rent out the town for a movie. But the desert reclaimed its own quickly, and whatever minor improvements they made had been wiped away quickly.

"Indigo," Ringo said, shaking his head. "Do you think that Jessy heard right? Why in hell was that Tanner Green's dying word?"

"I don't know. Has to mean something," Dillon said. He looked at Ringo curiously. "Do you remember yours? Did you have a dying word?"

"If I did, I'm sure they were something like 'Fuck you, sucker,' " Ringo told him wryly. "It was all too fast, though. I don't remember."

"What the hell could Tanner Green have to do with Indigo?" Dillon wondered aloud.

"Nothing to do but start looking around," Ringo said with a shrug.

"Think those movie people changed the place much?" Dillon asked.

"Looks to me like they put all the dust back exactly where it had been," Ringo told him.

Dillon laughed and said, "I'll take the bank."

"All right, I'll start with the livery," Ringo said, then paused, shaking his head as he pointed farther down the street. "There she is—the old Crystal Canary. Some of the gals they had there could actually sing. There was one pretty little thing . . . Oh, well. That was a long time ago. Okay, you take the left side, I'll take the right." Then he stood still for a moment, looking around.

"What?" Dillon asked him.

"We can meet in the saloon." Ringo pointed to the building in question, where one of the swinging doors now hung lopsidedly from a single hinge.

"When the sun goes down, the rays reach right into the saloon. That was when it happened. Right when the sunset began."

"Good. We can go check it out in a few hours."

"Why?" Ringo asked.

"Why? Because we're here—for some reason," Dillon told him. He found himself remembering his discussion with Timothy Sparhawk. Was this what he'd meant when he said they were all coming together again? It made no sense. Ringo had been here, and so had John Wolf, but what did any of that have to do with Tanner Green?

He didn't know.

Ringo, spurs clinking, walked off toward the livery stables.

Dillon started with the bank.

His eyes had to adjust to the sudden shadow when he stepped through the doorway—an easy maneuver, since the door itself was gone. He almost stepped through a hole in the floor left by a broken floorboard, but he saw it at the last minute and avoided it.

The windows facing the street were a dusty, grimy gray. The counter remained, and the bars that had separated the tellers from the customers were still in place. A locked gate separated the outer area from the inner workings, but it was low, and Dillon easily leaped over it. There were drawers at all the tellers' stations, but whatever adding machines they might have used were long gone. In a back office he came across a desk with a broken swivel chair. Opening one of the drawers, Dillon found a dead scorpion and a pile of rat droppings.

There was a safe in the back, but the iron door was open, the lock was broken, and the safe itself was completely empty.

In short, there was nothing in the bank to tie Tanner Green to the place.

Next he checked the doctor's office. The examining room still held a table but nothing else, and the windows were mostly devoid of panes. The wallpaper had once been rose patterned, but the design was almost impossible to discern anymore. Several old photographs were hanging at skewed angles in the entryway. There was one that seemed to be of the doctor, standing unsmilingly next to his equally unsmiling wife.

After checking out the lower level, which held the doctor's office, the examining room and a small waiting room, Dillon carefully climbed the stairs, testing each step before he placed his weight on it, and found only empty rooms where the doctor and his wife had once lived.

Next on his side of the street was the pharmacy, and he found it oddly appealing. Ornate Victorian grillwork framed the counter, and behind it, there was an old blown-glass candy dispenser, although the dead insects in it broke the old-time illusion. Still, if you ignored the insects, it was a pretty piece. Dillon imagined that, long ago, useless tonics as well as prescriptions for laudanum, had once been handed across this counter from seller to buyer. Upstairs—where he decided he probably shouldn't have ventured, given the rather spongy state of the floor—he found nothing, just as he had at the doctor's house. No furniture, no photos, nothing. Just three empty rooms.

He moved on. There were four more buildings to

explore before he reached the saloon. One had been the general store, and another appeared to have been a dentist's office. A reclining leather chair—mostly eaten away by worm rot or other tiny predators—was surprisingly suggestive of the modern-day dental equivalent.

The third building had been the undertaker's parlor. Once Dillon's eyes adjusted to the dim light, he saw that, unlike what he'd seen elsewhere, many of the artifacts of the time still remained. There was an outer office, and right behind it, a large room that was still filled with cheap coffins. They were mostly just plain wooden boxes. One was leaning up against the wall, and closer inspection revealed that it was stained in a number of places with what might have been blood. Dillon wondered if it had been used to display the unsavory characters who had been apprehended and shot for their crimes, a graphic warning to everyone else to behave.

The last building, right next to the saloon, was the newspaper office. The faded but still legible sign informed him that, at one time, the *Indigo Independent* had been quartered there.

At first glance, there was nothing left in the front room but broken desks, swivel chairs and—Dillon discovered, after gingerly inspecting a mass in one corner—a torn canvas hat, the type a harried typesetter might have worn.

He was pretty sure that the rotting machinery in

back had once been a printing press, and up the stairs, he came across nothing other than two offices. One desk yielded several sheets of yellowed paper, but when he went to touch them, they fell into dust. He made a mental note to get to a local library and see if any past issues of the *Indigo Independent* had been preserved in any form.

He looked out a window and saw Ringo coming from the sheriff's office across the street, and went downstairs and stepped outside to meet him.

"Anything?" he called to Ringo.

"Nope. How about you?"

"Nope. Let's go check out the saloon," Dillon said.

Dillon entered ahead of Ringo, and there was something eerie in the clinking of Ringo's spurs behind him.

"The poker table is still here, and the chairs," Ringo said. "Look, pieces of the broken chair are still piled up by the wall. Hell, they left the old piano, too. Can you believe it?"

Dillon narrowed his eyes, trying to imagine what had taken place here a century and a half ago.

The bar still stretched across one long wall. There were several tables, and then, against the wall, the old piano. At the far end of the room there was a small stage.

A staircase led to the second story, where a balcony lined most of the second floor, the wooden railing leaning precariously, the handsome carved posts broken in places, completely gone in others. Once, he thought, saloon girls had plied their trade in those rooms up the stairs, decked out in their frilliest—and sexiest—attire as they stared down at the clientele, trying to find the least repulsive cowhand or miner.

Or the one with the most money.

He returned his gaze to the poker table, where Ringo was standing and gazing down ruefully.

"My cards sucked," the ghost said. "That day, the real competition was all between John Wolf and that fool from the East. Mark Davison, that was his name."

There were no longer cards on the table, only a thick layer of Nevada sand and the dust of time.

"Tell me about that day," Dillon said. "I've heard the stories, but you were there, and I need to know details."

"I hadn't been out here all that long," Ringo said, taking a seat. "Milly was singing. She wasn't great, but she was all right. All-right singer, good barmaid, lousy whore. But with the pickings around here, beggars couldn't be choosers."

"Ringo, I need you to tell me what happened, not rate people like they were contestants on *American Idol*," Dillon said.

"Sorry," Ringo said, leaning back in the old chair until it rested on two rickety legs. "Although I have to say that George Turner, the mixed-blood who played the piano, was damn good. Ahead of his time. He should have been born today. He'd have been rich and famous."

"That's good to hear," Dillon said dryly. "Now tell me what happened."

"I can't tell you the whole thing. I died, remember? I wasn't afraid of dying. I'd been in the war. I'd seen people die bad. It was just bad in general, in those days, especially in the South. That's why so many of us came West. That's the thing with war . . . they teach you to use a gun and tell you to kill. Then it's all over, and what the hell do you know but how to use a gun? That's why Varny took control so easy. Folks were used to the fellow with the biggest gun controlling the situation, you know?" He noticed Dillon's impatient look and said, "All right, all right, I'm getting to it. Let's see . . . I got here first. I think Grant Percy, the so-called sheriff—though he was really just Varny's lapdog—came in when I was at the bar, and then that Mark Davison. He was a real wannabe, as you call it these days. He'd thrown his lot in with Varny, but I think Varny knew he was a useless shit. Anyway, then your great-great-grandpa comes in. It was like he was geared up from the minute he got here. You know, you remind me of him a lot. Same eyes. And you could see in his eyes that there was something besides cards on his mind, but he could hold his peace real good. He had patience.

"So we all start playing—George is at the piano,

Milly is singing, the bartender is dishing out the whiskey. We're here—I'm in the same chair I'm taking up now, so to speak. We're all kind of angled, cuz in this town, no man worth his salt ever turned his back on the door. The last hand came down to Davison and Wolf, and the sheriff and I were kind of just waiting to get back into it. Then Varny showed up. Here's the thing. Wolf intended to see Varny. But I don't think he was expecting him so soon. John Wolf had a real poker face, and still, cool as he was, I could tell Varny took him by surprise that day.

"Wolf's clan didn't live far from here. I'm thinking they were coming in that evening, maybe, so he wouldn't be taking on Varny and his thugs alone. Who the hell knows now? Anyway, Varny shows up, and he and Wolf get into a thing over the gold. You know. The gold everyone thought was just outside town somewhere. They started arguing over who owned the land. Then the gunfire started. I took out a couple of Varny's hired guns, but not before one of them got me. I remember dying. I was hit hard and fast, and I was thinking, hell no, I'm too young to die, this can't be happening. I remember all the guns. All the blood. I was already dying, maybe even already dead, when they dragged the girl in. Mariah."

"My great-great . . . however many greats, grandmother."

"Yes. I don't know if I really saw her then, or if

I've just heard the story so many times that I think I did. You know how it is. We hear things often enough and they turn into memories. Did I really see her as I was dying? I don't know. But I do know that John Wolf would have died a thousand times over to save her. And that there was something he needed to tell her. I've had a long time to think about it, and I think it must have had to do with the gold everyone thought was here. That's what they were fighting over. Land. Gold. Wolf had made sure this was Paiute land, but no one ever found the gold. So we all pretty much died over nothing."

"All the poker players died that day, right?" Dillon said after giving Ringo a moment for reflection.

"Dead as doornails," Ringo agreed. "Along with Varny and a bunch of his henchmen. Mariah lived, though. Of course, you already know that. She was pregnant, and that's why you're here now. And that's the end of the story."

Dillon stared at him. "Except that it's not— because a twenty-first century man whispered the name of the place right before he died."

Ringo looked toward the door. "It was just like it is now. See the way the sky is turning all bloodred and gold? I remember thinking, before Varny walked in and everything went to hell, that this town might be a stinking disaster of sand and sagebrush, but when you looked out at a sunset like that, it made everything around you all beautiful. And then the shooting started and the blood was real, and pretty soon all I saw was darkness. Not even the fires of hell," Ringo said.

Darkness. Dillon felt inexplicably uneasy that night was coming quickly. Night—and darkness. He felt a stirring in his mind, an elusive idea that teased and then disappeared. Was something Ringo had just said a clue of some kind? If so, the word *elusive* was dead-on. Dillon couldn't shake the sudden feeling that he needed to get back to town. He dismissed the idea that he had nearly been onto something. After all, he'd already known what happened here; it was clan lore.

"I'll come back out here and explore again another day," Dillon said suddenly.

Darkness.

The idea haunted him.

It was time to be getting back. Jessy had finished work hours ago now, and even though she'd sworn she wouldn't go anywhere alone, that she would call her friend Sandra to pick her up, Dillon didn't want her out in the dark without him to take care of her.

He left the saloon, and Ringo rose at last and took a last long look around the place before following him out.

At the car, Ringo paused before getting in.

"What?" Dillon asked.

"That's the old cemetery over there. Can't see

much anymore. Looks like the crosses are all broken or long gone. But you can see some of the stones ringing the graves. They carried me over there. Took a look at me and said, 'That bastard's dead, just dump in him the ground.' No, that's not fair. Some preacher did say a few words over me."

"We'll bring flowers and set up a cross next time we come," Dillon assured him.

"Whatever. I think my pa was half-Jewish."

"We'll get a star of David *and* a cross, how's that?" Dillon said.

"I like it. And you can add whatever mumbo jumbo your people do, too, huh?"

"You got it," Dillon assured him. "Now get in the damn car, will you? It's an hour's drive back."

"So you admit you like him?" Sandra teased, speaking up to be heard over the crowd in the restaurant. "I think that's great. Now tell me all the details. Well, no, not *all* the details, but . . . a few of them, okay? Is he as fantastic as he looks? You know, sometimes the pretty boys aren't so hot in bed. I mean, they're so accustomed to being adored that they think it's all about them. They like the rabbit thing. Wham, wham, wham. I'm done, let's light up a few cigarettes."

"He's not a pretty boy," Jessy protested, laughing, happy to realize that the world seemed right again. Sandra always had that effect on her. The other woman was down to earth and funny, and even when she was serious, it was with a grain of irony. Life was what it was. Ups and downs, the good and bad. Sandra had perspective, and it was one of the things Jessy treasured about her.

In fact, the minute she had seen Sandra pull up in front of the casino, she had felt better.

Safe.

No longer so certain that a *living* stalker was following in her footsteps, that she might suddenly be whisked away, unnoticed. That she might disappear, with no one to tell her story.

Now Sandra leaned across the table and said, "Okay, no pressing on the sexual details. As long as he was good. I mean, if you're only going to break down and have one affair a *decade*, it at least ought to be hot."

"Sandra!"

"Okay, okay. So tell me about the ghost-busting thing," Sandra said. "Does he find ghosts? And what does he do then? It's not like he can call the cops and have them arrested. Tell me. I'm an inquiring mind, and I want to know."

"Sandra, he didn't go into details with me. It's not like he's allowed to talk about his cases." She hated lying to Sandra, but she just wasn't sure if she was ready to spit out the fact that, yes, there really were ghosts, and in fact she was being followed by one, and Dillon Wolf was trying to help her.

"I'll bet he could tell some amazing stories,"

Sandra told her. "I would love, just love, to hear a few of them."

"As soon as he tells me some, I'll share," Jessy promised.

"Do we actually have a waitress here, or what?" Sandra frowned. "I'm in the mood for a margarita." She looked around, trying and failing to catch a waitress's eye, then said, "I'll be back. Looks like I need to go to the bar if I'm thirsty. Salt or no salt?"

"I'm not sure I should—"

"Humor me. Salt or no salt?" Sandra asked.

"Hell, might as well go all the way. Salt," Jessy told her.

As Sandra walked through a growing crowd to the bar, Jessy drummed her fingers on the table and looked around. She could see out to the street, where nothing suspicious seemed to be going on, so she took a minute to look around the restaurant. The place was open and airy, but busy, its reasonably priced food and proximity to several major casinos making it popular. It had to be one of the safest places in the world to be.

Not too many people were sitting at tables this early, though, she realized. Most people seemed to come in and just mill around. She saw Sandra hand a bartender her credit card, then turned back to study the room at large again.

And there they were.

Tanner Green.

And, beyond him, Rudy Yorba.

It felt as if her heart skipped a beat, but she wasn't afraid. Tanner Green was seated at a little round-topped table just a few feet away. Rudy Yorba was two tables behind Green. Both of them were just watching her. She wasn't sure that Green even knew Rudy was there, because the smaller man seemed to be trying not to be noticed.

This was crazy, she thought. Did one ghost automatically see another? Did some ghosts hide from other ghosts? Dillon seemed to think that Tanner Green hadn't accepted the fact that he was dead. What about Rudy Yorba?

She glanced quickly back to the bar. Sandra looked back, smiled and waved, then turned to watch the bartender mix their drinks.

Jessy rummaged in her purse, and found her address book and a pen. She pretended to accidentally drop the pen. She wasn't a coward by nature, and it was time to be proactive. She pretended to reach for her dropped pen but instead kicked it closer to Tanner Green's table, then stood and walked to where he was sitting.

How the hell did she talk to a ghost without appearing to be stone-cold crazy?

She ducked down and picked up the pen, speaking softly and swiftly as she did so.

"I want to help you," she said. "I need to know what you know. And, by the way, there's a young man sitting just beyond you who apparently knows something or needs something, too. I'd really like to help you both."

"Jessy, is everything all right?"

The voice startled her so badly that she almost slammed her head into the underside of the table as she stood.

Tanner Green was gone, and once again, Rudy Yorba had apparently followed him.

The man standing above her was real. She knew him casually because she'd chatted to him around both the Sun and at the Big Easy, where they'd sat and talked once after her show.

His name was Darrell Frye, and he was a pit boss at the Sun. In fact, he'd been running the craps table the night she'd made her money, though he'd been spelled by another man before Tanner Green had come in.

He was ambitious, she knew. He might be a pit boss now, but wanted to move up to entertainment manager at the Sun. He had told her as much when he had come to see the pirate show. It had been flattering when he told her that people from the Sun had seen her work, and he'd heard them talking about the idea of her moving over to one of their shows. He'd admitted that if he was the one who brought her over, it would help his own career.

"Darrell, hi," she said, rising. "I just dropped my pen, that's all. How are you?"

"Good, thanks, and yourself?"

"Fine."

He was tall, six feet or even six-one, the kind of man who wore a suit well and was attractive without being drop-dead gorgeous. In fact, with sandy hair and eyes the same color, he wasn't the kind of man you really remembered. He had always been nice to her, and honest, so she didn't really mind that he had hoped to lure her over to the Sun at least as much for his own benefit as hers.

"You sure?" he asked her, concerned. "I heard that guy died right on top of you the other night."

"Yes, he did, but I'm okay now."

"It must have been horrible."

"Well, I wouldn't want it to be my usual evening, no."

"Are the police bugging you about it?"

She shook her head. "No one is bugging me. I didn't know the man. He walked in and fell on me, and that was that."

"I'm just glad you weren't hurt. It's been a shitty few days. First, Tanner Green. Then Rudy Yorba. He was a really nice guy. I hope you won't hold it against the Sun."

"I won't and I don't," Jessy assured him.

"So you might still consider coming over to the Sun? I bet they'd let you help develop a project from the ground up," Darrell told her.

"Thanks, I really appreciate the offer."

"Margarita?" Sandra interrupted. She had two glasses and was standing next to Jessy like a guardian Amazon, tall, beautiful and obviously ready to go to war if Jessy was being harassed in any way.

"Thanks," Jessy said, taking her drink from Sandra. "Sandra, I'd like you to meet Darrell Frye. Darrell, my very good friend Sandra Nelson."

"How do you do?" Darrell said formally, smiling and offering his hand with obvious appreciation.

Only a blind man wouldn't appreciate Sandra's appearance, Jessy thought.

"I'm fine, thanks, nice to meet you," Sandra said.

"Darrell is a pit boss over at the Sun," Jessy explained.

"Oh," Sandra said. "It must be tough there right now."

Darrell shrugged. "I began my vacation the day after Tanner Green died, so I haven't had to deal with any of it. They've asked me to come back in, though—they're extra busy. Seems people are intrigued by everything that's happened. Sick, huh? Anyway, it's been a pleasure meeting you, Sandra. And, Jessy, please remember me if you ever want a change of scenery."

Darrell just stood there, then, as if hoping to be invited to join them. Sandra, however, made it clear that the two of them were enjoying a girls' night out. She stared challengingly at him, waiting for him to leave.

"Well, have fun," he said at last, and headed for the door.

"You're tough!" Jessy said, laughing, as Sandra set her drink down and pulled out her chair, a frown creasing her forehead.

"I don't like his vibe."

"His *vibe?*"

"He wants something from you, and you can do much better," Sandra said. She grinned. "You *have* done much better. Can't forget tall, dark and handsome."

"Trust me, I haven't. But you don't need to worry about Darrell. He just wants me to leave the Big Easy and work for the Sun," Jessy explained.

Sandra stared out at the street as if she was still watching the man, though of course he was long gone. Finally she shook her head and said, "That's not it. Not to take anything away from your talent, honey, because you know I think you're great, but—this is Vegas. Beautiful, talented women are everywhere here. He doesn't need to go stealing people to work for his casino. You need to watch out for him. He wants something. And like I said, I don't like his vibe. Trust me, I've been around a few blocks."

"He's an opportunist, I'll admit, but so are lots of people."

Sandra shook her head. "I'm telling you, there's something about him. He's bad news. I'm sure of it."

Jessy started to reply, but before she could, she heard a familiar voice call her name. "Jessy!"

She turned to see her fellow pirate queen, April, on the arm of a handsome stranger.

"Denny, meet my friend Jessy and her friend . . . Sandra, right? Guys, this is Denny," she said proudly.

Sandra and Jessy smiled and shook hands with April's new man.

"We were just heading on over to Harrah's when I saw you two," April said, "and I just had to stop. I was worried about you, Jessy. Did you report the incident?"

"I did, and Ron said he'd look into it," Jessy told her.

"What incident?" Sandra asked sharply.

Jessy waved a hand in the air. "Nothing, a piece of the set came down when it shouldn't have, that's all," she said. "I talked to our stage manager, and he's going to have it checked out. All's well that ends well, just like they say."

"Well, good, I just wanted to make sure you were okay. See ya!" April said, and left, waving. They waved back.

Sandra leaned in. "Exactly what fell?" she demanded, frowning fiercely.

"One of the big sails that's supposed to fall during the battle scene. It scared me, but I wasn't hurt."

"That's not good," Sandra said firmly.

"Well, of course it's not good. And I reported it," Jessy said. Before either of them could say anything else, her phone rang. She answered and was glad to hear Dillon's voice on the other end. She told him where she and Sandra were, and when she hung up, Sandra was watching her excitedly.

"I'm going to get to meet him?"

"Yes."

Sandra sat back then and sipped her drink, still eyeing Jessy. "I'm very worried about you."

"Why?"

"Vibes," Sandra said knowingly.

"Sandra, listen to me. Darrell's a perfectly nice guy, and what happen with the set this afternoon was an accident—*just* an accident."

Sandra leaned forward again, her expression intense. "You're too trusting. What if it wasn't an accident? What if someone was trying to kill you?"

"If someone really was trying to kill me, I doubt his weapon of choice would be a big canvas sail."

"It didn't hit you?"

"No, I heard it falling."

"It could have beaned you."

"Seriously, Sandra. It was an accident, not a murder attempt. I mean, I might have been hurt if I'd been a bit slower, but I wouldn't have been killed."

"It could have been a warning, then," Sandra said sagely. "Someone wanting you to back off from . . . something.

"Sandra, any member of the cast could have been out there," she said.

"But it wasn't *any* member of the cast, it was

you." She shook her head. "This is scary, very scary." She stood suddenly, looking past Jessy, smiled and said, "Hi, I'm Sandra Nelson. And you must be Dillon Wolf."

Jessy turned and smiled at Dillon as Sandra continued to talk.

"Maybe you can talk some sense into her, since she thinks I've gone off the deep end just because no matter what she says about it being an accident, I think someone tried to kill her this afternoon."

11

The lights were neon and garish, the streets wild and busy, and the bar was doing a bang-up business in cocktails, while the sober, semi-sober and downright drunk laughed and talked around them.

Taking a seat at the table, Dillon frowned at Jessy. She should have been safe at work, surrounded by other people.

If Rudy Yorba hadn't died in what had clearly been meant to be mistaken for an accident, he might not be so concerned. But Rudy Yorba was dead, smashed almost beyond recognition.

Other people had seen the security tapes of the night Tanner Green had been murdered. Cops, casino personnel. What if someone—someone complicit in the murder—had noticed that Green had opened his mouth, had said something to Jessy before dying.

Indigo.

Would that mean something to the killer? Because it sure as hell didn't mean anything to *him*. The place was a ghost town, nothing but a ghost town.

"Tell me what happened—*exactly* what happened," Dillon said to Jessy.

"It was nothing. You've seen the show. When we attack Port Royal, the guns of the port fire back and we lose a sail. The sail fell again after the show was over and I happened to be walking by, that's all." In an effort to change the subject she looked more closely at Dillon and asked, "What have you been up to? You're all dusty."

"I took a drive out to the desert today," he told her. "I guess I could use a shower and some clean clothes."

"Want a margarita?" Sandra suggested.

He shook his head, smiling. "No, I'd rather have that shower, I think."

As they walked Sandra out to her car, she plied Dillon with questions about his job with Harrison Investigations, which he answered politely. There were so many things, he said, that no one could be sure of, but he *could* assure her that he'd never personally seen any evidence that a ghost had harmed anyone who was innocent of wrongdoing.

"Does that mean a ghost *will* harm a bad guy?" Sandra asked him eagerly.

He laughed. "It means exactly what I said. We're called in when inexplicable things are happening, but there's usually an explanation that's completely real-world. I suppose that if a ghost could manage to move objects, it could also manage to hurt someone with them. But we usually find a real perp behind whatever's going on."

They'd reached Sandra's car, which she'd left in a casino garage. Dillon opened the driver's side door for her and checked out the interior as she settled herself behind the wheel. "Drive safely," he told her.

"Will do," Sandra said. "And *you*—watch out for Jessy. Please."

"I intend to," Dillon assured her.

They watched her drive away, and he was silent as he slipped an arm around Jessy, leading her back toward the elevator. Finally he said, "I think maybe Sandra's right to be worried about what happened to you today."

"Dillon, Sandra is a good friend, and I love her for worrying about me, but nothing that happened this afternoon was anything other than an accident."

He frowned and let that go unchallenged, asking, "What's your work schedule, anyway?"

"I usually have Mondays and Tuesdays off."

"So you work tomorrow, then you're off for two days," he said thoughtfully, feeling an unwelcome sense of urgency. Maybe it was paranoia. Maybe he shouldn't be so afraid for her. But he was. He had barely spoken to Rudy Yorba, and Rudy had died. He and Jessy . . .

"Let's go to your place," he said.

They walked to his car, which he'd parked in a public lot by one of the huge shopping plazas. They were halfway back to her place when she turned to him excitedly. "I forgot to tell you! Tanner Green was back."

"Right," he murmured.

"Right?" she said, surprised. "I thought you'd be happy. Weren't you hoping he'd come back?"

Dillon gave himself a mental head-slap as he realized that she didn't know that Ringo had been watching Tanner Green watch. He really did need to tell her about Ringo.

"Sorry. I was sure he would come back. He's trying to reach you."

"Well, he was at the show. And then, when Sandra and I were at the bar, I saw him again, and Rudy Yorba was behind him, acting like maybe he didn't want to be seen. I tried to talk to Tanner, and I'm pretty sure he heard me, but then we were interrupted."

"Oh?" Dillon asked, his attention sharpening. This was news—very interesting news. "Who interrupted you?"

"It was just Darrell Frye. He's a pit boss at the Sun. You've seen him. He was there the night I won all that money. He wants to get a job in entertainment management, so he talked to me a few weeks ago about going to work over there. Do you know him?"

He nodded. "He went off shift right before Green died. I've been wanting to speak with him, see if he remembered anything, saw anything. They told me he was on vacation, and I haven't had a chance to track him down yet."

"Well, when he came up and started talking to me, Tanner Green and Rudy Yorba both disappeared," she told him.

Did that mean anything? Dillon wondered. He didn't know, but now he wanted to talk to the man more than ever.

Right now, though . . .

"I'm not sure what any of this means," Dillon told her, looking at her thoughtfully. He was glad she was no longer frightened about seeing the ghosts, had even sounded excited about it. But he was worried that even at work she might have been in danger. The puzzle pieces were starting to connect, but the final picture was still a mystery.

They reached her house, where he went through every room before heading into the shower.

He'd barely been there for ten seconds when she joined him.

Her presence was a piece of earthly magic that seemed to drive away all thoughts of puzzles and fears, and even the world around him.

He didn't know if it was the fact that she had entranced him at first sight, or if it had to do with the sleek, lean, beautifully muscled elegance of her body, the blue of her eyes, the tone of her voice, or even the essence of her soul, but she aroused him in a way that went beyond the sexual, beyond the instinctive rise of his libido in an animalistic reaction older than time. He wouldn't say that he loved her; love took time. But he knew that he was falling in love with her, and that she touched the core of him in a way no other woman ever had.

The look of mischief in her eyes was his undoing, followed by the sight of the steamy, hot water sluicing over the ivory perfection of her skin, shoulders and breasts, back and buttocks. It was the erotic feel of flesh against flesh as she pressed against him. It was finding her lips beneath the spray and exploring the recesses of her mouth, hotter than the water falling over them.

It was touching her. His hands sliding down her naked flesh, cupping her breasts, slipping between her thighs into intimacy.

She moved against him, the friction of her body irresistibly erotic. All so seductive, driving him to an agony of excitement and arousal. Her hands were on him then, kneading his muscles, her nails scraping teasingly over his skin. His lips broke away from hers, and he forced her back against the tiles, his mouth moving frenziedly against her flesh.

They made love in the heated steam, with him lifting her as she wrapped her limbs around him in wicked splendor. The roar of the water pounded in his heart and lungs like a tempest, and after they climaxed, he fumbled for the taps, then stumbled out of the shower, still holding her against him as if he wanted to keep her there forever.

He carried her to her bed, where they fell together onto the mattress and began anew, devouring one another with hands and lips and tongues, taking time, savoring each other's wet, clean and hot flesh, touching and tasting again and again, and reveling in the complete intimacy they had found with one another. She knew how to move, how to seduce, but it was never calculated, never planned, just an instinctive part of her beauty and being. Even when she wasn't beneath him or atop him, she was somehow rubbing against him, sliding along him with supple movements that aroused him all over again. She met his mouth with her own at just the right moment, showered his body with kisses, took his sex in her mouth and teased him until he was ready to explode. When he couldn't take any more, he rolled her beneath him, desire raging inside him again as she responded to his touch, as he caressed her breasts, her belly, her thighs, then moved between them, first with his hands, then with his mouth, until he possessed her, body and soul.

Sometime in the night, exhausted and spent, they slept at last.

He woke early. She was still asleep, and like any new lover, he spared a few minutes to watch her.

He found himself entranced anew by the fiery cascade of her hair over the pillows, the fine structure of her face, the way her lips were slightly parted as she breathed. He tucked the covers carefully around her and rose, then dressed quickly before heading into the kitchen and started making coffee. He didn't do anything about food, since he had a feeling she would want to join her grandfather again at the home and eat something there.

As the coffee brewed, he took out his cell phone and started making calls. This was no longer a one-man job.

Dillon could tell that Jessy was both surprised and pleased that he and Timothy got on as if they had known each other forever. When she took advantage of that fact and went to speak with her grandfather's doctor, he got a chance to talk to Timothy by himself, without having to worry about upsetting her.

"So, Timothy," he began casually, "you can see the ghost dancers, huh?" he asked.

For a moment the old man just looked out the window, as if he hadn't heard. Then he turned to stare challengingly at Dillon. "I know why you've come back. You're here because the desire for riches never ends. Men are greedy. They don't care what they do to other people if it makes them richer." He shook his head sorrowfully. "Man has always been greedy, quick to slay his fellow man if it will bring him material gain."

"Once," Dillon said carefully, "many of our people called themselves simply the Human Beings. We wanted to be good, as the Great Spirit asked. To care for the children, the injured, the needy. Yes, greed has existed for as long as man has been here. But we strive for more."

Timothy nodded.

"Timothy, you spoke of Billie Tiger. Is he . . . your guide? Does he help you understand the messages from the ghost dancers?" Dillon asked.

Timothy nodded, and when he spoke, his words seemed to be coming from far away. "Billie Tiger can see what was, and he knows that the world spins, time moves on, and what happened once will come to pass again, unless it is stopped. And now something terrible threatens to return, so it can be relived. It must be stopped."

" 'Those who cannot remember the past are condemned to repeat it,' " Dillon quoted. "George Santayana," he added. "Timothy, does the name Indigo mean anything to you?" Dillon asked.

Timothy nodded. "It's a town. An evil town."

"I don't think the town was evil, but I do I think evil men lived there," Dillon said.

Timothy nodded. "Greedy men."

"Yes, they were. The other day you told me 'they are assembling.' Timothy, are people from the past assembling somehow?"

"Evil keeps going unless it is stopped," Timothy said. He turned and stared out the window again, then looked back at Dillon and smiled. His voice changed and his features relaxed. "Did you mention Indigo, young man? I know Indigo. Sandy old place out in the desert. Some movie company rented it maybe five or six years ago. They filmed a few scenes and then they left. They didn't like the place. Said things moved around at night, and they went off to film somewhere else."

"Really?" Dillon said, intrigued. "I didn't know that."

"Some people said some of our people were sabotaging the shoot because they didn't think the movie company had paid enough to rent the town. Other people claimed it was because of the old burial ground out there, but nobody really knows. I'll tell you one thing, though. There's something wrong with Indigo, always has been. There was an awful shoot-out there. An Indian named Wolf was involved. Kin to you?"

"A great-great-great-something," Dillon told him.

"Jessy and me, we go back to Indigo, too," he said.

"Oh?"

"My grandmother was related to a mixed-blood who played piano in a saloon there," Timothy told him. He stared at Dillon, his gaze clear and focused. "The world can be strange. Life and death are not always what we think. The souls of the ancients slip into the living. Some are good, and some are evil. As to why they come, sometimes it's because the descendants of those who fought, the winners and the losers, are assembling. Do you understand?"

Dillon wasn't sure that he did. Not entirely, anyway, though certain connections were starting to become clear. An ancestor of Jessy's had lived in Indigo. His own ancestor had died there. And Ringo was still hanging around to this day.

But what did all that *mean?* What the hell did it have to do with the murders of Tanner Green and Rudy Yorba—or the casinos business and Emil Landon, who had been the starting point for everything?

"Timothy, the ghost dancers—how long have they been talking to you?" Dillon asked.

"I don't really remember when they came. A while ago now. But when I saw the blood," Timothy said sadly, "that's when I knew they were here to warn me. The cycle needs to be stopped."

"Timothy, where did you see blood," Dillon said, then asked, "Where?"

"On Jessy," the elderly man said, his eyes bleak. "I saw blood on my granddaughter. But I knew they didn't want to kill her, they wanted to save her. They told me that you would come. They said she would open the door, but you would come and guide her through it." Then he winked conspiratorially and inclined his head.

Dillon turned.

Jessy was on her way over, and she smiled when she caught his eye, then sat down next to him.

She looked across the table at Timothy and smiled. "I hear you've been playing a lot of Scrabble."

"It's good for the mind. Sally and I play almost every night."

"Is she all right? I don't see her," Jessy said.

Timothy smiled. "It's hair day. She's over in the main building, at the salon. How about you, young lady? Don't you need to get to work?"

She glanced at her watch. "I have time."

Timothy shook his head and looked at Dillon. "Whatever you do, make sure she eats a real lunch before you drop her off, will you? She burns a lot of energy onstage."

"Thank God," Jessy said. "I have an affinity for chocolate shakes. I'm grateful I get to burn all those calories, because I'd hate to have to cut down on the ice cream."

"Take her to lunch," Timothy repeated, staring at Dillon. "I'll be here tomorrow."

"I'll look forward to seeing you," Dillon said, rising.

Jessy followed suit. "You could come with us this morning. We could take you shopping or something, and then Dillon could drop me at work after lunch and then bring you back here."

"No, thanks. I appreciate the offer, but I don't really need anything. I think I'm going to take a nap, so I'll be ready to go when Sally comes back from getting her hair done," Timothy said with a wink.

"Okay," Jessy agreed, and kissed him fondly on the cheek. Dillon shook his hand, and then he and Jessy left.

She glanced over at him as they drove.

"Thank you," she said.

"There's nothing to thank me for," he assured her.

"He can seem perfectly fine . . . and then his mind wanders into another zone."

"I think he's very intelligent and insightful, and I enjoy his company," Dillon assured her.

"I wish he could live with me," she said. "But once he thought he was in a sweat lodge, and he kept trying to make a fire in the kitchen. The fire department had to come out. I knew then that he couldn't live with me anymore, not so long as I have to work."

"He's in a good place. He's happy, and he's still pretty independent."

She nodded. "I know, but I still can't help feeling guilty sometimes."

They were quiet after that, until Dillon asked her what she wanted to do to kill time before lunch. They settled on a movie, and by the time it let out, they were both ready to eat again.

He took her to a place he liked not far off the Strip. It was quiet and elegant, and he thought

Timothy would have approved. They were seated quickly, and the waiter brought over water for them to drink while they perused the menu. Just as it was served, Ringo entered and stood just behind Jessy.

Dillon heard the clink of his spurs and saw Jessy frown as she looked up from studying her menu. Obviously she'd heard them, too.

"Jessy," he said softly.

She met his eyes, and he cleared his throat. "You know how you see Tanner Green? And Rudy? Well, they're not the only ghosts in town. In fact . . . I have a friend who wants to meet you. I asked him to wait to show himself until I was sure you'd be all right with it."

She reached for her water glass and took a long swallow.

"Where is he?" she asked, visibly steadying herself.

"He's sitting next to you," he told Jessy as Ringo took the chair beside her.

She turned and gasped loudly enough that their waiter came running over.

"Is anything wrong?" he asked anxiously.

She shook her head. "I'm sorry. I just . . . swallowed the wrong way."

"So, Jessy, what would you like?" Dillon asked, defusing the tension. "The salmon here is delicious."

"Salmon it is, then," she agreed, trying not to stare at Ringo.

"And would you like the rice or the scalloped potatoes?" the waiter inquired.

"Rice," Jessy managed to say.

"I'll have the same, please," Dillon said.

The waiter left at last.

"You're a real jerk!" Dillon said.

Jessy stiffened. "Excuse me?"

"Not you. I'm talking to Ringo. He shouldn't have scared you that way."

"Sorry," Ringo told Jessy. "I didn't mean to upset you, and I'm delighted to make your acquaintance. At—last," he added pointedly, staring at Dillon.

"At last?" she whispered.

"I've been suggesting a formal introduction for a while now. I think I could have been helpful before now," Ringo said.

Jessy tried not to look in his direction. Ringo reached for one of the menus, which the waiter had forgotten to pick up. Dillon snatched it out of his hand before someone noticed that a menu was floating in thin air.

"Salmon," Ringo said in disgust. "You're a wuss. This is Nevada. You should have ordered a nice rare steak."

"He enjoys being aggravating," Dillon said, his eyes on Jessy.

She stared back at him, her own eyes wide. She might have adjusted to seeing Tanner Green and Rudy Yorba materialize right in front of her, but she clearly hadn't been ready for this.

"I'm wounded," Ringo said. "I was just anxious to meet you, Jessy."

"Did you let Clancy out?" Dillon asked.

"You're asking a ghost if he let your dog out?" Jessy said, and took another long drink of water. She noticed that her hand was trembling. "But you said ghosts couldn't hurt people, so how could he—"

"I said I didn't know of any ghosts who hurt people," he said. "I didn't say they couldn't touch objects or move them. Ringo here has been around a very long time, and he's mastered the art of using his energy to affect the physical world. And, despite your first impression, he's actually a nice guy."

"Thanks, partner," Ringo said.

"He's your *partner?*" Jessy asked.

"No, that was just an expression of speech," Dillon assured her.

She played with her napkin, not looking at Ringo even though she was addressing him. "So, Mr. Ringo—"

"It's not Mr. Ringo," Ringo corrected. "Name is Ringo Murphy, just Ringo to my friends, and I'm hoping you'll be one of them."

She looked at Dillon. "He's around—all the time?" she asked faintly.

"No, not all the time," Dillon said firmly, staring at Ringo.

"Trust me, ma'am. I am a perfect gentleman,"

256

Ringo promised her, then turned to Dillon. "I just want to help. I want this solved."

Jessy was about to answer him, but their salads arrived, so she kept quiet.

"Ringo died at Indigo," Dillon explained once the waiter was gone.

Jessy, blue eyes narrowing, stared at him. "So 'Indigo' *did* mean something to you. It meant a *lot* to you."

"I don't know what it means, not yet," he told her.

"You know, your grandfather isn't so crazy," Ringo told Jessy. "Maybe he's somehow seeing Indigo in his visions, or whatever you want to call them."

She turned to stare at him indignantly. "I never said my grandfather is *crazy*. And no one really knows *what* he sees."

"I'm sorry, no offense meant," Ringo said. "I just meant . . . well . . . maybe he does see those ghost dancers he says he talks to."

"Don't look at him when you talk to him," Dillon cautioned her. "It unnerves people, and Ringo always gets a kick out of that."

"Just how often is he around?" she asked.

"When he's needed, usually," Dillon told her.

She spoke to Ringo again, this time without turning to look at him. "What do you know about my grandfather?"

"I know he's a nice old man," Ringo said. "And that he may be very important to figuring this out."

257

Jessy frowned at Dillon. "What is he talking about? What's 'this'?"

"Jessy, I honestly don't have all the pieces yet."

"But you do know *something,* and you've chosen not to share that with me," she said, trying to keep her growing anger under control.

"Jessy, I know that Emil Landon called Adam for help, afraid that his life was in danger. I met with him, met Tanner Green and Landon's other bodyguard, Hugo Blythe, and then Tanner Green was killed, but not before saying something to you."

"So you hounded me," she said.

"I didn't mean to hound you, but I needed to know what he said. And I was afraid for you," he said softly.

"What else do you know?" Jessy demanded.

"Jessy, if I had all the answers, Green's killer would be awaiting trial right now," Dillon assured her. "But I *don't* have all the answers. I know that—somehow—your grandfather's ghost dancers seem to know that you'd have a link with—a link with the dead. And that, because of it, you'd be in danger. They knew that I'd be drawn into the mystery, too. That I'd be here to help you."

He met her eyes across the table, and it was all she could do to stop herself from leaning in for a kiss.

Ringo groaned. "Get a room, would you?" he said. "Hell, I'm out of here," he said, and rose, but then he lingered.

258

"Jessy?"

She looked over at him then, deciding she didn't care if the other diners thought she was crazy.

"I really will do my very best to protect you," Ringo swore.

"*You* can protect me?" she asked skeptically.

"Well, I can watch out for you," he said.

"Then stop scaring me," she ordered him. "The noise of your spurs has been driving me crazy."

"Excuse me, but I died with my boots on," Ringo said indignantly, then walked away.

Someone cleared his throat, and Dillon looked up, cursing himself for not paying attention.

"Is everything all right?" the waiter asked.

"Fine," Dillon said, as the waiter served their salmon, then left.

"The other day, at your house . . . I heard his spurs. When we . . . did he . . . ?" Jessy asked, and she could feel herself blushing.

"He left, I swear," he told her. "I promise you, Ringo isn't a voyeur."

She flushed even deeper and said, "The other night, before you came to my room . . ." Her words trailed off, but then she forced herself to go on. "I'd been dreaming about you—rather erotically. I mean . . . then . . . we weren't being watched, were we?"

He lowered his head, trying quickly to hide his smile.

"Jessy, you were dreaming, nothing more. I

259

swear. Ringo had already left to look into some things on his own."

"Like . . . ?"

"He went back to hang around the casino, see if he could pick up any new info."

She still looked unhappy, he thought. He wondered how she was going to react later tonight, at the arrival of the reinforcements he'd called for.

"Jessy, he may be able to get Tanner Green to talk. And if Green talks, maybe we can find out how Indigo is involved in all this."

She shook her head. "What is it with that place?"

"I'm still not sure, but the pieces are starting to fit. An ancestor of mine was killed there, and so was Ringo—both of them in the same shoot-out. This morning, your grandfather told me that you two had an ancestor who was there at the same time."

"Oh?" she said coolly. "Was he a bad guy or a good guy?"

"He was a piano player."

"A piano player?"

"Yeah. And no, I don't know how he fits in. I just know that you're in danger, and that whoever killed Tanner Green is probably the same person who ran down Rudy Yorba, and somehow, everything is tied to Indigo."

She eased back in her chair, staring at him. "I think . . ."

"What?"

She shook her head. "I think I've lost my mind."

"You haven't."

She poked at her salmon with a vengeance. "Where the hell does Emil Landon fit into all this?"

"I don't know."

"So where do we go from here?" she demanded.

"I'll keep investigating until I find out what's going on."

She shook her head. "No way am I letting you push me out of this investigation. Thanks to you, I've had to face the fact that I see ghosts. I may even be making friends with a dead man in a ten-gallon hat and spurs. Don't think that you're not going to inform me of every move you make."

"All right, here's what's happening next," he told her, pushing his own food around on the plate. "*We're* going to the Big Easy, where we're going to go to the stage manager and find out what happened yesterday. Then I'm going to leave Ringo to watch over you, and I'm going to have a discussion with Emil Landon. Next I'm going to head over to the Sun to chase down your friend the pit boss, Darrell Frye, and find out why he conveniently managed to go on break just when a murdered man came stumbling into the building. Then, if there's time, I'll call Jerry Cheever and find out if he's got any new info. And maybe I'll drop in on Doug Tarleton—he's the medical examiner. Also, there's a young woman in the crime lab who has been very helpful, so I can take the opportunity to catch up with her."

"Wait a minute. I never said Darrell was my friend. And I think you're way off base if you really do suspect him. He just wants to lure me over to the Sun so he can climb the corporate ladder."

"And I hope you're right. Anyway, while I'm doing all that, Ringo can hang out with you, and maybe see something, hear something . . ."

So much for a nice lunch, he thought.

"We should go," she told him. "You do know that I'm not entirely incapable, right? I'm smart, and I know how to be careful."

"I do know that. But, Jessy, everyone is vulnerable, and you haven't been trained in self-defense nor do you carry a gun. It won't hurt to have someone—even a ghost—there to help if help should be needed."

She digested that, then nodded stiffly. "All right. Point taken. But I *will* be going with you to talk to *my* stage manager."

"Not a problem," he told her, and signaled the waiter for the check.

"Here's the thing," she told him. "I've already been crushed by a dying man who bled all over me. I've seen ghosts. And maybe I *am* in danger. So I don't want you keeping *anything* from me, anything at all. And *you* don't have a plan, *we'll* have a plan. I'm not a delicate flower. This is *my* life, and I intend to be just as involved in saving it as anyone else."

He stared back at her, trying not to smile, glad to see her anger and her courage.

He just didn't want her so courageous that she forgot to respect her fear—not to mention logic and self-preservation.

"Well?"

He let himself smile then. "It's a plan," he told her.

They rose, and he rested his hand on her back as they left the restaurant. He heard the jingling of Ringo's spurs as they neared the car.

"Shotgun, if you don't mind," Jessy said to Ringo.

Ringo laughed, catching Dillon's eyes, and slid into the back.

12

When they got to the Big Easy, Ron Pearl was actually up in the rigging, checking the machinery that controlled the sail that had fallen. He saw Jessy with Dillon and called down to tell them that he would just be a second. A moment later he was on the ground, facing them.

He was an agile man of about fifty, and he'd been in Vegas working on shows forever. He'd done it all, worked props and sets, even acted on occasion. His delight, however, was in managing a cast and all in the technical details that went into a show. Jessy had worked with him before, and she adored him.

"Hey," he said. "I'm Ron Pearl. And you're . . . ?"

"Dillon Wolf. Jessy told me what happened. What went wrong?" Dillon asked.

"I actually called the cops about this, because I think we had a prankster up in the rafters. Someone who lost big in the casino and wanted to shut us down, put management out some money themselves," Ron said, looking at Jessy. "I'm hoping it was a prank, anyway, and they didn't know anyone was down there. So the cops came and took some prints off a backstage door, but I don't know how much that will help. There were some weird scuff marks up there, too, and they took some pictures. They're still checking it out, and I've made sure everything's been resecured and is totally safe. I put a security guy up on the catwalk today, just to make sure nothing goes wrong."

Jessy noticed that Dillon didn't look entirely satisfied. "Mind if I take a look for myself?"

Ron started to frown; the rafters could be dangerous, and Dillon wasn't one of his own. But Dillon didn't give him a chance to protest. He leaped on stage and started climbing the rigging as if he'd been trained by Cirque du Soleil.

"Where the hell did you find him?" Ron asked Jessy.

"He found me," she said with a shrug.

A few minutes later Dillon rejoined them on the ground. "It's got a safety catch. Someone had to undo it on purpose."

Ron stared at Dillon, clearly worried.

"Shit. I guess it's a good thing the cops are on it. I don't suppose you're hanging around for the show?"

"No, he's not," Jessy answered for him. "He's busy. He has a lot of things to do."

"Well, see you later, then," Ron said. "I'll let the security guy know to be extra vigilant. Jessy, you ought to be back in costume and makeup."

"I'm going right now," Jessy said. "I'll see you later," she told Dillon coolly as she passed.

"I'll be back," he assured her.

"Take your time," she said. "I can keep myself busy."

"Good-looking guy," Ron told her as soon as Dillon was out of sight.

"He is that," she agreed.

Jessy headed backstage to her dressing table. April was already dressed and almost finished with her makeup. "Hey, there. Did you hear? Someone really was messing with the rigging."

"Yes, I heard. But they've added security. I'm sure we'll be fine."

"Go figure," April said as she powdered her nose. "I was afraid to be a flight attendant. Who would have thought you could be in danger doing a kids' pirate show?"

265

She left, ready to take her position backstage. They would be opening the doors soon.

Jessy followed her a few minutes later. She shifted the curtain slightly to look out to the audience. She could see kids filing in, along with a number of adults. She looked past them to the glass partition separating the theater from the lobby.

Grant Willow, one of the security guards, was at the door, watching the last people filing through the door. Next to him, Tanner Green was standing with his face pressed to the glass.

Behind Green, leaning against the far wall, one leg cocked for support and arms crossed over his chest, stood Ringo Murphy, keeping an eye on the proceedings.

He saw Jessy peeking out from behind the curtain and lifted his hat to her.

Oh, Lord, she thought. This was crazy. She was being haunted by one ghost and guarded by another.

"Places!" Ron called, and she stepped back, ready to make her entrance as Bonny Anne, queen of the pirate ship *Treasure*.

Once again, Emil Landon was waiting in his office, anxious to see Dillon.

"Well? Have you found out what's going on?" Emil asked impatiently. "What have the cops found over at the Sun? Someone over there is guilty, has to be," Emil said. "And I'm sick of holing up in here, afraid to go out."

Hugo Blythe was just outside the door, Dillon knew. He had been surprised to find that other than the big bodyguard and the boss, the penthouse was empty. Not even the huge-breasted secretary had been in sight.

"The latest attack took place right here in your own casino," Dillon told him.

"What?"

"There was an incident at the pirate show yesterday," Dillon told him.

Emil Landon stared at him as if he'd lost his mind. "You think that was an *attack?* It's a kids' pirate show. Some joker broke in and messed with the set. Nothing was broken, so what's the big deal?"

"The 'big deal' is that one of your players could have been seriously injured," Dillon said coldly.

Landon bristled at Dillon's comment. "Don't go mistaking my words for a lack of concern. I had the incident investigated immediately, but that's all it was—an incident. That actress should have been offstage with everyone else by then, so no one could possibly have meant to hurt her or anyone else. This was probably some bored kid's prank. What the hell does it have to do with someone being after me?"

"I'm still not sure why you're so convinced that someone wants to kill you," Dillon said, drawing a small notebook from his pocket. "When we first met, you said you were being followed. Green and Blythe both worked for you for some time, right?"

"Right, but . . . hell, that's why I finally called Harrison Investigations. I kept feeling I was being watched, even when I knew there was no one around. It was eerie. Even with those guys around, you know? And I figured you guys don't just prove there are ghosts around, you debunk them, too, right?"

"Right," Dillon agreed. "So what about Green and Blythe? What did you have them doing? And what was Green up to the night he died?"

"When one was on, the other was off," Landon agreed. "Where the hell Tanner Green was before he was murdered, I have no clue. It was his night off."

"All right. But these men were there to protect you, and you still felt unnerved enough to ask for outside help because your car was followed a few times when you went out to dinner. What else? A man of your position and power . . . it had to take more than that to convince you that someone was trying to kill you."

"Someone shot at me one night," Landon told him uneasily.

"Someone shot at you? And you didn't inform the police? Why?"

"What the hell were the cops going to do? I was in the parking lot of a restaurant. I heard shots.

Blythe threw himself on top of me, and we heard a car speeding away."

"What kind of car?"

"I don't know. I didn't see the car, I only heard it."

"If you'd called the cops, they might have found the bullets."

"Look, my bodyguard is dead, and you haven't found a damn thing. The cops are working on it, you're working on it, and what the hell do I have? Zilch."

Dillon wanted to tell him to go to hell then and there. There had to be something more going on, and Emil Landon just didn't want to talk about it.

If it weren't for Jessy, Dillon would have told Landon to stuff it then and there.

But Dillon wasn't going to find himself barred from the casino on some trumped-up charge when he needed to be there to keep an eye on Jessy.

"I'm going to head back over to the Sun later today," he said, rising. "I just wanted to make sure you knew you had trouble in your own casino first."

"Trouble? This is a casino. We throw angry drunks out on a daily basis, and the cops are in here at least once a week because some asshole gets nasty. This was some prankster messing around where he didn't belong," Landon said, but he must have seen something in Dillon's eyes, because he quickly added, "I value my employees. Trust me,

I've made sure that the situation has been taken care of. I'm not a great humanitarian, but that pirate show makes money hand over fist—not just on ticket sales, but because it brings people into my casino. What do you think the parents are doing while their kids are being entertained? Losing money, that's what. My security staff are good. Interview them at your leisure, and you'll see that I'm telling the truth. It's me I'm worried about. I'm getting cabin fever, afraid to leave my own penthouse. Get out there and find out who the hell killed Tanner Green—and who the hell is gunning for me."

Dillon left, bidding Hugo Blythe a cheerful goodbye as the goon saw him to the outer door.

But as he rode down in the elevator, he reflected grimly that he didn't believe Emil Landon, and he didn't trust him.

But he didn't want a showdown with the man.

Not now.

Soon, but not now.

The show went smoothly. The entire cast had been a little on edge, she had realized during the performance, which had somehow made *her* feel calm. The sail fell right on cue, with everyone in proper position, and then it was returned to its original position just as it was every day, seven days a week. When the show was over, Jessy did notice that the techs hurried backstage more quickly than usual, and Ron Pearl himself was there, keeping an eye on everything as the cast posed for pictures and gave autographs to the children. Ron was still there as the last of the audience departed, and when he shooed the cast back to the dressing rooms he seemed both relieved and happy.

Ringo didn't follow her back to her dressing room; now that she was aware of his existence, she was certain that she would know if he was there. Although, she realized, now that the show had gone off without a hitch and she'd had some time to calm down, having a hundred-and-something-year-old ghost in her corner might not be a bad thing.

She found herself actually wanting to have a discussion with him.

As she had the night before, she gave Sandra a call on her cell, then was surprised when Reggie answered the phone.

"Hey," she told Jessy, approval in her tone. "I hear you're dating Mr. Hottie."

"Reggie, please. Your mom has already tortured me enough on that score. And speaking of your mom, where is she?"

"I don't know, and she forgot her phone here when she went out, so I couldn't call and ask her. I'm sure she'll be back soon. What's going on?"

"Nothing. I just wanted to see what she's up to."

"Don't know. I just came in from school. But I'll tell her you called."

"Okay, thanks." She hung up, wondering what she should do. A second later her phone rang and she answered it, even though she didn't recognize the number.

"It's me calling from a pay phone," Sandra said quickly in response to Jessy's cautious, "Hello?"

"Where are you?" Jessy asked her.

"I'm down the street," Sandra told her. "I suck as a friend—sorry. I was going to meet you right there at the show, but I stopped in at the Rainbow, and a new slot machine sucked me in. I just realized the time, so don't worry, I'll be there in five minutes, and we can hang out until tall, dark and stunning returns."

"Sandra, you really don't have to babysit me," Jessy said, but in fact, she was glad that Sandra was on her way. Just in case she really was in danger, she would rather not be alone.

Of course, now she had a ghost watching out for her, as well. Or maybe he'd been there all along. Although apparently Ringo went off on his own periodically, and she was pretty sure he could only be in one place at a time. She wondered what rules, exactly, ghosts had to follow.

"It's not babysitting to spend time with a friend," Sandra assured her. "Consider me on my way."

"No," Jessy said, suddenly sick of everyone— including herself—seeing her as a potential victim. "You're just down the street. I'll come to you."

"Are you sure?"

"The Strip is crawling with people. I'll be fine." *Besides, I have a cowboy ghost following me,* she added silently.

"Okay, but come right here."

"Yes, ma'am."

Jessy hung up, smiling.

She gathered her personal belongings and left her dressing room.

Tanner Green had departed somewhere toward the end of the show, but Ringo had remained, so she looked around for him when she got back out front. She was surprised that he was nowhere to be seen and wondered if he had tried to follow the elusive Tanner Green.

It didn't matter. The Strip was crawling with people. She would be just fine.

It was time to find Darrell Frye, which proved to be easier than Dillon had thought, because the pit boss was back at work. All Dillon had to do was wait fifteen minutes and Frye would be on break. He headed off to the casino's coffee bar to wait.

The Strip was crowded with people.

As she walked down the street, staring at the neon and glitter that defined Vegas, Jessy found herself amazed that someone had come to the desert, started with nothing and ended up with the fantasy playground that was Vegas. Sure, a lot of it was false and plastic, but underneath the facade, it was just like any other place. Lots of people came to play—but others came to work. People built homes, and raised families, and it was a mecca for young entertainers.

And for her, it was—and always had been—home.

Suddenly that comfortable thought fled from her mind, driven out by the realization—immediate and absolutely certain—that she was being followed.

She told herself that it was Ringo, but she knew it wasn't. She realized that she'd always known when Ringo was around, even when she hadn't been able to see him, because of his spurs.

This wasn't Ringo. This was someone who was stalking her. She hadn't seen anyone when she left the theater, so this had to be someone who knew when she got off work, someone who had timed her movements and waited in the crowd to pick her up when she left, someone who knew exactly where she was right this second and could easily attack her if he chose.

She stopped dead in the street. No one would take a chance on attacking her with hundreds of people around, would they?

Then she remembered that Tanner Green had suddenly appeared out of nowhere, a knife in his back.

There was a large group of tourists ahead of her. She hurried to join them, looking for safety in numbers.

• • •

"Hey, Wolf," Darrell Frye said, approaching Dillon at the table where he was sitting. He offered Dillon a broad smile and a handshake, looking as if he didn't have a care in the world. "I heard you're working on Tanner Green's murder. Horrible business."

"It was. And since you were there that night, I was hoping you might have noticed something that could help me."

"I doubt I can help you. Martin was running the table when Green actually died."

"I know," Dillon told him. "Can I get you a cup of coffee?"

"I'll grab some—it's a freebie for me. No alcohol on the job—but we get all the coffee we can drink. Do you want a refill?" he asked, indicating the cup Dillon had in front of him.

"I'm good," Dillon said. "Thanks."

"Be right back."

When Darrell returned with his coffee he sat down across from Dillon, glanced at his watch and said, "I'm good for nine more minutes."

"That should do," Dillon told him.

"You were there, too, so you would have seen everything I did. Although . . ." Darrell said, frowning with the memory. "Who left first, you or me? Me, I think. I remember the night pretty well. Coot, he's a regular. There was a skinny woman there who looked like she was on her last legs.

There was the drunk who didn't know if he wanted his chips on or off the table. And . . . Jessy, of course. Jessy Sparhawk. You must know her—I saw a tape of the two of you leaving the casino together on TV."

"I just met her that night," Dillon said. "But you know her fairly well, I gather."

Darrell shrugged, shaking his head. "Wish I did. She's not a gambler. I did talk to her once after I'd seen her show. I want off the floor and into enter-tainment—everyone who knows me knows that—and I'd heard some of the brass talking about the pirate show at the Big Easy. They liked Jessy, so I figured if I could get her over here . . . well, that would look good for me."

"Where did you go when you left the floor that night?" Dillon asked him.

"The employee cafeteria," Darrell replied.

That would be easy enough to check out, Dillon thought.

"Why?" Darrell asked.

"I was hoping maybe you'd stepped outside, maybe seen something you didn't even know you'd seen. Something important," Dillon said.

"I wish I could help you."

"Me too. I did talk to some of the guys outside, at the door and at valet parking," Dillon told him.

"Oh?"

Darrell Frye suddenly looked wary. His smile wavered for a moment, or at least it looked that way to Dillon. No matter how willing to help the man seemed to be, there was still something about him that seemed wrong. As if he was being *too* willing.

"Yeah," Dillon said. "Anyway, one of the guys *thought* maybe he'd seen Tanner Green stumble out of a white super-stretch limo."

"Really? Who?" Darrell Frye demanded. "Did you tell the cops?"

"Yeah, the cops know. But it won't help them much."

"Why not?"

"Because the guy I talked to is dead. It was Rudy Yorba."

Frye let out a whistle. "Imagine that. The one person who actually sees something winds up dead in a hit-and-run."

"Yeah, imagine."

Frye glanced at his watch. "I gotta get back. But if I think of anything, I'll call you. I promise."

"Darrell, one more quick question. Does anyone at this casino have access to the security tapes? Other than security, obviously." "I thought the tapes went to the cops," Frye said, frowning. "Those were copies, right?"

"You'd have to ask security. I gotta go," Darrell said. "But I'll be happy to talk to you again, though. Anytime."

"Thanks, Darrell. I appreciate that," Dillon said. "Sure."

As soon as Frye left, Dillon got up to leave himself, wondering what the other man had been lying about. Because he *had* been lying. A thin sheen of nervous sweat had appeared on his upper lip, and his eyes had kept shifting toward the left.

The tourists turned en masse, heading down a wide one-way alley alongside one of the casinos to the parking area where buses dropped off and picked up their passengers.

But Jessy was so sure that she was being followed, she turned along with them.

Great, she thought. What the hell was she going to do? Board the bus?

She decided—too late—that she was probably making a big mistake. If she really was being followed by someone who meant to harm her, she should have stayed on the Strip and caught up with some other group to hide in.

Unable to think of anything else to do, she tried to board the bus, but the tour guide stopped her. "Miss, I'm sorry, you must be lost. This is a chartered bus."

"I know. But I think I'm being followed."

The young man looked around. There was no one around except the rest of the tour group—who were all wearing name tags, explaining how he had known she didn't belong.

"Can I call someone for you?" he asked, looking at her as if she were an escapee from a lunatic asylum.

She had a phone, she realized. She could call someone herself. Like Dillon. Where the hell was he? Why hadn't she heard from him yet?

"Miss, you'll have to step aside. The people behind you need to get on."

She stepped aside, hoping they boarded slowly, and dialed Dillon's cell, praying that he would pick up.

He did.

"Jessy?"

The concern in his voice made her take a deep breath. She told herself she was being ridiculous.

"Where are you?" he asked her.

"About a block from the Rainbow. I'm walking over to meet Sandra. Where are you?"

"At the Sun. I never got any farther. I'll come find you. Is Ringo around?"

"He was at the show, but I haven't seen him since," she said, amazed that she was talking so casually about seeing a ghost.

"Are you all right?" he asked.

"Yes. I'm sorry, I was a little nervous before, but . . . I'm okay now." She had panicked, and she didn't want him knowing just how afraid she had been. She absolutely couldn't allow herself to become paralyzed by paranoia.

"Okay," he said slowly. "How was the show?"

"It went fine, no problems."

"Good. Okay, I'm on my way. Where are you?"

"About three blocks from the Big Easy."

"I'm on foot," he told her, "but I'm already on my way."

She hung up. The last tourist was about to board the bus, and she needed to get moving.

She turned and started walking briskly. She heard the driver rev the engine and realized that the last tourist had gotten on and the door had closed.

The broad alley looked empty. All she had to do was walk quickly and she would be back on the Strip, surrounded by the crowd. It was insane to think that whoever had been following her—if anyone even had—was still out there.

She neared a clump of bushes the casino must have worked hard to maintain in this desert climate. She hadn't even noticed it when she had passed it with the group.

She kept to the far side of the alley as she went by, thinking she was going crazy.

But she wasn't.

As she walked by, she saw that the bushes started moving.

She swore and started walking more quickly.

She turned back and saw two men emerging from the cover of the bushes. Two men she would never recognize, because even in the warmth of a Vegas spring, they were wearing dark ski masks and were clad in black from head to toe.

She started to run.

She had to make it to the Strip before they caught up to her. Had to. If she could just get there, there was no way they could attack her without people noticing.

She heard footsteps coming up behind her.

They were moving like lightning, and she was wearing pumps. The heels weren't high, but they were hardly running shoes.

She could feel the energy behind her, the force. A hot wind seemed to be reaching out for her as the footsteps drew closer.

"Help!" she screamed.

She could see the crowds just ahead, where the shadows of the alley ended.

"Help!" she screamed again.

And that was when she felt someone grab her arm. She screamed again, tearing at the gloved fingers that held her.

"Help!"

The second man reached her then, but she barely saw him because she realized that the first man had something in his hand and was pressing it to her face. A cloth. And it had a sickening-sweet smell. She felt dizziness rising and realized that the cloth was drugged.

"Help!" This time her scream was weaker.

There were people on the sidewalk just ahead.

Couldn't they see her?

She started to fall. . . .

And that was when something happened. When someone seemed to plow into the man holding her and wrench him from her.

"Run, Jessy, run!" someone yelled.

It was Dillon's voice.

Run. She had to run.

But she could barely stumble.

She tried to move, but she had no strength and the night seemed so black.

The second man was reaching for her and she . . .

She was falling.

13

Dillon moved without thinking as he tackled the first man, ripping him away from Jessy. With the element of surprise in his favor, it was an easy feat to bring the man down hard enough to keep him there, fighting for breath. A right hook to the jaw bought him more time.

Dillon had been a punk as a kid. He'd gotten his eyes blackened a dozen times in idiotic fights he'd started himself, but in the end he'd learned how to take care of himself.

But though the first man had gone down without much effort, the other now had Jessy, who'd fallen limp to the ground, and was tossing her over his shoulder as easily as if she were a bag of feathers.

Where would could he be planning on taking her?

He couldn't dwell on the question. He disentangled himself from the man on the ground and went straight for the second assailant, using all the force he could muster to chop the edge of his hand against the man's nape.

The guy was a gorilla; a smaller man might have gone straight down, but the giant shuddered, then finally started to stumble to his knees, but at least he dropped Jessy, who landed directly between his feet. She roused, blinking rapidly as she tried to escape, but her movements were erratic, her limbs unable to obey the commands her brain was sending. Then her knee jerked hard and high as she flailed in her struggle to rise, and her assailant let out a bellow, rolling to his side and clutching his groin. Dillon dived after him.

"Jessy, get to the street!" Dillon ordered.

There was a moment when her eyes met his and he was afraid that she wouldn't obey, would try to stay and help him.

But apparently she knew she was too weak to be any good in a fight. She staggered to her feet and moved toward the street, screaming for help. Her voice was weak, but she was getting away.

She reached the sidewalk at last, and that changed everything. People heard her, saw her, and someone called 911. In seconds police-car sirens filled the air. Dillon turned to rejoin the fight. The first man had turned to run, heading for the other end of the alley. But the big man remained, glaring at Dillon, before running in the opposite direction. Toward Jessy.

Dillon raced after him, but the man ignored

Jessy, who was sinking toward the pavement once again, and just tore past her, shoving people out of the way, and disappeared into the traffic. Dillon tried to follow, but it was impossible to break through the crowd of people surrounding Jessy. Frustrated, he gave up and cursed the fact that the attacker was no doubt even now doing a chameleon change, discarding the ski mask as easily as he'd donned it earlier, blending in with everyone around him.

Dillon dropped down to the sidewalk next to Jessy and put his hands on her shoulders. "Can you breathe?"

"What did he dose me with?" Jessy asked him, inhaling deeply.

He could smell a hint of the drug. "Ether, I think," he told her. "Are you all right? Did they hurt you?" he asked anxiously.

She shook her head. "No, no . . . I'm fine. But I might have been. . . ." She trailed off with a shudder. Neither of them knew what might have happened. Had the men been out to kidnap her—or kill her?

A police car wailed as it came to a halt. A uniformed officer made his way through the crowd. "Move back, folks. Let me get to the victim."

"I'm not a victim," Jessy protested.

"Yeah, you are," Dillon corrected her.

An officer was speaking into his radio, ordering an ambulance for Jessy.

"I don't need an ambulance," she protested. Using Dillon's shoulder for support, she rose. "I don't need an ambulance," she repeated.

"Jessy, you might have been hurt," Dillon told her.

Her blue eyes narrowed mutinously. "I'm not hurt." She turned to the cops. "Thank you. You came along just in time. But I'm an adult and in my right mind, and I'm not going to the hospital."

"Your knee is bleeding," Dillon pointed out.

"And I have Band-Aids in my purse," she snapped.

"Excuse me, but we need to find out what happened here," one of the officers said. He turned to face the crowd that was milling closer. "Folks, back off. I need everyone to just move on, unless you saw what happened here."

A young man stepped forward. "Lisa and I heard her scream, and I called 911."

"Did you see anything?" the officer asked.

"Someone must have seen something. One of the men ran right through the crowd," Dillon said.

A dozen people started speaking at once.

"One at a time," the officer said politely. "Where did he go?"

A girl pointed toward the street. "There."

"There" meant six lanes of traffic.

"Officer, I had the sense that someone was following me as I was walking down the street," Jessy said.

The cop's brows hiked. "On the Strip?" he asked.

"Yes."

"So you ran down an alley?"

Jessy flushed. Dillon looked at her, because that was certainly a question in his mind, too.

"I was with a bunch of tourists."

"What?" the officer said.

"There were about twenty-five tourists ahead of me when I felt I was being followed, so I tried to blend in with them. But they wouldn't let me on their bus, so I hoped maybe I had shaken whoever it was, and I headed back to the street. And then they . . . they came at me out of the bushes," she explained. "They were dressed in black, and they were wearing ski masks."

"Do you know who they were?" the officer asked.

"She was attacked, and you're grilling *her* like that?" an older woman demanded.

"We have to try to catch the perps," the officer said. "And that means getting all the information we can." He looked at Dillon. "And you?"

"I had just talked to Miss Sparhawk on the phone and I was on my way to meet her. I'm pretty sure it was a kidnap attempt. They tried to drug her," Dillon explained.

The crowd in the street was growing. The ambulance, which had been called whether Jessy wanted it or not, was pulling up. A second set of officers arrived and began cordoning off the scene.

"Get in the ambulance—please," Dillon whispered to Jessy. "We can get out of here, the crowd will clear, and the crime-scene team will be able to get to work."

Jessy looked at him and then, unwillingly, agreed.

Her phone rang, and Dillon took it out of her hand and answered it. Sandra was on the other end, and she quickly became hysterical when Dillon explained what had happened and where they were going. He told her to meet them at the hospital and hung up.

In the ambulance, stretched out on the gurney with a med tech asking her questions and taking her vitals, Jessy complained about how ridiculous it was to send her to the hospital for a scraped knee.

Ridiculous or not, Dillon still thought it was the right call. As they headed to the hospital with the siren blaring, he called Jerry Cheever. The call went straight to voice mail, but Cheever must have gotten the message right away, because he called back just as the ambulance pulled up to the E.R.

Dillon tersely told him what had happened. "I'm homicide," Cheever reminded Dillon. "This was a mugging, Wolf."

"That's bullshit and you know it. They didn't want her purse—they wanted *her*."

"All right, I'll be down," Cheever agreed.

Sandra arrived while Jessy was in with a doctor.

Sandra had tears streaming down her cheeks, and Dillon tried to calm her down, assuring her that none of it was her fault. She finally calmed down when the doctor came out to say that Jessy had suffered no lasting effects from the attack and was free to leave. As soon as Jessy herself arrived, Sandra hugged her and started apologizing all over again.

"Sandra, stop it. It's not your fault, and if you don't stop, I'm going to have to beg someone to give *you* a sedative," Jessy told her firmly.

Just as they started to leave, the news came on the waiting-room television with a report on the attack. There were no pictures from the scene; everything had happened too fast.

But a picture of Jessy did go up on-screen, her promo shot, which Dillon couldn't help thinking was absolutely stunning. The reporter went on to say that Jessy's condition was unknown, then added that Miss Sparhawk was certainly having a rough time lately and went on to remind people of her unintentional role in Tanner Green's death.

Jerry Cheever came through the emergency doors just as they were preparing to walk out. He looked at Jessy with what seemed to be genuine concern and asked if she was all right.

"A scrape on one knee, and that's it," Jessy told him.

Cheever stared at Dillon. "I'm still not sure—"

"Get serious, Cheever. She was followed down

288

an alley and attacked. Not robbed. Attacked. I'm assuming they had some way of spiriting her off. They wanted something from her, or they wanted her. . . ."

"Dead," Jessy said flatly.

"Oh, God," Sandra moaned.

"Let's take this to the station," Cheever suggested.

"Better idea. Let's take it to my house," Dillon said. "That will be a lot easier on Jessy than dragging her down to the station."

"Get in the car," Cheever agreed with a sigh. "We'll do it."

At Dillon's house, they heard Clancy the minute they reached the house. She might be big and furry and lovable, but she was a guard dog all the way. As he opened the door, Dillon spoke to her, and she wagged her tail, certain not just from his presence and his voice but from his manner that everything was all right.

"I can make coffee, if you want," Sandra suggested. "So you guys can talk."

"Thanks. That would be great," Dillon told her.

Just as Cheever sat down in the living room with Dillon and Jessy, his phone rang. When he got off, he said, "That was the crime-scene sergeant. They found two separate blood types, so one of you must have nicked one of the guys. If the DNA is in the system, we can find the guy. Otherwise, broken branches and scuff marks, that's it."

Dillon nodded. "Here's the thing, Cheever. It was a planned attack. I think that whoever killed Tanner Green thinks he said something to Jessy before he died, and that whatever he said is worth . . . silencing her. Rudy Yorba talked to me, and Rudy wound up dead. You need to get subpoenas on both of those limos. We've got to find the killer before people wind up dead."

Cheever frowned, looking at Jessy. "If these events *are* related, then Wolf is right and you're in danger. And here's the thing—I saw the tape. I know Green said something to you, and I'm willing to bet other people know it, too. Care to tell me what it was?"

Jessy glanced at Dillon, who shrugged.

"Indigo," Jessy said.

"Indigo?" Cheever echoed, confused and disappointed.

"Indigo," she repeated.

Cheever stared at her blankly. "Like the color?"

"Yes. I forgot it at first, because there was so much going on. And then, even after I remembered, it didn't seem to mean anything," Jessy explained. "And then . . . I didn't know it was a town."

"It's a town?" Cheever asked, looking at Dillon.

"I'm surprised you haven't heard about it. It's kind of a faded legend in these parts, a bump in the timeline of history. There was a shoot-out there, and soon after, the town went down. It's on Indian land, but it's just a pit out in the desert now. A movie outfit rented it from the tribe a few years back, and they filmed a few scenes and got out—it was too creepy for them," Dillon explained.

"You're sure he meant the town?" Cheever asked, perplexed.

"I'm not sure of *any*thing," Jessy told him.

"Same here, unfortunately," Dillon added.

"Coffee," Sandra announced from the doorway. She came in with a tray holding four steaming cups of coffee and all the necessaries.

It took a minute for them to fix their cups, and then they sat back down and started talking again, with Sandra sitting on the sidelines trying to look invisible.

"I'll be damned if I know what it means, either," Cheever said, and looked at Dillon. "Why would anyone commit murder because of a ghost town?"

"I don't know," Dillon said. He certainly wasn't about to tell Cheever that ghosts—including one with ties to Indigo—were real, or that he and Jessy both had ancestors who'd lived—and presumably died—in Indigo, since what that meant was still a mystery, as well.

Cheever sighed. "All right, both of you need to think. Do you remember anything about these guys that might help us find them? Tell us where to look for them?"

"Green," Jessy said.

Cheever looked at her. "First Indigo, now green?

I need something more than colors here," he said wearily.

"The big one had green eyes," Jessy said.

Dillon looked at her, surprised and pleased. He hadn't noticed either man's eye color, but then again, he'd been busy pulling them off Jessy, more concerned with how well they fought than what they looked like.

"The other guy, I don't know . . ."

"There's someone out there running all this, and I don't think he's as scary as he'd like to be. This is the second time he's used drugs. LSD on Green, and ether just now with Jessy. He hires guys with real muscle, but he goes one better and drugs his victims. He doesn't want to meet with resistance," Dillon said.

"Great. I need to look for a rich guy with a drug problem in Vegas. That narrows it down," Cheever said sarcastically.

"Bring in those limos," Dillon said. "And do it soon."

"What the hell would I find in one of the limos at this point? Even if Tanner Green *was* in one of them, any evidence would have been sanitized away by now," Cheever said.

"People miss things," Dillon reminded him.

Cheever stared at him. "You've been in at least one of those limos, haven't you?"

Dillon started to answer, but Cheever lifted a hand and cut him off. "Never mind. If you did

292

something illegal, I don't want to know. Which limo am I tearing apart first? And what should I expect to find? In your *educated opinion*, of course."

"A button," Dillon said. "You know how easily buttons fall off."

Cheever rose, setting his coffee cup down. "Thank you," he said to Sandra, and offered her his hand. "We haven't been introduced. I'm Jerry Cheever."

"Oh, sorry. Sandra Nelson. It's a pleasure—I think," she said.

"I'll get a car to keep an eye on Miss Sparhawk's place," Cheever said, turning to Dillon.

"She'll be with me," Dillon told him.

"Right. Well, I can get a car out here in—"

"That's not necessary. They're not going to come here, and even if they do, I have a few protective devices of my own."

Cheever groaned. "Yeah, I'm sure you do. Well, then, if you hear anything, call me . . ."

Sandra stood. "I have to get going, too. I have a teenager waiting for me," she explained to Dillon.

"We'll get you home," Dillon assured her.

"I can take you," Cheever said. "If you'd like."

"Yes." Sandra looked at Jessy, then walked over and reached for her hands. "You're sure you're okay? You know I'd stay, but Reggie will be home alone."

"Go. It's fine, honestly, and thank you."

Dillon and Jessy walked with Cheever and Sandra to the door, where Sandra paused to give Jessy a hug and look questioningly into her eyes one more time.

"Sandra!" Jessy laughed. "I'm fine, and I'll see you tomorrow."

Sandra and Cheever left at last, and Jessy and Dillon turned to look expectantly at each other. But before either of them could speak, they heard the clink of spurs.

Ringo walked into the entryway from the hallway that led to the bedrooms and office.

"Where have *you* been?" they demanded in unison.

"Sorry to be late, but I was following your man Green until I heard what was going on with Jessy," Ringo said. Hands on his hips, he stared at them for a minute, then shook his head in disgust that was clearly aimed at himself. "I thought it was important to know what he was doing when he wasn't stalking Jessy. And you—" He looked at Dillon. "You didn't tell me to stick with her like glue. You never said that."

Dillon gritted his teeth, seething with anger at himself. He'd known Jessy was in danger. He'd known it in his gut, and he had left her alone anyway.

It wouldn't happen again.

Jessy was staring at Ringo. "So—where did Tanner Green go?" she asked.

"Now, that's the odd thing," Ringo said. He walked over to the sofa and sat down comfortably, resting his arms on the back of the couch and resting one booted foot on the opposite knee. He stared at them for a long moment and then said, "The craps table."

"And . . . ?" Dillon persisted. "What did he do at the craps table?"

"He watched it for a while. Didn't try to touch anything, didn't interfere. He just stared at it, looking really sad."

"And that's all he did?" Jessy asked.

Ringo shook his head. "After a while he went to the penthouse elevator. He couldn't make it work. Eventually one of Landon's people came down, and he got in when they got out. You need a key card to make it go up, though."

"Wait," Jessy said. "Tanner Green couldn't just . . . um, materialize up there?"

Ringo shrugged. "Green's only a novice ghost. He knows he's dead by now, but he hasn't accepted it, and he isn't dealing with it very well. I don't know what powers he's figured out yet. I know I wandered around Indigo for a few years before I even learned to travel any distance."

"So?" Dillon asked, interrupting impatiently. "What happened then?"

"He just stood there in the elevator. I think he sees me but doesn't trust me. Anyway, I hung with him a while, and then made my way back here.

Turned on the television and saw what had happened, then heard you coming, so I turned off the television—and listened while you guys talked to that cop. I'm so sorry I wasn't there to help when you needed me, Jessy."

"You should have pushed the button and followed him up to Landon's place," Dillon said.

"I told you. It needs a key card, and I didn't have one. The only way I've ever been up there was on my own power, and that wouldn't have helped Tanner any. Plus, with him refusing to see me, I couldn't explain to him how to get up there."

"Right, sorry," Dillon said.

"Whatever Landon is up to, he's careful. I didn't see anything but business going on in that suite when I was up there," Ringo said. "I may not be much of a spy, but I *am* a damn good ghost." He looked at Jessy. "And I'll prove it to you. I won't leave your side again until this whole mess is over."

"It's all right, Ringo," Dillon said. "I plan to be with Jessy."

"You can't be with her all the time," Ringo said, then looked at them and started laughing. "Okay, let's not go that route again. I don't intrude in the bedroom or the outhouse. But I'll be with you everywhere else, and I won't fail you."

"Maybe Green was in the suite before he died. Drinking spiked drinks with his boss before going for a ride," Dillon said.

"Maybe, maybe, maybe—we need something that isn't maybe!" Jessy said forcefully, then looked at Dillon. "I need fresh clothes and some dinner," she told him, smiling suddenly, as if she hadn't been in mortal danger just a few hours earlier.

She stopped speaking and stared across the room, then said softly, "Dillon, look."

He turned. Fading in and out as he sat in one of the wingback chairs by the fire was Tanner Green.

"It's all right, Mr. Green. Please, don't leave," Jessy entreated.

Dillon kept his own voice low and calm, "Tanner, we're trying to help you. Everyone in this room wants to help you."

But Tanner Green faded away, despite their pleas. They all stared at the chair as the seconds ticked by, but Tanner didn't reappear.

"Why won't he stay?" Dillon murmured.

"He's trying. It's just not as easy as you'd think," Ringo said.

Clancy woofed suddenly, and Dillon frowned, listening. Finally he heard what the dog had already sensed: a car coming down the street and pulling up in front of the house.

In the police car, Sandra tried to pull herself together, but she couldn't help feeling as if she'd let Jessy down.

"It's all right, Ms. Nelson," Cheever said when

she confessed her guilt to him. "No one can know ahead of time that this kind of thing is going to happen."

"I should have been with her," Sandra said.

"Think about it. Even if you'd been there, what chance would two women have had against two trained thugs?"

"It's just all such a mess. I mean, poor Jessy. First a guy just ups and dies on her, and now she's in danger herself," Sandra said.

"You've got to stop worrying or you're going to make yourself sick. Dillon's with her, and he seems pretty capable of protecting her. Now, how about some directions so I can get you home?"

She looked at the cop. He came on as gruff, but he had spoken so gently just now.

"I'm over in Henderson. Just hop on the highway, and I'll show you where to get off," Sandra said. "And thank you. My girl is pretty grown-up, but I don't like to leave her alone at home too late." She sighed. "You just never know what can happen."

"You sound like a good parent," Cheever said approvingly.

"She's everything to me," Sandra told him. "What about you? Your job is pretty dangerous, huh."

He shrugged, and a slight smile crossed his face. "Not so dangerous. Narcotics, now, *that's* dangerous. Drug lords and junkies. Those folks are scary. In homicide—well, by the time I get to them, they're not going to hurt me."

"That's not true," Sandra warned. "The victims may be dead, but whoever killed them is still out there. Take this case. Whoever killed Tanner Green is still out there and going after Jessy."

He cast her a glance. "Are you an entertainer, too, Ms. Nelson?"

"Call me Sandra, please. And I was, but now I'm a writer. Which I guess means I'm still an entertainer, in a way." She pointed to a sign along the highway. "There . . . Take this exit."

"So are you . . . still married?" Cheever asked.

"No, not anymore. What about you?"

Cheever shook his head. "Believe it or not, dating is not such a breeze when you're a homicide cop. Go figure."

"The right person will come along for you, Detective. I'm certain," she assured him. "There, that's my house on the right."

Cheever pulled up in front of the pleasant little ranch-style dwelling she'd pointed to. "I'll see you into the house," he told her.

She smiled. "Thanks."

She got out of the car, glad that he was staying until she'd locked the door behind her.

"Reggie?" she called as she opened the door.

"In here, Mom, on the computer!" Reggie called.

Sandra thanked Cheever for the ride, then leaned back against the newly locked door. She was still worried sick about Jessy, but at least Jessy had Dillon now. Reggie was her world. And Reggie was safe. Life was good.

Timothy lay in bed, staring up at the ceiling. This had been a good day. He enjoyed spending time with Mrs. Teasdale. True, she needed her medications, but she was bright and her mind was still clear, and she made him feel young again. Not this week, but soon, one day when Jessy was free, they would plan their trek out to the reservation.

For now, he was feeling fine. Usually everyone, even Jessy, did nothing more than humor him when he talked about the people in the wall.

But today . . .

Today Dillon Wolf had come by to see him, looking so much like the man in the image the ghosts in the wall kept showing him.

Right now, Billie Tiger was up on the ceiling. At first Timothy had seen only the patterns in the plaster. Then, as they always did, they began to take shape, almost as if there was a movie playing on the ceiling.

Billie Tiger was a handsome man with his feathered headpiece and clothes in traditional bright Seminole colors. His skin was deep brown, in color, and he had large almond-shaped eyes.

"Brother Hawk," he said gravely to Timothy.

"Tiger," Timothy returned.

"The time grows near, the time when times collide," Tiger said. "They are gathering, but I have not seen the men at the door, the men who come with evil purpose, driven by greed, who care not what danger they bring to others." Tiger's voice faded, and the movie began. Timothy saw the dusty roads of an old ghost town. He saw the buildings, faded almost to the color of the sand. Timothy felt as if he were there, as if he were walking down those streets. He strode along a wooden sidewalk toward the swinging doors of the saloon. He pushed them open, and then he was inside. A man was playing the piano, and when Timothy sat down next to him, it was as if he somehow slid into the body of the other man. The keys felt so real beneath his fingers. There was a woman standing at his side, leaning against the piano. She was pretty, but she would have been prettier if she hadn't looked so tired and worn. She began to sing, but it was clear that her heart wasn't in it. Once, when she'd been young and filled hope, she had probably sung in a rich soprano. She might even have smiled back then, and her smile would have lit up a room. But she was tired, he knew, and so was he. They had both been in Indigo too long.

He turned and saw the bartender wiping down the bar with a rag, while several patrons were pouring whiskey down their gullets, neat.

He looked around and saw the poker players. John Wolf had a quiet strength that marked him as a

301

leader, though he wasn't a chief. He was a half-breed, a man who had learned that he would never be accepted in either world and had become stronger from having to make his own way in the world. If anyone could save Indigo, it was John Wolf.

All this he knew because, in some strange way he was not only himself but the piano player. And as the piano player, he knew he had a Lakota wife and three children, and that his oldest son had a white wife who hadn't wanted to stay in Indigo. The two of them had set up housekeeping on a patch of land closer to the river. They were near the bigger town of White Rock but still near a reservation, and they were somehow managing to straddle the line between those two worlds, heedless of the slights some cast their way, in love despite them. That was the definition of hope, he thought. Hope also resided in John Wolf because Wolf had returned from the territorial capital earlier that day, and something had happened there, something Wolf wasn't talking about but that had clearly given himself a sense of power that practically radiated from him. And now Wolf was waiting, waiting for Varny, but also waiting for someone else. Mariah. He had something to tell her, he'd said, and he wasn't going to tell anyone else. Clearly it was connected to the business he'd transacted in the capital. And as he waited, his guns were always within reach. He was a man of peace, but he knew how to shoot.

The other players at the table were the sheriff, Grant Percy, who wanted to be brave but had already been cowed by the man whose malignant presence had infected the whole town. Frank Varny ruled Indigo. He'd used money to bribe and to bully until he'd created a gang of men to do his bidding, and from the labor—even the deaths—of others, he had created his own kingdom. But if money had built him up, then money could also bring him down.

And he knew it.

The town idiot was at the poker table, too.

Mark Davison was a buffoon. He had cast his lot with Varny as soon as he came to town. He swaggered and pretended to be brave, but at heart he was a coward.

Then there was Ringo Murphy. Freewheeling, and too young to know that confidence and a sense of one's own immortality wasn't always enough to combat the power of greed and evil. Ringo thought he'd seen it all. He'd fought in the war. He'd watched everything he'd known and loved go up in ashes. He thought his weariness was a bullet-proof cloak, but it was not.

The saloon doors suddenly burst open. A man stood in the doorway, silhouetted by the setting sun. Just the dark figure of a man, nothing more, and still he was somehow the epitome of evil.

Varny had shown up before Mariah. The timing was off. Out of kilter. And it would change everything.

"Get the hell out," he told Milly. And in the dream he was the piano player as he spoke to her.

And then he rose from the piano and slipped out the back.

As he did so, the movie began to fade away and Timothy felt himself sinking back into his own body, his own consciousness. The swirls in the plaster were once again nothing more than swirls in the plaster. Not even Billie Tiger, who was trying so hard to find the truth and reveal it to him, remained.

"Where are you, Tiger, my brother Tiger," Timothy asked.

He thought he heard the whisper of an answer.

"I am trying very hard to see, brother," Tiger told him. "Time shifts, the years pass, and what happened once happens again, but what was is hidden by what is, and still I seek the truth."

Then even Tiger was gone and there was nothing but the ticking of the bedside clock.

But one certainty remained. Timothy knew he had to keep seeking the truth. With Billie Tiger's help or alone, he needed to find the truth.

Because *they* were assembling. . . .

And the bloodbath was coming again.

14

Clancy suddenly passed them and raced to the front door, where she set up a racket. Jessy looked instantly to Dillon, alarmed and alert.

He offered her a smile. "Right on time," he told Jessy. "Down, girl, it's all right," he added, addressing the dog as he headed for the door.

"It's all right?" Jessy asked, rising. "How do you know . . . ?"

"Because it's Adam Harrison," Dillon told her.

Jessy stared, her brows rising. He hadn't told her that *the* Adam Harrison was on the way, but then again, she couldn't really fault him for that because he hadn't had much of a chance.

"Adam? That's great," Ringo said.

Jessy looked at Ringo. "You know Adam, too?"

"Yes. And no," Ringo told her. He sighed and rose. "Adam isn't a nightwalker like Dillon here. He can see things sometimes. But he can't really see me, though he hears my spurs pretty clearly. We talk sometimes, through Dillon."

Dillon had opened the door, and Jessy could see Clancy wagging her tail. "Leave it to you, Adam," Dillon said. "Every other plane in the sky may be late, but you always land right on time. And it's good to see the rest of you, too."

The rest of them? Jessy looked toward the door and saw that three people were entering.

305

The first was clearly Adam Harrison. He was around Timothy's age and had snow-white hair and beautiful light eyes, a lean face and, again like Timothy, he stood ramrod straight and was a tall man, though shorter than Dillon.

He was followed by an extremely beautiful young woman, lithe and slim, with long golden hair and brilliant aqua eyes.

Jessy was surprised when Dillon picked her up and hugged her.

A spasm of jealousy flooded through Jessy and she deplored herself for it. Of course Dillon had friends, and some of them were bound to be women.

She kicked herself for being even momentarily ridiculous when the woman was followed by a man who warned, "Dillon, go gently there, I prefer my wife unbroken."

Dillon grinned and unabashedly greeted the tall man with an embrace, as well. "Come in, come in. . . ." He turned to smile at Jessy, and that smile warmed her all over, conveying as it did that she was important, important enough to be introduced to his guests right away.

"Jessy Sparhawk, Nikki and Brent Blackhawk— and Adam Harrison, of course," Dillon said. "Brent, Nikki, Adam, this is Jessy."

Adam took her hand first. "Of course?" he asked teasingly. "Does everyone know me right away because I'm old?"

"Never old, Adam, just distinguished," Nikki assured him, taking Jessy's hand. "Nice to meet you. And I hope you'll forgive the intrusion. After Dillon called Adam, Adam called us."

Her husband stepped up next. He had long black hair, but his eyes were light, indicating that there was probably some white blood somewhere in his heritage. "Jessy," he said, taking her hand and studying her openly. "Sparhawk, huh? With that hair?"

"Lakota Sioux, just a little further back," she told him. "You'll have to meet Timothy, my grandfather. He's half."

"Brent is Lakota Sioux, too," Dillon said.

"Looks like it's you and me against the assembled tribes," Nikki said to Adam, but her grin made it obvious that she was teasing.

Jessy laughed along with everyone else and realized that she already felt comfortable with the newcomers, and she hadn't known any of them for more than a few minutes.

Clancy started barking for attention then, and Brent hunkered down to pet her. "Clancy, old girl. What's up? I heard you need some help around here, but the house looks in good shape to me."

Clancy barked happily, then bounded over to Nikki for more petting.

"Ringo, you can come out now," Brent called over his shoulder.

Ringo made his appearance from the hallway. He

ignored Brent and walked straight to Nikki, giving her an ethereal kiss upon the cheek. "Hello there, beautiful," he told her.

"Ringo, behave," Dillon warned.

"He's all right," Nikki said. "So, cowboy, how's it going?"

"I wasn't a cowboy," Ringo said indignantly. "I was a decorated war hero and a gunslinger, I'll have you know."

"Lord, this is frustrating," Adam said, and turned to Jessy. "So you see Ringo, too?"

She nodded.

"Would someone mind telling me what's being said?" Adam asked.

"He just wants us to know that he was a civil war hero and a gunslinger, not a cowboy."

Jessy looked at Adam curiously. He was looking in the right direction, but she had a feeling that was only because he saw where everyone else was looking.

"You never . . . see? Is that frustrating?" she asked him quietly, wondering whether seeing ghosts was really much of a gift anyway. It was simply a . . . phenomenon, one that came to you. You couldn't buy it, steal it or simply wish it into existence.

Adam smiled serenely. "I've learned to see Josh, my son. That's what matters to my heart. When I can't help others because I can't see them, *that's* frustrating."

"It's all right. You always know how to find us," Nikki told him affectionately.

"So she's a nightwalker, too?" Brent asked Dillon, inclining his head in Jessy's direction.

"Yes, but only very recently. Her ability seems to be connected to Tanner Green's death," Dillon explained.

She was a nightwalker. The word was terrifying, in a way, and yet it also filled her with a strange sense of pride and belonging.

"You guys will have to fill us in on exactly what's going on," Nikki said, then looked probingly at Dillon and Jessy. "You two look like you've been in a fight."

"Jessy was attacked earlier tonight," Dillon said.

All eyes turned to her with concern.

"I'm all right," she assured them quickly.

"Tell us about it," Adam said, walking into the living room and taking a seat.

As soon as everyone else was comfortably settled, too, Ringo groaned. "It was my fault."

"It was not," Jessy said.

"What wasn't what?" Adam asked, and Dillon told him what Ringo had said.

Then, between Dillon and Jessy, they explained the events of the evening.

"Two men, obviously a planned assault, using ski masks. I'd say someone out there is getting scared," Adam commented. He looked at Dillon. "The police are investigating the obvious leads, right?"

Dillon nodded. "And I appreciate the fact that you're all hereto help with the . . . less obvious angle. There are things I need to do, but now that we know Jessy is in danger, I want someone with her every minute."

"What are you doing about work?" Nikki asked her.

"I have two days off," Jessy told her.

"That's good," Brent said. "It will help us if we have fewer fronts to cover and fewer crowds to deal with."

Dillon looked at Adam and said, "Emil Landon is involved somehow. I know it." He went on to recount the story of Tanner Green dying on the craps table, then counted off the people involved in the case. "As soon as possible, I questioned all the workers who had been out front that night. A guy named Rudy Yorba *thought* Tanner Green had come out of a current-model super-stretch white limo, but he was killed in a supposed hit-and-run before I had a chance to talk to him again. I'm certain he was killed because someone realized he'd talked to me and didn't want him saying anything more. Anyway, I checked, and there are two limos fitting that description in use right now—one belonging to the Sun and one to the Big Easy. Strangely, they both ended up in the garage. The *same* garage."

"You broke in to that garage, I take it?" Brent said.

Dillon nodded.

"I found a button in the one belonging to the Big Easy—Landon's casino—and I think it could have come from Green's shirt. I left it where I found it, though, and planted a bug in Cheever's ear, so I suspect it will be rediscovered any time now. Anyway, Landon's remaining goon, Hugo Blythe, showed up at that point, so I got out of there."

"Did he see you?" Brent asked.

"Yes, but I'm certain he didn't know it was me. He chased me, but he's as big as an ox, and that makes him slow," Dillon explained. "I got away clean. And then there's Indigo."

"Indigo," Brent repeated. "We went out there years ago." He shook his head. "It's a ghost town. In fact, it was a ghost town almost from the moment it was conceived. It's too far from water, and even then, it was a long, dry haul back from there to anywhere worth being. It served the miners who were working the claims owned by a nasty piece of work named Frank Varny. He went down in a rain of gunfire, along with some of the locals, and the town didn't last long after that. You think something's going on out in Indigo that's connected to this case?"

"I do. And I also think it's connected to something Timothy, Jessy's grandfather, warned me about. He said that 'they' are assembling," Dillon said.

Jessy turned to him, startled. She realized that

Dillon hadn't been pretending to listen to Timothy; he honestly believed Timothy had an ability to divine information from the people in the walls or . . . somewhere. She felt a little tremor in her stomach. Had she been too quick to think her grandfather was slipping? No, his ramblings had seemed genuinely bizarre. Then again, she was seeing dead men, and most people would call that crazy, too.

"So what you're saying is that we're looking at a number of things," Adam said. "First, there's Indigo. We need to find out what we can about the town. Next, there's Jessy. We have to keep her safe. Then there are the two casinos, and I'd like to take a closer look at the Sun to start with. So first thing tomorrow, I'd like to spend some time with Timothy, then play some craps over at the Sun. Dillon, you keep researching Indigo. Dig deep. Find all the old records you can and see what we *don't* know about the town."

"Right now, I say we need to decide what to have for supper," Nikki said. "I'm starving."

"Me too," Jessy admitted, smiling.

"It's awfully late. Will anything be open?" Nikki asked.

Brent, Adam and Dillon looked at her, and simultaneously said, "This is Vegas!"

Nikki laughed. "Good point. So should we go out or order in?"

While the others were debating their options,

312

Jessy turned to Adam. "Emil Landon is anything but a poster boy for ethical behavior," she told him. "Why did you suggest that Dillon take on this case?"

Adam was silent for a moment, then said, "Emil Landon called me and asked specifically for Dillon. He said someone on the police force had told him that Dillon could find out what was going on."

"Yes," Jessy argued, "but don't a lot of people ask for your help? I'm sure you don't take on every case, so why this one?"

"I was curious, for one," Adam said. "Ringo told Dillon that he should take the case, too. Even so, I was going to turn him down, but then, I had a . . . well, a gut feeling that we should pursue it."

Jessy swung on Ringo. "Why?" she demanded.

Ringo lifted his hands. "I don't know. Maybe it was the same thing, a gut feeling. I just had a sense that there was something going on here and we needed to be involved in it."

"It's certainly turning out to be intriguing," Adam said, his eyes lightly sparkling. "And I think it's going to be important, too. Just because I'm not a nightwalker, that doesn't mean my intuition isn't reliable."

"Your intuition certainly seems just fine to me," Jessy told him.

"Right," Adam said. "Now, let's see what the ravening horde has decided to do about dinner."

Brent had rented a car, and since Dillon's was still on the Strip, they decided to squeeze into Brent's to retrieve Dillon's, then grab something to eat. After dinner, Brent and Nikki would head out to stay at Jessy's house, keeping an eye on things there, while Jessy and Adam would stay at Dillon's.

"There's plenty of room for everyone to stay here, you know," Dillon pointed out.

"But Tanner Green might come looking for Jessy at her place, and he just might decide he likes Nikki or me better than he apparently likes you," Brent pointed out.

"True," Dillon admitted, grinning ruefully.

"This is a good plan," Adam said. "I can keep an eye on Jessy when you're not around, Dillon, and this house is safe." He grinned. "Ringo can bunk with me if he wants to. After all, if he kicks or snores, it won't bother me."

"I resent that," Ringo commented.

"He doesn't care," Dillon translated, shooting a warning look at Ringo, who snorted disdainfully.

"Please," Nikki begged. "Let's eat."

They were settled at an all-night buffet and it was nearing 2:00 a.m. when Dillon's phone rang. The cops? he wondered.

It *was* a cop—-but not one Dillon would have expected.

"Dillon?" The voice was feminine.

"It's Sarah. Sarah Clay, from forensics."

He sat straighter. "Sarah. Thanks for calling me. Have you found something out?"

"Yes. They've just brought in a corpse, and. . . . I saw the news tonight that you were there when Jessy Sparhawk was attacked by a couple of guys wearing black. I could be way off base on this, but they've just brought in an apparent suicide. A guy took a dive off the roof of the Rainbow. He's about thirty-five, no ID, but we're running his prints through the system."

"You said an *apparent* suicide," Dillon said, frowning.

"That's what it looks like, and I'd even believe that's what it was, if he weren't dressed all in black. I thought you might want to know. I don't know, maybe I'm way off base, but the black clothing made me think there might be a connection."

"Who's there right now?" Dillon asked quickly.

"The place is pretty quiet. I think Tarleton is around somewhere, doing the autopsy. I can meet you at the entry and let you in."

"I'll be right there," Dillon told her.

Even though Adam would be with Jessy—and Clancy was guarding the house, plus he had a few homemade alarms—Dillon didn't want Jessy and Adam going back to his place without Brent and Nikki. No one minded.

315

Dillon left them with the rental and took his own car out to the morgue. He saw Sarah Clay waiting just inside as he parked.

She opened the door and let him in, then told him that since a few people were still around working, it would be smart if he put on scrubs, which would make him less noticeable.

As soon as he was dressed, she led him to one of the freezers and pulled out a drawer.

She explained that the M.E. hadn't done more than a cursory inspection of the body as of yet. It had probably been photographed, and probed to determine lividity and time of death, but otherwise it was pretty much in its original state.

The man's own mother wouldn't have recognized him. He had apparently landed facedown, so there was no face left.

Not that that really mattered from Dillon's point of view, since he hadn't seen the attacker's face, because of the ski mask. The man's build seemed to be the same as the slighter attacker's, though, and when Sarah showed him the man's shirt, which she pulled from a pile of neatly folded clothes on a nearby table, the style appeared to be the same.

He stared at the corpse, then at Sarah. "Anything on the prints yet?" he asked her.

"Yes," she told him, then picked up a file folder and began to read. "Harold Miffins, alias Nigel Tombs, alias Burt Tolken. He's got a record a mile long, but mostly for petty theft and breaking and entering. Thirty-five. No known family. He's moved around a bit. Hailed from Flagstaff, started on his petty-crime spree in Los Angeles, came to Vegas, went to New York, returned to California, then came back to Vegas. No drug arrests. Looks as if he just couldn't hold down a job, so he kept returning to a life of crime."

"Anything about what he'd been doing in Vegas before he took his plunge?"

"So far, if the cops have gotten anything, I don't know," she told him.

He looked at the body for a moment longer. It was a twisted mass of blood and bruising. Whatever his past crimes, he had just paid a hefty price.

Dillon thanked Sarah, and as she led him back to the front door, she promised to call him if she heard anything. "I'd really like to know who he was working for," he said.

She laughed. "I don't think they hand out social-security forms when they hire you for a hit."

"He was connected to someone here in Vegas. You don't plan a coordinated hit like tonight's on your own, not when your past crimes are pretty much limited to knocking over convenience stores. He was no master criminal."

She smiled. "No."

"You're really burning the midnight oil," he told her.

She grinned. "I'm going places," she told him confidently. "The more tech knowledge I can master, the better a detective I'm going to be. I'm aiming for homicide detective, then I'm going to be a lieutenant in homicide, and from there I'm going to make my way to the top."

"I'm sure you will," he said.

She let him out. "I'll keep in touch."

"Thanks, Sarah. Thank you a lot."

Jessy was glad that Clancy was friends with Brent. She barely barked when they arrived, then went over to both Brent and Nikki looking for attention. Brent left Jessy with Nikki, then took Adam, and together they went through every room in the house. They declared the house clean. "Still, I think we'll hang around a while," Brent said.

It was well past 3:00 a.m., and Jessy could hardly keep her eyes open. They had stopped by her house on the way to dinner so she could show Brent and Nikki how to work her alarm, and she had picked up a bunch of her own things, so there was really nothing to keep her from going to bed.

She yawned, and Nikki laughed and said, "You should get some sleep."

"I'm certainly going to bed. I'm too old to stay up this late," Adam said with a grin.

"I think I'll have a cup of tea, and if Dillon isn't back by then, I'll call it a night, too," Jessy said.

"I brew a great pot of tea," Brent said, and

shrugged. "My father was Sioux, but my mother was off-the-boat Irish. I come by my talent honestly."

So Adam went off to bed, and Jessy and Nikki sat down in the living room to wait while Brent did his thing. Ringo joined them, his spurs jingling as he rested his feet on the coffee table.

Jessy turned to Nikki. "Were you . . . born with the ability to see the dead?"

Nikki shook her head and leaned back, closing her eyes for a minute. "No. One of my best friends was murdered, but I saw her standing at the foot of my bed just after it happened. I went through all the usual. I thought I'd been dreaming, that I'd had a nightmare. Anyway, that was a while ago now, but I still don't have all the answers." She glanced at her husband, who was in the kitchen. "Brent was very young when he first saw . . ." She paused, looking at Ringo, who appeared to be sleeping, his hat pulled low over his brow. "The past," she finished.

"Ghosts," Ringo corrected, clearly not asleep after all.

"Brent was just a kid, on a trip through the Dakotas with his parents, when he saw the Battle of the Little Bighorn being played out all over again right in front of him. After that, it became a natural occurrence for him. But it's not easy. Just because you can see a ghost, that doesn't mean the ghost wants to interact, which, I imagine, is part of the problem here."

"Ladies, ladies," Ringo said, rising. "Think about it. What did you know when you were born? Or when you were a toddler? Some ghosts are quick learners, some struggle. Some are afraid because they can't accept what's happened to them. Some play out their lives over and over again, some move on and others stick around and make new friends."

Brent came out of the kitchen with the tea, but it was Ringo he addressed. "Adam said that Dillon thinks the strangest thing about this case is that Rudy Yorba seems to be following Tanner Green. When Green takes off, Yorba takes off."

"He's afraid," Ringo said firmly. "I think they both are. I've been careful to stay out of sight when I'm following Green. He may not even be disappearing on purpose. He may not even know how to communicate yet. We'll have to keep hoping."

"What about Rudy Yorba?" Brent asked.

"He might be afraid of Tanner Green, or he might not know the ropes of being dead yet. Hard to say," Ringo mused, then leaned toward the teapot and tried to inhale. "You know, I don't miss whiskey, but I sure do wish I could taste that tea." He stood. "I'm going to go to bed and snore as loud as I can, see if I can bug Adam," he said.

He clinked his way to the hall.

Jessy stared after him. "It's as if he's really here," she said softly.

"He *is* here—somewhere. He's made of energy, and one of the few things scientists agree on is that energy can't be destroyed," Brent explained. "So where does a person's energy go after death? Maybe heaven and hell really exist and that's where it ends up. I've never met a ghost who knows the truth of it, so . . ."

"Some of them choose to stay to help," Nikki said. "Maybe it's a form of karma. Who knows?"

Jessy sipped her tea, which was both delicious and soothing. Then she yawned again and gave in to exhaustion. It was hard to believe she could sleep after the events of the day—and night—but she was quite certain she could. She rose and said, "Thank you both for everything, but I think I have to get some sleep now. I can't tell you how much I appreciate not having to be afraid when I do."

"For what it's worth, I think you're doing pretty damn good learning to deal with the whole ghost thing," Nikki said, smiling.

"Because now I know it's the living I need to fear," Jessy told her, then headed for the hallway and the comfort of a soft mattress.

It felt wonderful to take a shower, as if she was washing away the horror of the attack.

Afterward, even though she had her own things, she found one of Dillon's T-shirts and crawled into it, towel dried her hair and curled up in bed.

It took only seconds for her to fall asleep.

321

Dillon knew he didn't need to worry about his house. He didn't have a high-tech alarm, but he had Clancy. Of course, she was flesh and blood, and she was a dog, dogs had to go out—and he never let himself forget the fact that dogs could be poisoned. He watched her carefully, but he counted on more than just Clancy to provide protection.

His windows were all discreetly rigged in his own adaptation of the old Paiute hunting style. If anyone tried to break in through a window, they would trigger a nylon net, which would fall over him, then tighten if the intruder tried to struggle free. At the same time, a buzzer sounded in the kitchen, loud enough to be heard through out the entire house. On top of that, he was licensed to carry a firearm, and he did: a small, specially equipped Glock with one extra shot, giving him ten bullets.

Even so, it was good to find Brent and Nikki waiting up for him when he got home. He immediately told them about the latest body and his theories.

"So because this guy was in the system, and his boss was afraid he'd left blood at the scene and we would find him, he took him down before he could talk?" Brent asked.

"That's the way I see it," Dillon told him. "We have to move on this. Jessy loves her job. I don't want it to end her life."

As soon as Brent and Nikki were gone, Dillon locked the door and secured the dead bolt, then headed to his room, yawning. No one was going to have more than a few hours' sleep before they started fresh in the morning.

He found Jessy sleeping, and a wealth of emotion swept through him. He wasn't sure how it was possible to care about someone so much so quickly. Even if this ended well, there was no guarantee that she wouldn't walk right out of his life.

He turned away and headed toward the bathroom for a shower. He glanced in the mirror as he passed and saw that his hair was in disarray, and there was a smudge on his cheek, and thought that it would have been nice if someone had told him about that.

Then he stripped down and stepped into the shower, closed his eyes and let the water rush down on him.

He heard a noise and instinctively turned off the water, tension filling him, then stepped silently out of the shower, reaching automatically for the first weapon he could find: the towel rack. If he needed to, he could rip it off the wall.

"It's me!" Jessy said quickly, her hypnotically blue eyes huge.

"You were sleeping," he told her.

"I know, but I heard you come in," she said, smiling.

"You must be exhausted."

"I am—but not that exhausted."

Heedless of the fact that he was dripping wet, he took her into his arms. The water on his heated skin quickly soaked the T-shirt, which seemed incredibly erotic. He kissed her, tugging off the shirt, which was only an irritating barrier between them. In a matter of seconds her eyes were on his again as her breasts rose and fell, and then she was back in his arms.

They kissed, the steam filling the air around them and adding to the rising heat in their bodies. Then he lifted her until she straddled his hips, and they both laughed as he carried her from the bathroom to the bed, where together they fell to the mattress. Their laughter faded then, and he shifted, moving into her, exhaustion fading away in his urgency to be with her.

They moved swiftly, climaxed violently, then drifted down and made love slowly. Eventually, they fell asleep, tangled in one another's arms.

To Jessy's astonishment, Dillon was still asleep when she woke up.

She tried very hard to slip out from beneath him without waking him up. It was early—especially considering that they hadn't actually gone to sleep until around eight-thirty—but she was a creature of habit, and she had been meeting Timothy for breakfast for so long that she was pretty sure it would be impossible for her to sleep late in the morning anymore, no matter how hard she tried.

She slipped on a simple T-shirt and jeans for the time being, thinking that she could shower and dress in something more presentable once Dillon was awake.

Clancy was waiting for a chance to go outside, so Jessy let her out, and then put on a pot of coffee. While the coffee brewed, she checked in the living room, but Adam was nowhere in sight, either. Feeling hungry, she made herself some whole wheat toast and realized that she hadn't eaten much the night before. She'd been starving when they got to the buffet, but her appetite had waned once Dillon received the call from the woman in forensics.

She realized that she hadn't even asked him anything about that when he had come in. She had needed to touch him, to be with him, and nothing else had mattered.

Her toast popped, and she found some butter and jam. With her plate in one hand and coffee cup in the other, she rounded the counter toward the living room, figuring she would watch the news.

But as she came around the counter, she froze.

The living room had been empty. Empty, and as quiet as the dead.

No longer.

Tanner Green was sitting in a comfortably upholstered chair.

Behind him, standing as if he was ready to run at any minute, was Rudy Yorba.

325

"Don't leave, please," Jessy said quietly, reassuringly. "It's just me. You've been trying to reach me for days, and now I'm here—just me, no else—so don't be afraid."

She had to admit that she was a little bit afraid herself. Yes, she was, just a little. She had gotten accustomed to Ringo, but now, faced with two of the newly dead, she felt herself begin to tremble.

She tried to remain perfectly calm as she took a seat on the couch.

"Excuse me." She spoke softly, and carefully set down her breakfast, then reached for her coffee cup, needing a sip, as if it were alcohol and might bolster her courage.

"Mr. Green," she said politely. "I apologize for being afraid of you at first, but I'm not afraid now. I want to help you. The people who killed you are trying to hurt other people." Her voice cracked for a minute. "They killed Rudy, and they're going to kill again if you won't help me. Please, talk to me."

Tanner Green's mouth worked as if he was trying to talk; then he started to fade away.

Suddenly she heard Ringo's impatient voice.

"Come on, you big coward. Be a man and talk to the lady."

"I can handle this," Jessy objected firmly.

But Ringo's approach had the desired effect.

Tanner Green seemed to stabilize in his chair.

"I'm glad you decided to stay," Jessy said, at a

loss for anything else. "Now, please, tell who ki—who did this to you."

"I don't know," he said.

"You have to find out." He seemed surprised that he had actually managed to speak. He almost smiled, then spoke again, his confidence seeming to grow. "I keep trying to remember the day, where I was. I keep trying to retrace my footsteps."

"That's a great idea," Jessy told him encouragingly.

"Mr. Yorba, you could sit down," she added quietly.

Rudy Yorba seemed startled to be addressed so directly, and Tanner Green stared at him curiously. She reminded herself that they hadn't known one another in life.

She took a long drink of coffee, set the cup back down and asked, "Rudy, why do you keep hiding from Mr. Green?" she asked.

"I've been watching him. I think whoever killed him killed me, too, so I thought if I followed him, I could find out who that was. But I was afraid for him to see me. He's . . . huge."

Jessy nodded. "He is, but I'm sure he doesn't want to hurt you."

Tanner look at Rudy quizzically. "Why the hell would I hurt you? I don't even know you!" His eyes narrowed. "You weren't part of this, were you?"

"No, no, we think Rudy was killed by the same

people who killed you," Jessy said quickly, then cleared her throat. "We're pretty sure Rudy was killed because someone knew he had talked to Dillon—Dillon Wolf," Jessy said. "We're all looking for the same answers, and we all need to help each other."

Rudy didn't speak, but Tanner Green frowned and said, "I remember . . . having a drink, and then . . . then it changed. Everything changed. There was so much neon. I saw the playground from when I was a kid in Philly . . . I saw . . . I saw lights. I saw you. *You* . . . Someone attacked me, and then I fell down and died on you."

"Yes. You did."

"I'm sorry."

"It's all right. It's not like you wanted to."

"Rudy, what about you? Did you see anything?" Jessy asked him.

"Lights. I saw lights. The bastard came at me like a bat out of hell. He meant to kill me, not just to hit me. It was murder, and I want the bastard who did it," Rudy said.

"Rudy, how did you run out of gas?"

"I *didn't* run out of gas," he said. "Someone siphoned my tank. They left me enough to get out on the highway, and they knew exactly where I'd have to start walking."

Jessy looked over at Tanner Green. "Mr. Green, how about you? Can you think of *any*thing that might help?"

The big man shook his head. "I'm trying. I knew someone was after Emil Landon, and I was ready to defend him. But who the hell—"

"Wait," Jessy said. "You said you knew that someone was after Emil. *How* did you know? Because he told you so?"

"No," Green said. "Someone shot at him one night. I wanted to call the cops, but Mr. Landon took care of it himself. He called some cop he's kind of friends with, and after, that's when he called Adam Harrison. He insisted on getting Dillon Wolf to find out what was going on. His friend at the station had him convinced he needed Wolf. So Wolf came on the job, but he was just investigating, we were protecting—Hugo Blythe and me. But I was off work when it happened. Was I killed so I couldn't protect Mr. Landon?"

"I don't know, but I suppose it's possible," Jessy said.

Green let out an aggrieved sigh.

"Mr. Green, there's something else. We need to know why you whispered 'Indigo' to me before you died."

15

Dillon awoke with a start. Despite the heavy drapes, he knew that day had come.

He reached out in anticipation, then realized that Jessy wasn't beside him. He jumped up and started toward the door, then realized he was naked and Adam was in the house, and went back for a robe.

He almost called her name, but it was always better to seek someone in silence, so he hurried down the hall as quickly and quietly as he could.

He reached the living room and stopped short in shock.

There was Jessy, all that long red hair streaming around her face in a red halo, a stunning contrast to her navy blue T-shirt. She was holding a cup of coffee, one of her legs crossed over the other, and she was engaged in what looked to be the most casual conversation in the world.

With three ghosts.

Ringo, a given, was at her side. But Tanner Green was there, too, sitting in a wingback chair, his expression one of intense concentration.

Rudy Yorba was there, too. He looked tense, standing behind Green, watching the others.

Ringo sensed Dillon's presence first. He interrupted Tanner Green just as he was about to speak and said, "Green, don't you go turning into a girlie-man again and disappearing. Dillon is a longtime nightwalker, and he's the one person here who can really help you. Stay, do you understand?"

Startled, Green looked up at Dillon and began to fade. Dillon silently cursed himself and spoke quickly and very softly. "Please, Green, I need you. We need your help."

Tanner Green took what looked for all the world like a deep breath and his image stabilized.

Next, Dillon looked across the room at Rudy. "I'm sorry," he said.

Rudy, to his surprise, seemed to release some of the tension that had held him so stiffly and said, "Don't be. Not your fault."

"You tried to help," Dillon reminded him.

"I was all over those tapes. Hell, if that cop hadn't been such a jerk, I might have talked to him right away, and then I probably would have been killed sooner. What is, is. But I want to know the truth. I want to know who did this to me, and then I want to watch the bastard fry. At the least, I want him locked up for the rest of his life, and when he is, I'm going to see to it that he doesn't have a minute of peace for as long as he lives."

Jessy cleared her throat, looking at Dillon. Her eyes were bottomless pools of blue, but she was clearly doing amazingly well.

"Dillon, I was just asking Mr. Green about Indigo," she said.

Dillon walked over to the couch, and Ringo moved to accommodate him as he took a seat next to Jessy.

"Indigo might be the key to everything," Dillon explained to Green. "We need to know what's so important about the place."

"There's gold there," Tanner Green said.

"How do you know that?" Dillon asked.

"There's been a legend about the gold for over a century, but are you telling me it's real?"

"I don't know," Green said, frowning as if the answer was just out of reach.

"Let's try this. Let's start with the beginning of your day."

"It was my day off."

"And what were you doing on your day off?"

"Sleeping late. I have a room up in the penthouse. Landon, he acts like a prick, but he's pretty decent to the people who work for him. I slept until noon. Blythe was on guard duty. I don't think he was that concerned. He didn't really think anyone was after the boss. The shots that were fired . . . they might have been fired at anyone in that parking lot. Most people thought it was just a backfire, you know?"

Dillon kept a rein on his temper. They finally had Tanner Green talking. He had to tell his story in his own time.

"Yes, I know, but when you know the sound of a bullet, you can tell it isn't a backfire," Dillon said. "So then . . . ?"

"So then . . ." Green paused for thought. He seemed pleased when he spoke again. "I was hungry, so I went and got something to eat."

"Steak and potatoes."

"Yeah," Green said. "How did you know?"

Autopsy reports, Dillon thought, but he didn't say so. "You just look like a meat-and-potatoes man," he fudged.

Green nodded again. "Then I went gambling."

"Where?"

"I hit a few places."

"Did you gamble at the Big Easy?" Dillon asked.

Green shook his head. "No. Can't work there and gamble there. It's not allowed."

"Okay, so where?" Dillon asked.

"Um, I hit some of the big ones. Bally's, Wynn, MGM."

"You stayed on the Strip?" Dillon asked.

"Yeah. I think I gambled at the Sun, too," he said, musing over his own answer. "Yeah, I was there."

Dillon made a mental note to check that out on the security tapes. Even if Green *had* been there, did it mean anything?

"And were you drinking in the course of the day?" Dillon asked.

"Yeah, here and there. I'm not a lush. But I did have something, and that's when the lights I was telling Miss Sparhawk about started up and . . . I was playing kickball in Philly again," Green said.

Rudy Yorba snorted.

"It wasn't his fault. Someone slipped him some LSD," Dillon said.

"For real?" Rudy asked.

"For real," Dillon repeated.

"Mr. Green, can we talk about Indigo again?" Jessy said, slipping back into the conversation.

Dillon could feel the tension in her. He gently set

333

a hand on her knee, a warning that they needed to be patient.

"I was in a car—a limo, maybe—and I heard people talking about it, saying there had to be a way to find the gold, that it was really there."

"Who?" Dillon asked quietly.

"I don't know. I was there, and at the same time I wasn't there," Green said.

Dillon rubbed his forehead in frustration. Green had overheard the conversation, but he'd been tripping and had no memory of the specifics.

"Please, try to think. This is important," Dillon said. "Do you remember being in a car?"

"A nice car. A limo, I think."

"Okay, that's good. Who else was in the car?"

Tanner Green frowned in concentration. "Friends. I think. The kids I played kickball with."

Dillon leaned forward. "Tanner, you weren't really with your friends from the old days back in Philly. It had to be someone you know from here. Think hard."

"I'm trying," Green said.

They were all startled by a cheerful whistle coming from the hall. "Good morning," Adam Harrison said as he walked into the room, showered and dressed and ready to tackle the day.

"No, stay!" Dillon said when Tanner looked as if he was about to disappear again. "It's Adam, my boss, and he can't even see you."

"I'm sorry. I didn't mean to interrupt," Adam

said. "I'll be in the kitchen. You all keep talking."

"I need to think," Tanner said, his image solidifying. "I need to think."

Dillon rose. He needed to do some thinking himself. "Rudy, go hang around the Sun and see what you can pick up. Tanner, you go back to the Big Easy and see what you can find out over there. Jessy, we need to go see your grandfather."

"Gotcha," Rudy said, nodding.

"I'm off, then," Green said.

"I'm going to take a shower," Jessy said to Dillon. "You can go fill Adam in."

Nikki and Brent met them at the home, and Timothy was delighted with the extra company. He and Brent talked for several minutes about the old ways, and it made Jessy smile to see Timothy so happy.

She was embarrassed when Sandra called and she realized that she had forgotten to call her friend that morning to assure her that everything was all right. She stepped out into the hall and told Sandra that some friends of Dillon's were in town, and said maybe they could all meet up that night.

Sandra was relieved to hear that Jessy was now surrounded by people who could be trusted. "Promise me you'll be with someone every second of the day," she demanded.

"I promise," Jessy assured her.

Sandra hung up, and Jessy wandered back to

Timothy's room, where he was happily holding court. A little while later Dillon said he had to leave to do some work at the library. Adam excused himself, too, and said he was going to take the rental car and head over to the Sun to see if he could overhear anything useful, maybe even find someone likely to know something and get him talking. The others seemed happy enough to spend time at the home with Timothy until someone was free to pick them up.

Once they were gone, Brent Blackhawk faced Timothy. "I'd like to hear more about the ghost dancers," he said gravely.

Timothy, seeming totally lucid, nodded, looking anxious, and glanced at Jessy. She went to his side and put her arms around him. "Timothy, it's okay. The rest of us see things that others don't, too. Brent has been seeing . . . ghosts for many years, and he believes in your visions."

"They are assembling," Timothy said.

"Who is?" Brent asked him.

"My ancestor, Dillon's ancestor. The others . . . I know their names. The singer is Milly, and there is a man named Ringo Murphy and another named Mark Davison. No one likes him. The sheriff is there, too. His name is Grant Percy. Or Percy Grant," Timothy said, frowning and shaking his head. "I'm not sure. But they're waiting. Something evil lives there. The posse is on the way, and Wolf is waiting, but he's been betrayed.

336

Someone told the evil man that he was there, because otherwise he couldn't have known so quickly that Wolf had returned. And now they're assembling again."

"Why, Timothy?" Brent asked.

"Because of the gold," Timothy said.

"But there *is* no gold. The veins they found were tapped out, and no one ever found the mother lode."

"But it's there," Timothy said gravely. "It's there."

"Where?" Brent asked.

Timothy ignored the question or maybe didn't even hear it, and said, "They'll assemble because they're searching for the gold." He shook his head. "It isn't theirs, and that's why they want to find it first. So they can steal it."

For the second time that day, Jessy wanted to scream in frustration. Half of what he was saying made sense, and the rest sounded like nothing but nonsense.

Were all these people really dying because of gold that might not even exist?

The Henderson Library not only offered state-of-the-art facilities but a coffee shop and, best of all, librarians who were helpful, knowledgeable and willing to tackle any challenge.

Dillon started out by researching the town itself. Indigo had been incorporated in 1857 by miners working a nearby goldfield that, sadly, didn't pan out as they'd hoped. Still, for years men kept looking for the vein that was rumored to be bigger than any other find. Frank Varny owned the mining rights on as much of the nearby land as he could grab and worked relentlessly to control the area. There were a few struggling ranches closer to the river, and the town had enough going on to support a bank, a doctor and a weekly newspaper. Every now and then a preacher even came to town and set up shop, but the preachers never lasted. The single church had pretty much crumbled into the dust, and it had never been repaired. The land the town stood on had not, oddly enough, actually belonged to Varny, but to an old miner who had moved on to the San Francisco goldfields. In 1876, a purchase, duly registered in the territorial offices, showed that one John Wolf had paid the measly sum requested by the old owner, and a deed had been written out, making the Paiute nation the actual owners of the land.

Dillon looked up and shook his head. He hadn't learned anything new. He started looking for articles on the gunfight that had killed John Wolf and Frank Varny, along with a number of others.

Blood Bath in Indigo, read one headline.

Dillon began to scan the accompanying article, Timothy's words running through his head as he read.

They are assembling.

338

The account of the incident said that there had been a history of bad blood between John Wolf and Frank Varny. It was a pretty good article, Dillon thought, filled with facts. Killed: Frank Varny, John Wolf, Ringo Murphy, Mark Davison, Sheriff Grant Percy and five hired guns who had worked for Frank Varny: Austin Makepiece, Riley Hornsby, Seth Bigelow, Drew Miffins and Tobias Wilson. Those who had survived the massacre and lived to describe it had been Mariah Wolf, Milly Taylor and the piano player, George Turner, who had left before the gunfire to raise a citizens' posse. Despite being afraid and armed with only a motley array of weapons, they had come as quickly as they could, but arrived only after the bloodbath. Since John Wolf had purchased and registered the claim to the land on behalf of the Paiute nation, the land underneath Indigo, as well as the nearby claim, had belonged to the tribe, and a later act of Congress had given it to them in perpetuity as reservation land. Any gold discovered would belong to the tribe. But the gold hadn't been discovered, and Indigo had become a town of dust and tumbledown buildings, soon to be abandoned completely.

They are assembling.

Dillon shook his head. He was a Wolf, Jessy was descended from the piano player and Ringo was still here. There were already three dead men—did they count for three of Varny's gunslingers? If so, it

339

meant there were two remaining—one gunslinger and Davison—along with Varny himself. And what about Rudy? Was he connected somehow?

He gritted his teeth, wondering if he was crazy. If he was right, Emil Landon was Varny. Two more henchmen would round it out. No, he was forgetting the sheriff, the bartender and the singer. But they hadn't taken sides in the deadly confrontation, nor had Mariah.

It still didn't make sense that the whole thing was connected to the search for gold. Men had searched the entire area, and no one had ever found the gold that legend claimed was there.

He read the article again, wondering what he wasn't seeing. And why in hell would Emil Landon hire Tanner Green as a bodyguard, then kill him himself?

On a hunch, he asked a librarian for local birth and death records. Emil Landon had claimed Paiute blood in his ancestry, which meant his lineage could be traced.

The librarian led him to a separate room, where he started to pore over long-ago records, some seemingly as dusty as the town of Indigo itself.

Finally he found exactly what he was seeking. Emil Landon could trace his bloodline back to a Paiute on his paternal side—and to Frank Varny on his maternal side. Did he believe that there really was gold in Indigo? That he could finesse it away from the tribe because of his ancestry?

Dillon closed his eyes and was rubbing them in exhaustion when his phone started vibrating in his pocket. He answered it quietly.

"Wolf here."

It was Jerry Cheever, and Dillon realized he should have expected the call. Cheever didn't know he'd already seen the latest corpse to wind up in the morgue.

"One of those guys you chased off last night is dead. At least, I think it's one of the men who attacked Jessy Sparhawk last night. Corpse came into the morgue last night, a jumper—or that's what it looked like, anyway. But you'll never guess what Tarleton found in his system when he ran the tox screen today."

"What?" Dillon asked.

"LSD. The fellow took a nice trip before he went for his flight straight to hell. Oh, he had a record, by the way."

"Why am I not surprised?"

"Well, here's something else to factor into the equation. We're bringing Emil Landon in for questioning. Go figure," Jerry said sarcastically. "We found a button in his limo. A button off Tanner Green's shirt. Imagine that."

Dillon smiled at Cheever's sarcasm. "Can you charge him?"

"I can keep him around a while. Charge him? I can try—but he'll walk. Tanner Green worked for him, and whether it's true or not, Landon will say that Green sometimes drove the car. There's no way a button from Landon's employee's shirt in Landon's own casino's limo will be enough evidence to satisfy anyone that the man's a murderer. A good defense attorney—hell, even a crap one—could tear apart a flimsy piece of evidence like that. But I'll hold him as long as I can. See if he'll inadvertently spill some info. I could be wrong, but he doesn't seem like he's that bright, certainly not bright enough to be behind this whole thing, so maybe we'll get lucky."

Mean, yes. Bright? Maybe not. Maybe Cheever was right.

"Just because he's not brilliant doesn't mean he's not in on it," Dillon said.

"I agree. But we need evidence."

"Right, and thanks. Jerry, mind if I come in and study the tapes again?"

"No problem. Give me an hour or so. I'll get you set up with a decent monitor and a tech."

Jessy was glad to answer her phone and hear Dillon's voice. When he suggested that they all have lunch together, she agreed, and he said he would be by shortly.

"I think we ought to take Timothy with us, don't you?"

"I think that would be great," he told her.

When they got to the restaurant, she and Nikki wound up at one end of the table—with Ringo—

while Brent, Timothy and Dillon confabbed at the other. Before long, she and Nikki—and Ringo—found themselves eavesdropping, and from there it was just a short step to joining the conversation.

"Timothy, you say there's gold out there?" Dillon asked. He was frowning, but he wasn't acting as if he thought Timothy was delusional in any way.

"It's there," Timothy said. "I saw what happened when I was there. Well, George Turner was there, and I saw it through his eyes. Wolf knew where the gold was, I'm sure of it. And then Varny came in, and . . . well, you know what happened after that."

"If that's the case, and all these deaths really have something to do with Indigo," Jessy said, "it means that someone out there believes in the gold, too. But he doesn't know how to find it. He thinks Dillon will figure it out for him."

"You think that's why he was looking for a paranormal investigator? Because he knows things are building toward a reenactment? You think it was all a scam, his life being in danger?" Brent asked.

"It's beginning to look that way," Dillon admitted.

They had barely finished eating at that point, and already he was looking anxious.

"We've got to go," he said, standing and reaching into his pocket for a piece of paper, which he handed to Brent. "Check out these names for me, will you? Start with the top name in the left-hand column. On the right I've listed the names of everyone in the saloon the day of the gunfight. I want to see if they all connect somehow, if each name from the past lines up with a descendant in the present. I'm going over to the police station. I want to see the security tapes again. I swear I'm missing something."

They left, and Dillon dropped them all at Jessy's house so they could pick up her car, since Adam had the rental. Dillon started to drive off, then stopped and called out to Jessy.

She walked over to the car and saw that he was smiling at her.

"What?"

"I . . ." He reached out and pulled her close, then planted a gently passionate kiss on her lips. "Be careful. Stay at the home until you hear from me. Stick with Timothy or Nikki once you're there. I'll be back soon," he promised.

She smiled. "I won't spend a moment alone. By the way, who's on the list?" she asked curiously.

"Everyone I've come across in the course of this investigation," he told her. "Cops—Jerry Cheever, Len Durso. Emil Landon and Hugo Blythe. Darrell Frye. I even threw in an M.E., my friend, Doc Tarleton, along with Sarah Clay, who works in forensics. And your stage manager."

"Ron?" she said with a gasp.

"And Sandra," he admitted.

"Sandra?" She felt her temper rising.

"Trust me, she's not a suspect," he assured her. "Humor me, huh?" Then he kissed her lips again and drove away.

"Jessy?" Nikki called, and Jessy turned around to see that Brent was already settled behind the wheel, with Timothy next to him. It was her car, but she decided it wasn't really the time for a feminist statement.

Jessy got into the backseat with Nikki, and in a few minutes, they were back at the home. Brent walked them in, and Timothy greeted Jimmy and a nurse named Liz, who he really liked. He admitted he was ready for a nap, but first he took them to the TV room and introduced them to Mrs. Teasdale, who took one look at Nikki and Brent and informed Nikki that she was going to have beautiful children.

Timothy and Mrs. Teasdale agreed on a Scrabble date for later, and then Jessy, Nikki and Timothy retired to his room. Brent left them at last, heading for the library where Dillon had spent the morning. To be on the safe side, Brent ordered Ringo, who'd tagged along, to stay with the women. "And call if anything—" he began. He shook his head. "Hell, Ringo, you're such a damn good ghost, I forgot you can't use a cell phone."

"Who knows, maybe I can," Ringo said. "It'll be a new challenge, anyway."

They left Timothy to his nap and retired to a

table in the empty breakfast room, where Jessy started doodling, and Ringo was standing off to the side, trying to dial Nikki's cell phone.

"It's bizarre, isn't it?" Jessy said to Nikki.

"What's that?"

" 'They're all assembling,' " Jessy quoted. She looked over at Ringo, who had managed to flip open the phone. "Ringo, tell me about the shoot-out that day."

He set the phone down and walked over to her. "The circumstances of my own death are beginning to bore me."

"Please, Ringo."

"Okay, okay. There was a bartender—and some townsfolk, but they had cleared out. At the poker table, there were John Wolf, myself, Sheriff Percy and Mark Davison. When Varny came in, he had four men with him. Now this I've only read, mind you, because I was dead at the time, but Varny had another of his goons, a particularly distasteful fellow named Tobias, with him, and he dragged in John Wolf's wife. They'd been married in some kind of an Indian ceremony, and I guess the law recognized it."

"Ten people," Nikki said. "Four poker players, Varny, five goons. Wait, and Mrs. Wolf. That makes eleven."

"Actually, there were really thirteen," Ringo pointed out. "Don't forget the piano player, and the singer."

"Okay, so you're you," Jessy said to Ringo. "Dillon would be John."

Ringo laughed. "Or Mariah. She was the one who carried on the line. She was pregnant at the shoot-out, or the Wolf line would have ended right there."

"I wonder if I play any part in this?" Jessy murmured.

"The piano player," Timothy said from the doorway, surprising them all.

In fact, Jessy was so startled by the sound of his voice that she jumped. "Pardon?"

"The piano player. George Turner. He was a distant relative."

Adam Harrison spent his time at one table.

It wasn't the craps table where Tanner Green had died, because that had been removed, but he played at the table that had taken its place.

The pit boss had a name tag that read Darrell Frye, and he kept looking at his watch as he walked around keeping his eye on the various tables. Interesting, Adam thought.

Adam waited until things were relatively quiet and then got the croupier talking.

"Hear you had some excitement in here the other night," he said to the croupier closest to him. "A man died or something?"

The croupier looked around and saw that Darrell Frye was hanging around by another table, then grinned conspiratorially and said, "Yeah, a fellow bought it right here, right where we're standing. Hell of a thing."

"Were you working?" Adam asked.

The other man nodded gravely. "I didn't see anything till the guy collapsed on some poor woman, though. Too bad about the cameras."

"Yeah? What happened to the cameras?"

"It's a big deal up in the executive offices, but they were glitching and not catching everything or something like that. It was supposed to be a big secret, but everyone working here knew it."

Adam filed that away to tell Dillon later and played for a few more minutes, then tipped the croupier and wandered away. He noted that Darrell Frye had finally gotten the break he'd obviously been waiting for. Adam spotted him in the coffee shop and went in himself, ordered a cup of coffee and took a seat, and then he waited.

His vigilance was rewarded when a pretty brunette in a clingy knit dress came up to Darrell Frye. She had a nice figure, long red-tinted hair that was poufed up like something from the sixties and huge sunglasses. Adam found her more than a little suspicious and wondered if the hair was real, or if she was wearing a wig.

She sat down across from Darrell Frye, and at first they spoke too softly for him to overhear their conversation. But in a minute their voices grew heated and their words were clear. "Today. Today, do you hear me?" the woman said, and then she rose and stormed away, stiletto heels clicking sharply on the terrazzo floor.

Dillon was surprised to see Doug Tarleton when he arrived at the station. Doug was wearing civilian clothing and sipping coffee in a chair in the conference room where Jerry Cheever had set up the screen and player so they could study the tapes.

"Doc, what are you doing here?" Dillon asked.

Tarleton grinned. "Taking a break. I've been up to my arms in blood and guts for too many hours in a row."

"You *are* an M.E.," Dillon reminded him.

Tarleton laughed. "Yeah, I know. But Detective Cheever here decided to humor me, so here I am. Okay with you?"

"Hell yeah," Dillon told him.

The technician today was another rookie officer, this one named Drake Barton.

"Where's Sarah Clay?" Dillon asked.

"Over at the morgue, working trace evidence," Tarleton said. "That girl has ambition, and she's one hard worker."

"She is," Dillon agreed. He studied the young tech, hoping that this guy was just as good. "Can you show the craps area for the time before the murder took place?" he asked.

"What are you looking for?" Cheever asked him.

"I'm thinking that maybe Tanner had been playing at the Sun earlier," he said.

"Sure. I'll roll it back," the tech told him. "How far? There are hours and hours of footage here."

"Go back about three hours, but fast-forward until I tell you to slow down," Dillon told him.

"Gotcha," Barton said.

The tape began to roll. Dillon watched the croupiers and clientele running around like something out of a cartoon but saw no sign of Tanner Green.

Then, suddenly, there he was, playing at the same table where he had died.

"I'll be damned," Cheever said.

"Hey, they say the man is good for a reason," Tarleton commented.

Dillon shrugged. "All we've done so far is see that Tanner Green was there before he was killed," he pointed out. "Back it up, please," he asked the tech.

This time Dillon kept his eyes on Darrell Frye. He went through the motions of his job competently, but he seemed nervous. Hell, he looked like a ferret, Dillon thought.

And he was constantly watching the time.

But Dillon knew that he just didn't like the guy, and that could be behind his impression of what was going on.

"Wait," he said again. "Back up again, then play it again, but slowly this time."

"He ordered a drink. Not exactly unusual at a casino," Cheever said.

"Play it again," Dillon insisted.

"There *is* something odd there. I see it, too," Tarleton said.

"What?" Cheever asked, apparently annoyed that he wasn't seeing what the other two did.

Barton, the tech, said slowly, "It's like one of those pictures where you see something different depending on how you look at it, or one of those 'what's different in picture B from picture A?' things."

"Play it one more time, please," Dillon said.

The tape began to roll.

"Stop!" Dillon said. "That's it."

"What?" Even Tarleton looked confused this time.

"The cocktail waitress," he said.

"What about her? She's cute—they try to hire cute girls," Cheever said.

"No, no. There's another woman in the background. They're both wearing little sarong things, but look at the difference."

The two outfits looked the same at first. On second glance, though, the waitress serving Tanner Green was wearing a slightly different version. On one, the parrots in the pattern were dark green and in perfect alignment with one another. On the other, they were more of a lime color and arranged at odd angles.

"Picture A and picture B," the tech murmured.

"Does it mean anything?" Tarleton asked.

Dillon looked at Jerry Cheever. "Can you get someone in personnel to let us know if there are any variations in the uniforms for the waitstaff?"

"I'm on it," Cheever said, reaching for the phone.

Tarleton had risen and was standing right next to the screen, staring at it pointedly and blocking Dillon's view.

"What is it?" Dillon asked him.

Tarleton stared a while longer. "Hell if I know. But there's something else. It's right on the edge of my mind. Maybe. . . ." He sat down but kept staring. "Ah, hell. I can't figure it out, and I've got to get back. Thanks for letting me play cop for the hour, guys. And I know I saw something. I'll call if I ever figure it out."

16

Jessy didn't remember crawling up on the bed with her grandfather, but she felt as if she were lying with him the way she had as a kid when they went to the lake. They would lie on the ground on big beach towels, looking up at the clouds and turning the rare wisps of white magic in the Nevada sky into fairy-tale creatures.

Today, the clouds were strange. They seemed to fill the sky. Timothy pointed up and told her,

"There. Do you see him? That's Billie Tiger. Don't be afraid of him. He's a Seminole, but he was captured and forced West, where he escaped and joined up with Sitting Bull."

"How do you do, Mr. Tiger," she asked politely, because, now that Timothy had pointed him out, she could see him, of course.

"He's a good friend," Timothy told her.

Something in her felt sad that he found his friends in the clouds and on the walls, but she wouldn't say so; she loved him too much to hurt his feelings.

"Billie Tiger shows me what happened," Timothy said. "He'll show you, too."

The clouds shifted as Timothy described a town with one long street that was all rutted sand. A breeze blew, but it had only hot air and desert sand to toss around. A tumbleweed danced across the road now and then. She saw a big sign on one building identifying it as the Crystal Canary. Another building was a bank. There were horses and a livery stable. People wore old-fashioned clothes, the women in long dresses, often in pastel flower patterns, and bonnets to protect their complexions against the sun.

"There's the newspaper office," Timothy said. "And there . . ." He pointed up to the sky. "There's the saloon."

She felt as if she walked with him through the swinging doors into the saloon, where she saw a piano player. He was a handsome man, more brown than copper, with beautiful green eyes, and might have been a deeply tanned white man, an Indian or even a black man.

She was suddenly sitting on his lap, but it was all right, because somehow the man had become Timothy. A young woman was standing next to them, singing.

There were four men at the poker table. She recognized two of them: Ringo—and Dillon. Except that it wasn't Dillon, only someone who looked a lot like him. The other two men weren't familiar to her. One had a goofy smile, and the other one looked mean, the sour and gaunt kind of mean. She didn't like him.

Then the doors burst open, and tall and dark and looming, and seeming to cover the sun, he *was just there. The clouds turned dark when he arrived and seemed to roil with anger.*

She was afraid.

"Hide," Timothy said. Except that he wasn't Timothy anymore, he was the piano player again. "I have to rouse the townfolk."

She crawled under the piano.

The man in the doorway entered and walked to the poker table, followed by four of the biggest men Jessy had ever seen. Then, suddenly, everyone was standing and guns were blazing. She wanted to scream, but she was hiding and was afraid to give away her presence . . .

Only two men were still standing at that point.
And then . . .

The swinging doors opened again. A huge man came in, dragging a beautiful woman in deerskin. But she wasn't an Indian, she was a blond-haired white woman.

Jessy looked at the man who was so like Dillon. His mouth was moving as he looked at the beautiful woman, and Jessy strained to hear what he was saying. She could see that the blonde didn't understand him, unable to hear his words over the bullets.

But Jessy could hear him.

And the word he said was here.

The guns stopped firing, and she looked around to see that both the men were dead, and the beautiful blond woman was standing alone, weeping.

Jessy woke abruptly. She wasn't lying on the bed next to Timothy but was sitting in a chair in the breakfast room. She must have fallen asleep with her head on the table, just as Nikki's was.

Jessy closed her eyes and groaned. Timothy wasn't crazy at all.

Billie Tiger had just shown her Indigo.

Had she really heard John Wolf speak? Great. Another cryptic one-word message that might mean nothing at all. *Here.*

Brent Blackhawk was coming up with some interesting connections. One of the most surprising was that Jessy's friend Sandra was a descendant of Milly Taylor, the singer in the saloon at the time of the shoot-out. He wondered if Sandra was aware of her heritage.

He kept searching, and another correlation fell into place. Tanner Green.

His father's side of the family might have come from Philadelphia, but his mother's family had been from the West, and their surname had been Hornsby. There were a number of Riley Hornsbys listed in the Nevada census, surely one of them could have been the goon who had accompanied Frank Varny and an ancestor of Green's.

Brent was growing more and more amazed. The hapless parking attendant, Rudy Yorba, could be traced, through the maternal line once again, to the gambler Mark Davison. Odd, though, that a bad guy in the past was connected to a good guy in the present.

An hour later he sat back and considered the amazing web of names and connections he'd discovered. Virtually all the names Dillon had given him had ancestors who'd been in the area at the time, including Darrell Frye, Hugo Blythe and Detective Jerry Cheever, whose genealogy could be traced back to the ineffectual sheriff of Indigo, Grant Percy.

The real jackpot was Emil Landon, though. He could claim a direct line right back to Frank Varny.

Brent kept searching and found something odd,

so odd that he wasn't even be sure it was relevant. It looked as if Emil Landon had more than the one child he acknowledged, who lived with an ex-wife back East. He'd accompanied a pregnant hooker to the hospital in Reno twenty-some years ago, when he had been just a kid of twenty himself.

Brent peered at the computer screen, reread the article he'd found and cursed. There was no mention as to whether Landon had been in the delivery room with the prostitute or had only been playing Good Samaritan, but he jotted down the hooker's name and quickly turned back to his search.

The hooker was named Celia Smithfield, and her maternal great-grandmother had been named Varny. Brent pulled out his cell phone and put a call through to Dillon.

Jessy left Nikki sleeping and went out into the hall to stretch her legs. She was startled to run into Sandra there, and stunned to see that her friend's eyes were red, as if she had been crying.

"What is it? What's wrong?" Jessy asked, worried.

"You've got to see this! Come on, hurry. It's just outside," Sandra said, tugging on Jessy's hand.

"All right, calm down, Sandra."

Since she was just going down to the parking lot—and with Sandra, not some stranger—Jessy decided against waking Nikki. She put a comforting arm around Sandra's shoulders and was shocked to realize that Sandra was trembling.

"Sandra, please, let me help you."

"Just—come," Sandra said. "Please."

Jessy followed Sandra downstairs and waved cheerfully to Jimmy. "I'll be right back," she told him.

"My car is right there," Sandra said when they reached the lot, and she threw open the door to the backseat.

Jessy leaned forward to see what Sandra wanted to show her and was stunned when Sandra suddenly shoved her forward, into the car. Her head struck the handle of the far door, and she felt a searing pain. She heard Sandra gasp and say, "Oh, shit!"

And then the pain in her head exploded and the world went black.

Dillon was still thinking about the cocktail waitress uniform that wasn't quite right. In fact, there was something not quite right about the cocktail waitress herself. Her hair was strange, for one thing. Too big and tilting oddly to one side. It had to be a wig.

And, according to Jerry Cheever, who'd talked to the personnel manager, all the waitstaff uniforms were made from identical fabric.

As he drove away from the station, Dillon realized that the woman was familiar. It was something about the way she stood, the way she moved.

His phone rang.

It was Adam. "I think your man Darrell Frye is in on it. I heard him in the coffee shop, talking to a strange-looking woman in a bouffant wig. She was angry, told him that 'it' had to be this afternoon. If you can get hold of your buddy Cheever, tell him he needs to find some excuse to pick up Darrell Frye."

"Got it. And I think I saw the same woman on the security tape from the night Green was killed. She was the one who slipped the LSD to him," Dillon said. "I'll call Cheever right now."

He had to leave a message, because apparently Cheever was in the men's room.

"Tell him he needs to find an excuse to pick up Darrell Frye—pronto. And he has to get back to me right away," Dillon said.

His phone rang the moment he hung up with the cops. Brent was on the line. "Get this. Just about all of your guys collide, just like you thought, even that Darrell Frye you weren't sure—"

"I've left a message for Cheever to trump up some excuse to pick him up right away," Dillon said. "Anyway, sorry for interrupting. What else have you got?"

"Here's the wildest. I think Emil Landon had a child."

"Yeah, he has a kid back East."

"No, in Nevada. Illegitimate."

"A son?" Dillon asked.

"I don't know, the kid just disappears. But guess who the mother's family line goes back to?" Brent asked him.

"Who?"

"Frank Varny. Bizarre, huh? Landon goes back to Varny himself. So he had an affair with a woman to whom he was distantly related."

Dillon finally remembered where he had seen the woman in the tapes before, and why she had looked familiar.

"It was a girl," Dillon said, cursing his own stupidity. He'd been led around by the nose like an idiot. "Get back over to the home and get Jessy and Nikki. And Timothy, too. I'm afraid something is going down right now. I'm going to call Cheever back and get out to the morgue. Brent, I'm scared as hell. Get over there quickly. Please."

When Jessy came to, her head was killing her. It took her a moment to realize that she hadn't been dreaming, that Sandra really had shoved her into the car and abducted her.

"Sandra, what the hell is wrong with you?" she demanded, trying to sit up, then failing in the face of the pain.

"Reggie!" Sandra cried.

"Reggie?" Jessy said, baffled.

"They couldn't get to you because you were with Dillon, so they kidnapped Reggie and told me to get you. They're waiting in Indigo, and if I don't hand you over to them in half an hour, they're going to kill Reggie."

Jessy swallowed hard. She understood, but she had to find a way to talk Sandra into doing the smart thing. The *right* thing.

"Did you call the cops?" she asked.

"I can't call the cops!" Sandra cried hysterically. "They'll kill her, don't you understand? She's nothing to them. Once they have you, they'll let Reggie go. And they swore they wouldn't hurt you, either. They just want you as leverage so they can get Dillon to tell them where the gold is."

"That's insane. Dillon doesn't know where the gold is."

"They think he does."

Jessy's head was spinning. Why would anyone think Dillon knew where the gold was? She thought back to Dillon's theory about the connection between past and present, and then she remembered Timothy's words. *They are assembling.* Did someone believe that by putting together the descendants of those who had died and re-creating the bloodbath, that would somehow reveal the location of the gold? That Dillon would somehow channel his ancestor's memory of the past and lead them straight to the treasure?

Jessy blinked, trying hard to clear her head and make sense of what was going on. "Have you got any aspirin or anything up there? You really hurt me—you bitch."

She was almost sorry for the last when she saw the tears streaming down Sandra's cheeks.

"I'm sorry, but I had to," Sandra said.

"Sandra, we have to tell the police what's going on."

"I don't trust the police!" Sandra insisted vehemently.

"Why?"

"Cheever took me home last night. He knows where I live," Sandra said. "How can I be sure he didn't tell them where to find Reggie?"

"But . . . Sandra, you're listed in the phone book, anyone could have found you," Jessy protested.

"Maybe. But it doesn't matter, because they said that if they saw the police, they'd kill her."

"Calm down and tell me about the whole thing," Jessy said, knowing even as she spoke that she was asking the impossible. Calm down? These people had already killed three times. What would Reggie's life matter to them?

Sandra drew a long shaky breath. "I went to the grocery store. When I came back, I could tell Reggie had come from school because—I found her knapsack. Then I got the phone call."

"Was it from a man or a woman?"

"I don't know! They used one of those things that disguise your voice."

"Are you sure they really have Reggie? That they're not bluffing?"

Sandra started sobbing even harder. "They put her on the phone. She was crying."

"Okay, so they have Reggie," she agreed. "But, Sandra, we have to call the police. Don't you see? Even once they have me, they won't let Reggie go. They can't. She knows too much. They'll kill all of us. Indigo's a ghost town in the middle of nowhere. If you don't trust Cheever, we can call the state police."

"We can't call the police," Sandra said.

"Why?"

"I forgot my cell phone again."

Dillon put through a call to Tarleton's cell, but the M.E. didn't pick up. He called the main number at the morgue, figuring Doug might be wrist deep in a corpse and unable to pick up his phone. Instead, he discovered that Tarleton was out but due back shortly, and Sarah Clay had taken the afternoon off.

The minute he hung up, his phone rang.

"Dillon, it's Brent. Jessy is gone, and so are Timothy and Ringo. Nikki's frantic. That orderly, Jimmy, said Jessy left with her friend Sandra."

"Sandra?" Dillon said incredulously.

"That's what the man said."

"Call the cops—I'm on my way out there," Dillon said, pulling a U-turn and ignoring the horns blaring at him.

"Where's 'there'?" Brent said.

"Indigo."

363

● ● ●

It had been a hell of a long time since Timothy had driven, but it really was like riding a bike. He was sorry that he'd sneaked out and left without them, but his time was coming to a close. He'd had a long full life, and he was comfortable with whatever came his way.

Billie Tiger had warned him that it was happening, that Jessy was in danger, and Timothy had known then that he had to get to Indigo. If it was going to play out again, it was going to do so with him, not with Jessy.

Driving was fun. He would never have predicted that an ambulance could be so much fun to drive—or that it could go so fast. It was good to be on the road. They would come after him soon enough, the minute they realized they had a vehicle missing.

Before long he could make out the town of Indigo just ahead, though it was so weatherworn it blended right into the desert, like a mirage.

He heard a voice in his mind and recognized it as Billie Tiger's. Billie warned him not to take the main road all the way into town and not to leave the ambulance where it would be seen—although if anyone was looking, they would have to see him. You couldn't hide something as big as an ambulance in the vast flat expanse of the Nevada desert.

He heard an annoying clinking sound. It had been plaguing him for the entire trip, and sounded like the constant jingle of a pair of old spurs.

364

It was time to slow down if he was going to make a quiet entry this way.

He veered off the road, and the ambulance shuddered across the uneven ground.

If they were looking, they would definitely see him.

But they probably weren't looking, he thought as he pulled up to the rear of the buildings on Main Street and was surprised to see that their vehicles were all parked back here, too. Three of them, so far.

They were assembling.

Sandra finally slowed the car as they neared the town; if she hadn't, Jessy thought dryly, they would have shot right through it.

Sandra brought the car to a halt in the middle of Main Street and leaped out, screaming her daughter's name.

Jessy was stunned when a woman came out of the building whose peeling sign identified it as a bank.

"You made it!" she cried cheerfully.

"Where's my daughter?" Sandra demanded. "Jessy is here. Now where's my daughter?"

Sandra started to rush the woman in a frenzy, but Jessy dragged her back when she saw that the woman was holding a small gun. Despite everything, she wasn't going to let Sandra get herself killed.

"Slow down," the woman said to Sandra, all the while looking Jessy up and down. "So you're Jessy Sparhawk."

"Yes—who are you?" Jessy asked.

"Sarah Clay," the woman told her.

The name meant nothing to her.

"Who the hell is behind this?" Jessy demanded. "Emil Landon?"

Sarah started to laugh. "Emil Landon? The son of a bitch who won't accept me as his child? Who claims my mother fooled around with so many people that half of Las Vegas could be my father? The guy who won't take a paternity test?"

"Emil Landon is your father?" Jessy said in shock.

"Where's my daughter?" Sandra demanded.

"Mom!" The cry came from the bank. Reggie came out then. She would have run, except that she was being held.

By Hugo Blythe.

He was followed out of the bank by Darrell Frye.

"Hiya, Jessy," he said.

She was too dumbfounded to say anything, and she felt like throwing up.

"Won't you let my daughter go now—please?" Sandra begged.

"Go to Mommy, kid," Blythe said, letting go of Reggie.

Reggie seemed to fly off the raised sidewalk and down to her mother. Sobbing, Sandra wrapped her into her arms.

"Now, if you will kindly move this way . . ." Sarah Clay said to Jessy.

"Who the hell *are* you?" Jessy demanded.

"I told you, I'm Sarah Clay," the woman said, frowning. "Hasn't Dillon ever mentioned me?"

"No, he hasn't," Jessy said, surprised that the fact seemed to upset the other woman.

"Well, then, he's just being a man," Sarah said. "I mean, if he's got a thing going with you, he wouldn't mention the fact that he's got a thing for me, too."

It had to be a lie, Jessy thought, but she felt her temper soaring nonetheless. She forced herself to rein it in and looked at the woman with as much contempt as she could summon. "Frankly, I just think he's never thought of you as anyone important—or sexy, for that matter."

She might have pushed it too far, she thought. It was one thing to aggravate the woman, another entirely to rile her to violence.

Too late.

Sarah Clay strode over to Jessy and slapped her so hard that her vision blurred, on top of the splitting headache she already had from being shoved into the car.

"Okay," Jessy said. "You have me, so now let her go. Let Reggie and Sandra get out of here."

"You need to give Dillon a ring first. And tell him to lose that old man and his friends before he comes. I want to know where the gold is," Sarah said.

"You're crazy. There isn't any gold," Jessy told her.

"There is. And it's here somewhere," Sarah insisted.

"She's right," Darrell said. "She found a letter that John Wolf wrote to some woman named Mariah saying he'd found it."

"Shut up, Frye. Get the phone down here so she can call Dillon, and tell him to get out here or I'll shoot her," Sarah ordered.

Darrell handed her a cell phone, and Jessy found herself wondering what service even worked out here.

Sarah punched in a number, then swore, and Jessy tried not to smile. Apparently the call had gone straight to voice mail.

Where *was* Dillon? Jessy wondered. Nikki would have awakened by now and raised the alarm. Jimmy knew she had left with Sandra. That wouldn't normally raise anyone's suspicions, but these hadn't been normal days.

Suddenly the sound of an old piano playing an even older tune came from the saloon, and they all jumped.

"Bring them and follow me," Sarah commanded, already hurrying toward the saloon. Blythe took charge of Sandra and Reggie, while Darrell grabbed Jessy by the arm and started dragging her with him. She bit down hard on her lower lip, forcing herself not to show any emotion.

So Emil Landon wasn't involved after all. Had his own daughter been trying to kill him?

They entered the saloon via swinging doors that didn't actually swing anymore. In fact, they seemed in danger of falling completely off their hinges at any second.

It took Jessy a minute to adjust to the dim light, and then she gasped aloud, unable to help herself.

Timothy was sitting at the old piano, his fingers resting on the keys.

"Milly, you made it," he said to Sandra. "Come on over here and sing us a tune."

"Who the hell is the old bastard and how did he get here?" Sarah demanded.

"Why, ma'am, what's the matter?" Timothy asked, stroking the keys again. "I'm Turner. George Turner. That there is Milly and her young'un. Some folks won't be joining us, on account of they're dead, like that fellow you've got stashed over in the bank. But they're here, the rest of them."

Even in the dim light, Jessy could see Sarah's face darken in anger. So there *was* a dead man over in the bank.

"It's the second thug who attacked me, isn't it?" Jessy asked.

Darrell gave her arm a painful twist.

"Look, if you're planning on me talking to Dillon for you, you'd better let me go. Now. You've all got the guns, and as I'm sure you can see, I haven't got a gun or any other weapon."

To her amazement, Darrell, uncertain, let her go, and apparently Sarah wasn't in the mood to fight him over it.

"All right, get them to the bank, all of them, for now," she said. "Geezer, get up!" she commanded Timothy.

"Well, now, that's just foolish," Timothy said. "If you'd let Milly come on over here, we could regale you with some old tunes."

Sandra stood there shaking, with Reggie in her arms, Timothy wasn't moving.

"Get that old bastard out of here," Sarah snapped at Hugo Blythe.

They would hurt Timothy, Jessy knew, and she had to stop them somehow. "Wait. I'll get him," she said, and walked over to the piano. Timothy looked up at her as she reached out a hand to him. "Grandpa, we have to go join the townspeople in the bank."

"All right, child, all right," Timothy said, and stood.

Sarah pointed toward the street, and they preceded her out the door and over to the bank.

They crossed the dusty road and stepped up onto the wooden sidewalk level again and stopped in front of the bank. "Told you that you should have come to work for me, Jessy."

She stared back at him. "What I don't get is why you threw Tanner out of a limo—with a knife in his back."

"Great touch, don't you think?" Sarah said. "My father has a limo identical to the one the Sun owns." She laughed. "You're all so stupid. Darrell got hold of the Sun's limo, and then I got the button off Green's shirt and flirted with a guy at the Big Easy so I could get into their limo and plant the evidence, in case someone figured out to check the limos. And someone did—Dillon, to be precise. We timed things so Darrell would be in plain view on the casino floor, and who in hell would suspect me or know I have any connection to this town or the gold or anything else? I drugged him, and then I killed him. He never knew what hit him. Darrell was great—he ran out and met us on his break, and he knew right where we needed to stop so we could push Green out into the crowd and not be caught on camera." She smiled. "Hugo was driving, but Landon would have sworn he was with him the whole time, because Hugo slipped a nice roofie into my dear old dad's drink, so he slept like a babe in arms and never knew that his loyal Hugo had ever left his side. It was brilliant."

"Why?" Jessy asked. "Why kill Tanner Green if all you wanted was the gold?"

"Don't you understand anything? *I* shot at that lame bastard who refuses to admit he's my father. Tanner had to die so my father would keep on thinking he was in danger. I even got Dillon this job because I saw the message that Daddy Dearest had called my boss, Lieutenant Brown, looking for a recommendation, so I pretended Brown had asked me to call him back and convinced him that he'd only be safe if he hired Dillon Wolf. Because I need Dillon so I can find the gold, but I also had this wonderful opportunity to make life miserable for my father. It was perfect."

"Say you find it—what good will it do you? It's on Paiute land," Jessy said.

Sarah started to laugh. "Exactly, it's Paiute land, and my father is trying to use his Indian heritage to get the rights to build a casino here. And if they come in to bulldoze and dig, they'll find the gold, so he has to die before he gets that far. That gold is mine, and I intend to have it."

"What makes you so certain that Dillon can find it?" Jessy demanded. The other woman was clearly insane and this whole elaborate scheme based on a crazy dream, but even so, she could leave them all dead. "I'm in forensics, in *research*," Sarah said.

"Precisely," Jessy told her. "Why would you believe—"

"John Wolf died here, and he was Dillon's ancestor. And I clawed my way through every word ever written about Adam Harrison, Harrison Investigations and Dillon Wolf. He has a power that science hasn't explained yet. He knows where the gold is, or if he doesn't, he'll find it," she finished stubbornly.

"But you can't—" Jessy began.

"Oh, shut up!" Sarah said, and shoved her into

372

the bank. As the door started to close behind her, cutting off the light, she realized that the others were all still outside.

Furious, Jessy screamed, "I want my grandfather and my friends—now! Dillon won't do anything for you unless I ask him to—nothing. And I won't ask him a thing unless I know my friends are safe."

As she waited for an answer, she stumbled over something and leaned down to see what it was. It was stiff and sticky . . . yet it gave. It felt as if it was growing cold. . . .

It was a body.

She jerked her hand away, remembering that they had killed someone else—probably the hired thug who had been working for them. Apparently this was supposed to be a three-way split.

She gathered all her resources, swallowing a scream, and was ready to repeat her demand when the door opened and Sandra stumbled in, followed by Reggie and then Timothy.

"Jessy?" Sandra said. "What are we going to do?"

"It's all right. We'll think of something. And Dillon will come," Jessy said, fervently hoping she was right.

His caller ID recognized the number as Sarah's, and Dillon knew without answering that she was calling to use Jessy's life as a bargaining chip. It took every ounce of willpower he had, but he didn't answer, because so long as they still needed her, Jessy's life was safe. She had to be terrified, but he couldn't answer. He'd been so blind. He'd suspected some of the right people, but not Sarah. Not until now, when he prayed that knowledge hadn't come too late.

How much longer until he reached Indigo? And then, how much longer than that before help came?

And even if help came, was there going to be another bloodbath?

Sarah was insane. A brilliant woman, but scorned by her father and driven mad by her demons. She had manipulated the action and the players—himself included—every step of the way. The limo-slash-murder scene had been the Sun's, and to his great humiliation, he had fallen for her planted evidence. Darrell Frye had to be part of it. And since Emil Landon wasn't involved, that meant that Hugo Blythe was. Anyone else in their conspiracy? Probably not. Sarah would know that the more people you involved, the more chance there was of someone slipping. The men who attacked Jessy had just been hired goons. They would never even have seen Sarah's face, and one of them was definitely dead, and if the second was still alive, it wouldn't be for long.

His cell rang again where it sat on the passenger seat. He debated whether he should answer or not just as he saw the first faint signs of Indigo rising from the sand.

Sarah was calling again. He hit the button, but he didn't speak. Maybe Sarah thought she'd gotten dead air, because she didn't hang up.

He heard voices, but not directed to him.

"We need to kill the other three now," Sarah was saying.

"You don't know Jessy. I do." That was Darrell Frye. "If you kill them, she won't help us. She's stubborn."

"How the hell did the old bugger get out here?" That was Hugo Blythe.

"He stole a car, how the hell else?" Sarah demanded. "You assholes are going to fuck this up, just like you've fucked up everything else. At least the idiots you hired to kidnap the girl are dead now. And you, you fool," she said to Darrell. "Maybe we were out of camera range, but couldn't you see that Rudy Yorba character staring right at the limo and Tanner Green? I studied the damn tapes, and I could tell what they'd see eventually."

"Oh, *we're* fuck-ups, are we?" Darrell challenged her. "Once you get Dillon out here, he'd damn well better know where the gold is so we've got the money to get out of here. Because someone will put the pieces together sooner or later and figure out that we were working as a team. Your stupid father is going to miss Hugo, for one thing."

"Relax. We have dead men who can take the blame," Sarah reminded him.

The line went dead then, so Dillon hit his own

end call button. He was close enough to the town now that if the phone rang again, he would answer it. Because he knew how he wanted to play out the scene when he arrived.

With a little help from the dead.

17

The door opened, and a flashlight blazed into the bank. Beyond the blinding light, Jessy could see that the sky was turning bloodred as the sun began to set.

"Jessy, get out here," Darrell ordered.

She didn't move.

"Jessy Sparhawk, get your ass out here or we'll start shooting," Sarah warned.

"Jessy," Sandra said, touching her shoulder.

"It's all right, Sandra. You just have to stay calm."

Jessy turned, trying to see Timothy in the darkness that shadowed the bank.

He must have sensed her movement, because he said, "It's all right, granddaughter. We are assembled."

Timothy's words and his preternatural calm were almost more unnerving than trying to figure out how to deal with Sarah so she didn't risk all their lives. Because she knew that Sarah really would start shooting, she walked to the door of the bank and stepped outside.

Sarah thrust a cell phone into her hand. "Call

Dillon and pray he answers this time. Make sure he knows that if he doesn't show up alone, I'll put a bullet through your head myself. I may go down, but I'll take you with me."

Without a word, Jessy took the phone from her and keyed in Dillon's number.

She half hoped to get his answering machine because that might buy them more time. But Dillon answered. "Dillon," she said.

"Jessy?"

"I'm at Indigo with a woman named Sarah Clay who says you know her. And Darrell Frye and Hugo Blythe," she added.

"I know," he told her quietly.

"She says that if you don't come alone and tell her where the gold is, she'll kill me."

"I figured that," he said softly.

"Tell him again—he comes alone. And he gives me the location of the gold," Sarah said.

"All right, I heard her. Listen to me, Jessy. Tell her that I'll be happy to let her have the gold. But I know that she also has Timothy, Sandra and Reggie, and they had better be all safe and in one piece when I get there. Tell her that she has to bring all of you into the saloon. Tell her that I can only figure out exactly where the gold is if we reenact the shoot-out. Tell her that I need all of you in the saloon."

Sarah ripped the phone from Jessy's hands. "Hello, Dillon," she said pleasantly.

Jessy couldn't hear his reply, but she saw Sarah frown.

"Don't tell me what to do. I have the guns—and your friends—and this redheaded slut you apparently find so attractive," she said.

Dillon answered with something that brought a furious "What?" from Sarah, whose eyes shot to Darrell Frye. "You don't need to talk to Darrell. I'm the one in charge."

"Sarah, we're all in this together," Darrell said, his own eyes narrowing.

"Who was the brain to put this all together?" Sarah responded furiously.

Then she stared at the phone incredulously. Dillon had hung up on her.

Sarah spun around. "Get the rest of them. He wants them all in the saloon. Move it!"

She shoved Jessy in front of her, pushing so hard that Jessy almost fell, but an unseen hand seemed to help her find her balance.

She heard the jingle of a spur, and she lowered her head and allowed herself a little smile. Ringo must have come with Timothy. He was here, and there was something oddly comforting in that fact.

She walked toward the saloon, aware that Darrell and Hugo had gone to get Sandra, Reggie and Timothy.

Sarah shoved her inside first, and to Jessy's amazement, Dillon was already there. He was seated at the poker table, one foot resting on it, as if he had grown weary waiting for them to arrive.

Sarah, coming in behind Jessy, gasped with surprise, but she collected herself quickly. "You're here. And you're an idiot. You might have taken one of us by surprise and improved your odds."

"Why? You're going to give me my friends back, and I'm going to give you the gold," Dillon said. "We've got to do this right, though. You've obviously researched your past, you know you're Varny's descendant—sorry, *double* descendant. What kills me is, you could have made it to the top. You aced the academy."

"I have no *money!*" she lashed out. "Oh, yeah. I researched my past. My idiot mother was in love with my father. She let him pay her off, then absolved him of any financial responsibility for *my* welfare. He refuses to recognize me. But he's a fool—he's going to lose every asset he has. I'll see to that. He's in debt, deeply in debt, and once I get the gold and set myself up, I can actually call in his banknotes. Then I can throw him out to the wolves—before I kill him. I've played this very carefully. My father is a jerk. He believed in Hugo, and Hugo has been with me for years. Hugo doesn't want to kiss my father's ass, he wants his share."

"What about Darrell?" Dillon asked.

"She . . . she knew about—" Darrell began.

"Shut your idiot mouth!" Sarah warned him, then sighed. "What the hell. He was skimming

379

casino profits, and I had him dead to rights. But he had the knowledge we needed to effectively stage Green's death. He knows the Sun inside out—including where all the cameras are. And I knew that once Green was killed, you'd stick with the case no matter what. I was brilliant, I really was. I convinced my father to hire you, then killed Tanner. And I could feed you information, and you believed in me, too. Now, if you want anyone to live, you'd better find my gold for me."

"I told you," Dillon said. "We need to reenact that night so I can get into John Wolf's head."

Sarah looked at him skeptically, then nodded just as the others entered.

"All right," Dillon said. "Let's see, Timothy—sorry, George—you go over by the piano. And you, too, Milly." He cleared his throat when no one moved. "That's you, Sandra. Reggie, you stay with your mom, and I need Jessy with Timothy. I can't be two people at once, so when we get to that point, we'll have to imagine Mariah standing at the door. Ringo, take your place at the table. Tanner, you were with Varny's men, I'm afraid. Rudy, you were at the table."

"Who the hell are you talking to?" Darrell demanded irritably, looking around nervously.

"Humor me. I'm talking to dead men," Dillon said cheerfully.

Ringo let Jessy see him then. He shrugged to show her that he didn't know what Dillon

380

intended, either. But he took a chair, scraping it against the wooden floor and making the others jump.

"What the hell are you pulling, Wolf?" Hugo demanded, an edge of fear in his voice.

"Do you want the gold?" Dillon demanded. "Then let me work through this. All right, we'll pretend that Cheever is here at the table—he'd be the sheriff. And you, Sarah, you'd be Varny, of course. Then there were the four thugs who died right away. I'm sorry, Tanner, that would be you, along with the two men you killed, the ones who tried to kidnap Jessy."

"You only saw one body," Sarah said.

"Yes, you were just so helpful, calling me about that so quickly," he said. "I guess they haven't found the other body yet."

"It's here," Jessy told him.

"I should have figured as much," Dillon said thoughtfully. "We really should get Cheever out here."

"I told you, no cops, or she dies," Sarah said. "All of you die, for that matter."

She was going to kill them all anyway, Jessy thought, and Dillon had to know that.

"I didn't call Cheever, so you can cut out the threats," Dillon said. "Okay, one of you is Tobias, and one of you is just another henchman." He studied Darrell and Hugo. "Which is which? I didn't get to talk to Brent long enough earlier, and

381

I'm not even sure he figured it all out, anyway. But no matter, we're all here except for the sheriff. Maybe Billie Tiger can take his place for now," he said thoughtfully.

Jessy barely contained a gasp when someone walked by her. It was the tall Seminole she had seen in her dream, the man Timothy talked to. And there they were, four men—well, three ghosts and one man—sitting at the table.

"Enough already," Sarah snapped. "Get on with it, Dillon. Quickly."

Jessy stared at Dillon, who was looking at her with an expression that offered strength . . . and something more. She remembered the word John Wolf had whispered in her dream, and suddenly, she understood.

Here, she mouthed silently to Dillon.

He nodded to show he understood.

Here. The gold was right here.

"Let's have a tune, George," Dillon said. "And a song, Milly."

Timothy began to play "A Bird in a Gilded Cage," and Sandra choked out the words.

"Good," Dillon said approvingly. "John Wolf had the winning hand. He and Mark Davison—that's you, Rudy—were the only ones still in the game. Ringo was bored, and Percy . . . he knew you were coming, Varny. He knew because he had warned you that I was heading back to town. He suspected that I knew where the gold was, and that

382

you had to get to it fast, before I could. You terror-
ized him into doing your bidding. Sad, because
deep down, I think he wanted to be a good guy. He
just wasn't quite there yet. You know, a lot of reli-
gions believe that we're reincarnated, and that we
grow with each life. I think Percy's finally found
his courage, and that in this life, he's going to be a
good man."

"What the hell is all this?" Darrell Frye
demanded. "Shut up already and get to the gold!"

Timothy suddenly pulled Jessy down to the
piano. He smiled at her and put her fingers on the
keys. She kept playing, kept singing in a low soft
voice. She turned and her heart froze; Timothy was
gone.

"Now you arrive, Varny," Dillon said. "You
come up to me and get in my face about the gold.
Come on, Sarah. If you want it, play it out."

As he spoke, Jessy found herself holding back a
gasp. Sandra let out a low moan and stopped
singing, and Reggie clutched her mother tightly.

Suddenly, everything seemed real. There *were*
four men at the poker table. There was cigar smoke
in the air. Beyond the swinging doors, the sun was
falling lower, a bloodred blossom in the sky.

The men around the table suddenly rose. Hugo
screamed, and Jessy knew that he could see them,
too: Ringo, Tanner and Rudy, all in period attire
and armed with six-guns. He screamed again, drew
his own gun and fired, but his shot went wild.

Dillon, too, had come to the gunfight—with a gun. He fired, dropping Hugo, then spun on a dime, and Darrell Frye, his hands shaking as he tried to aim, went down next. Then Dillon turned to Sarah.

But she had her gun leveled on him. "Not yet, cowboy," she said smoothly. "And I don't care what visions you've conjured. *They're not real.* And I still want my gold."

The saloon doors suddenly swung open with a vengeance, drawing Sarah's attention. She shot wildly at the doors, but there was no one there.

Ringo took a step forward, and Sarah's eyes darted in the direction of his clinking spurs.

Dillon took advantage of the moment, but he didn't shoot her. He slammed his fist into her gut, and she cried out in agony, dropping her gun as she crashed to the floor.

Suddenly there was a silhouette in the doorway, and an authoritative voice said, "I'll take it from here, Dillon. Good thing Mr. Sparhawk slipped out the back to warn me not to come charging in or I'd be shot full of holes now. The shooting's all over for the night, folks."

"Dillon!" Jessy screamed. It wasn't over. Sarah had reclaimed her gun and taken aim at Dillon again, a crazed glint in her eyes. "They're not real!" she screamed.

Gunfire exploded. Dillon had no chance to take aim and fire, but Sarah made a shocked, gurgling sound, and a pool of blood was staining her shirt.

Ringo Murphy was standing a few feet away, a small trail of smoke rising from the barrel of the Colt he had leveled at Sarah Clay. She stared at him, seeing him and finally believing in him, as the glare of fury, hatred and bitterness faded from her eyes until there was nothing there at all. Ringo might be a ghost, but he had taken a real gun from the fallen body of Hugo Blythe, and with it and the legacy of the past, he had dealt justice with it in the present.

Sandra started to sob, hugging Reggie. Timothy went over to her, taking her into his arms. "It's all right, Sandra, it's over now."

"What . . . the hell just happened?" Cheever asked.

"Just a trick of light and energy—and time," Dillon told him. Cheever would know, if he thought about it, that it couldn't have been so simple, but he would accept the explanation, because the reality would be just too hard to acknowledge.

As Jessy stood and walked unsteadily over to the table, she heard the sounds of sirens, car doors slamming and the voices of Adam, Brent and Nikki, as well as a number that she didn't recognize. People would be all over them in a minute. She threw herself into Dillon's arms, and he held her tightly, whispering against her hair before pulling away and kissing her lips.

"Oh my God, Dillon, you did it," she whispered.

"With help," he said, smiling.

"Ringo was brilliant."

"Yes, he was. But I meant you. You kept everyone alive until I could get here."

She laughed. "Only because she believed you could find the gold."

"As a matter of fact, I think I have a pretty good idea where it is," he told her.

She drew away, smiling. "I know," she said.

"You do?"

"I walked with Timothy's ghost dancers in a dream, and I saw John Wolf. It's here. He looked at his Mariah, and that's what he said, 'Here.'"

He laughed. "That's it. The exact answer. Here in the saloon. We're standing on it."

Epilogue

A month later, Jessy was fiddling with her bouquet when Dillon came over and stood next to her. The organist was getting ready, the crowd had assembled and the service was about to start.

"They found it," he whispered.

"Who found what?" she whispered back.

"The excavators found the gold. The vein was right there, running under the saloon. Now the Paiute nation will have the gold, and the town will come back to life."

She rose on her toes and kissed him. "That's

great. Now, please, get out of my way. I have somewhere to be."

It was a simple ceremony, but Jessy wanted everything to be right. When the music began, she looked back. Sally Teasdale, hiding behind the door, gave her a wink and a wave. Jessy started down the aisle, tossing flower petals as she went, until she reached the makeshift altar. The music changed, and to the traditional strains of "Here Comes the Bride," Mrs. Teasdale, in simple but elegant pale blue with a matching veil, came walking down the aisle, smiling radiantly.

Timothy, tall and handsome, was waiting for her.

The ceremony was presided over by a minister and a shaman. Words were spoken in English and in Sioux, and Jessy was certain that the guests understood everything that was said, no matter what language. The ending was traditional, as the minister and shaman spoke together and said, "You may now kiss the bride."

Timothy kissed the new Mrs. Sparhawk, and the assembled group of fifty or so—friends and anyone from the home who wanted to attend—applauded mightily.

It was time for the meal. Jessy took her seat next to Dillon, and Adam, Brent, Nikki, Jerry Cheever, Doug Tarleton, Sandra and Reggie all joined them at the table.

"It was a beautiful wedding," Jerry Cheever said.

"Absolutely," Sandra agreed. They'd been on two dates already; this was their third.

"I should have been the flower girl," Reggie said, shaking her head.

"I was the maid of honor," Jessy told her. "I just happened to throw flowers, too."

"And you're too old to be a flower girl," Sandra said.

"You can be a bridesmaid at my wedding," Jessy told Reggie.

"Are you getting married?" Reggie asked.

"Well, if I ever do," Jessy said.

"If you want us to stick around for that wedding," Nikki said, "it had better be soon. We can't stay here in Vegas forever."

"Actually, if Jessy agrees, you might still be here for our wedding," Dillon said. His dark eyes flashed as he looked at Jessy.

"Is that a proposal?" she asked him.

He nodded.

"It wasn't a very good one."

Dillon laughed and slipped to his knees by her side. "Jessy, will you marry me? I know we haven't been together long, but I also know I'll never love anyone as much as I love you or want to spend my life with anyone else." He paused. "Was that better?"

She laughed. "Yes, yes, you can get off your knees. Why the hurry?" she whispered for his ears alone, but he just shook his head.

"Later," he whispered back.

"She'll be Jessy Sparhawk Wolf. Sounds like a zoo," Reggie said, shaking her head.

"I'll be going with you to pick out the bridesmaids' dresses. I do not wear pink or anything ridiculously frilly."

Everyone laughed, and the talk turned to planning and guest list.

That night, as they lay in bed together, she finally found out why Dillon was in such a rush.

"Ringo is leaving," he told her.

"What? Why?" she asked, distressed.

"He says he's a third wheel. But the truth is, he's finished what he's tried to do for over a hundred years. He told me he can feel the light calling to him, says he can see it in a way he never did before. And he's longing to go."

She nodded. She was sad, but she understood.

Six weeks later they were married. It ended up being a huge affair, with all the entertainers and casino friends Jessy had ever worked with in attendance, along with friends of Dillon's from Nevada, and beyond. Sandra and Nikki had gotten together to do most of the planning, and the end result was both traditional and contemporary. None of the trimmings that came with a wedding meant much to Jessy, though. She was in love with a man who was also her best friend and her strength.

• , •

Two days after the wedding, Jessy and Dillon made another drive out to Indigo. Ringo was with them, squishing Jessy in the middle between himself and Dillon. She tried not to cry, but the tears came anyway.

He tried to comfort her. "Don't be sad. It's just time."

Construction equipment was everywhere around town. The old ghost town was coming into a life it had never known before. Whatever was being dug or built, however, the cemetery wasn't to be touched. The Paiute had a great respect for the dead.

At the cemetery, Ringo directed them to his grave. He gave Dillon a solemn handshake, then said, "What the hell!" and hugged him. He kissed Jessy one last time. "Be happy," he told her. "Keep strong, and be brave, just as you are. And never forget kindness. Be generous and kind to *all* around you, nightwalker," he said.

She nodded and set flowers on his grave as he turned away. The sun was setting, but the evening was suddenly ablaze with a beam of light. Ringo walked toward the light as Dillon and Jessy watched him.

Then the light faded and Ringo was gone.

Dillon tilted Jessy's chin and brushed her lips with a kiss. "We'll do as he asked," he told her softly. "We'll live bravely and generously, and remember the lessons of the past."

She smiled. "Live, learn and love," she told him. He smiled and brushed her lips with his again. Then, hand in hand, they walked away and left Indigo behind them.

Center Point Publishing
600 Brooks Road ● PO Box 1
Thorndike ME 04986-0001 USA

(207) 568-3717

US & Canada:
1 800 929-9108
www.centerpointlargeprint.com